THE TRIBE OF TSULIB

A STORY OF SURVIVAL

By
Helen Quinn

National Library of Australia Cataloguing-in-Publication entry:
Quinn, Helen
The Tribe of Tsulib
9780646549965 (pbk.)
A823.4

ISBN: 0646549960
ISBN-13: 9780646549965

In memory of
Jhon Alid Diomedes Corisepa Shimbo

Contents

Pachakuti ... a moment when history ended

There once was a time when the earth was consumed by human greed for power and total dominance over their fellow man. The great political powers saw the possession of all natural resources on the earth as a tool for total control of financial institutions and governments. This fight for power was fought under the guise of freeing poverty-stricken and religiously restrained groups in lands of rich natural resources.

After many thousands of years of politically motivated wars initiated by greed, the earth was slowly contaminated and the very basic requirements for life —fresh water and oxygen — became more precious than any other resource.

The tools of war had become more destructive as man became increasingly intolerant and thirsty for total control until destruction of the planet became inevitable. Four major politically orientated countries were increasing their stores of weapons and began a race to develop the ultimate weapon of mass destruction which would give them a deadly advantage. These weapons would be launched from space craft, submarines, aircraft and land-based missile launchers to cover every corner of the planet.

The countries in conflict were willing to destroy the planet in preference to being overpowered by another government. This selfish inconsideration led to plans for defence systems which would automatically launch weapons continuously for possibly months after they themselves were annihilated, leaving all the waters, lands, and air of the planet extremely contaminated for a long period of time.

Small enlightened groups all over the planet foresaw the inevitable and took it upon themselves to study ocean currents and wind patterns, making plans to retreat to isolated pockets of distant lands which they hoped would be spared from shock waves and poisons carried by the winds and oceans.

They collected only a few basic tools, many seeds, and books that recorded indigenous peoples of the earth and their cultures with the intent to learn the traditional ways of survival. They educated themselves about edible plants and indigenous herbs of many countries. Knowing the inevitable, they harvested and consumed many plants such as kelp from the ocean to prepare their bodies for the impending assault.

As the final ultimatums and cross threats were delivered to and from the major governments on the earth, the people put into action any plans for survival of a terrible fate, knowing that a peaceful outcome would not eventuate.

A huge exodus to safer destinations began. Some boarded planes to remote destinations, and others locked themselves down in their own homes with stores of water and dehydrated and canned basic foods.

One group set to sea in a fleet of sailing boats, launches and houseboats, trusting in the sea to carry them to safer destinations. These reluctant sailors planned to head directly out to sea and try to stay as close together as possible hoping that after the crisis had passed, they would have the company of others to help recover and build a new life.

As the distance between the boats and the mainland increased, the grim reality of their fickle existence became overwhelming but the anticipation of the unknown kept them alert. They watched as smoke plumes began to rise from the horizons,

2

knowing that they were not a result of bombings but possibly the looters who had begun their pointless raids on businesses in the large commercial areas as cities were abandoned.

The underlying sentiment was hopelessness, but many believed that they had to attempt to survive the impending doom for the sake of humanity and were not willing to submit to the fate depicted by selfish leaders.

As predicted, the day came when all the skies were lit up with the colours of fire and hot, violent winds rushed into every corner of the earth.

Everyone on the boats responded by tying themselves onto their vessels and braced themselves for the ride of their lives. Parents tied themselves to their children and gave them sleeping drugs to lessen their inevitable trauma. All they could do now was to watch the mushroom plumes rise above the horizon and wait. The children in their innocence were entertained by the missile vapour trails criss-crossing in every direction from east to west and some headed south.

The seas finally responded to the shock waves, violently carrying its passengers on the angry currents, throwing and tossing them in giant tides that sucked them out to sea before throwing them back to the shores, delivering them to a multitude of destinations, some habitable, some not.

Many boats and their passengers were unmercifully pounded into rocky shores while others were sent surfing on the top of huge waves into the open seas. Boats were thrown against each other, causing critical damage and unbearable grief and a sense of helplessness for the people witnessing the tragic loss of lives.

The resilience of the human body was severely tested by days and nights of relentless punishment before intermittent periods of calm settled the seas.

It was during these periods of calm that the occupants on the surviving boats comforted and assisted each other with their injuries and sorrowfully cast away members who had died as a consequence of the battering waters. They soon became adept at reading the seas and skies and to recognise the signs of another cycle of violent seas. This gave them a small sense of control as they could prepare themselves for what was now a known element.

After many weeks at sea and constant battering, small blessings such as seeing another boat brought great cheers and uplifted their spirits as they manoeuvred their boats to join each other.

As the weeks of constant abuse grew into months, more boats became visible as they were caught in the same currents regardless of being thrown apart again; the seas had developed a pattern that accumulated many boats and had held them on the same path. As each violent cycle passed, excitement was abound as they looked for their companion boats and shared their depleted food and water supplies. The loss of lives was now minimal as they learnt from their experiences and adapted.

It was during a particularly violent cycle that a group of fortunate exiles were forced into a bay on the west side of a large southern land mass.

The group of boats were then sucked out into the open sea once more to be thrown on the crest of a massive wave back into the bay. They saw the land mass, which jutted out like an arm reaching out into the ocean beckoning the seas to enter. Everyone watched in fear and prepared for the worst outcome as they were heading for a large wall of rock.

Suddenly, the waters began forming a whirlpool and the boats were one by one forced into a funnel of water sucking them into a very large cavern and sending them on a furious journey deep into an underground river. The waters were fierce and dragged the boats deeper into the bowels of the earth through deep rapids, tossing them around in large whirlpools which formed in open caverns.

As the waters receded with the tidal forces, the boats in the underground waterways became still and calm until the thundering noises of more water warned of another surge of water coming into the caves. The only defence was to tie themselves down again and hope for the best.

After many surges and wanes, the waters finally slowed down and the damaged boats and their occupants settled into a passive drift in the slowly descending cavernous river, which was dimly lit by reflected light.

Once more the people slowly gathered on the decks and for the first time, took a long look at their new environment and tried to ascertain who had survived and agreed that they once more had no choice other than going with the hand they had been dealt and hoping that it would eventually carry them back to the surface of the earth in a hospitable place.

After many hours of continuous drifting, light became sparse and eventually the darkness became overwhelming as they sunk further into the caves and daylight was totally obliterated. Not knowing what fate awaited them, they chose to rest while the river carried them in darkness to its destination.

The loud sound of crashing water brought everyone back to attention as they realised a large waterfall or rapids was only minutes ahead of them as the waters began to flow faster and the tunnel narrowed. They were totally at the mercy of the darkness and the waters. As they approached, the roar was deafening and without warning, they were thrown over the edge of a watery precipice and the feeling of falling into the unknown was terrifying, causing everyone to scream in fear not only for themselves but their families and companions.

The sound of people moaning and coughing was the first sounds which a young man called Dean heard as he gained consciousness while realising that he was on hard ground but still in complete darkness. He called out for other survivors and was answered by many screams of fear and pleadings for help. Calls for help were coming from many different places; some became more distant as if the waters were carrying them away in different directions. Dean realised that this was an impossible situation with no light, no knowledge of their surroundings, and no way of surveying the situation. He felt around his immediate area on his hands and knees and found that he was a few metres from the water's edge and the thunder of the falls was in the distance behind him. He put his hands into the water and mentally analysed his bearings in relation to the direction of the falls and the current of the flowing waters which was still strong but not violent.

Dean then called out to anyone who was fit and able to do the same to yell out their position in relation to the falls, which he designated as west. There were many survivors, both unharmed and injured, and the expected hysteria was deafening as people realised that some of their family members and close companions were not answering the calls.

After many hours of talking to each other, Dean and a few others decided to get everyone to slowly find their way downstream which they all agreed was the only option. Using their hands and crawling, some found the walls of the tunnel and decided to walk using the wall as guidance. Others decided to crawl using the edge of the water to guide them onwards.

Those who were injured or traumatised were advised to stay where they were after being reassured that the river had to go somewhere as it was still flowing, the temperature was pleasant, and the air was fresh.

The water at this point was quite salty but diluted, which indicated that fresh-water was coming in from somewhere and merging with the sea-water. They were encouraged to talk to each other even though they were not together.

The pace was slow as they proceeded to follow the river but were always talking and waiting as one encountered difficulties falling into the water and finding a grip to drag them back onto firm ground. After many hours, a boy named Joel fell into the river and yelled as he was washed downstream, leaving the others feeling helpless to offer assistance to him in the darkness.

The remaining people did not move or speak for many minutes as they realised that they could all perish the same way and

6

thought about the injured people left behind who were counting on them to come back for them.

Joel gained consciousness with the severe pain of a headache. He opened his eyes to be blinded by a ray of bright light which was being reflected to many places into the large area which he now found himself in. He lifted his head and took in his surroundings, totally amazed by what he saw.

The area was as large as five or six playing fields, with the river running through the centre of this large cavern.

Light appeared to be generated by the reflection of a single ray of light which appeared to be reflected around the cavern by many polished surfaces on the roof and walls.

He was trapped in a dam of rubbish which had accumulated on one side of the river, but he carefully dragged himself out of the river and sat on the rock edge. He stood up and checked himself for injuries, which appeared to be minor bruising and scratches. The more he surveyed his surroundings, the more uneasy he became as he realised that this was a dwelling of many people but no people were to be seen. He saw small individual constructions and what appeared to be overgrown gardens of strange plants. He wondered if he should call out and wait for an answer.

"Hello," he called.

He was hoping that he was alone because the thought of confronting unfriendly people was making him feel very uneasy and he had to admit that his call was not loud enough for anyone further than ten paces away to have heard him anyway.

He then remembered his companions back up the river. He felt very excited and began to follow a well-worn path against the wall alongside the river to share his findings. Once again the progress was slow but he eventfully heard the sounds of his companions as they scrambled over the rough, dark terrain and shouted out to them in excitement.

Everyone screamed with sheer delight knowing that he had survived and that they may have an end to their trauma. Their pace increased until they saw a faint stream of light downstream. They rushed for the remaining distance and stood motionless, absorbing the view in front of them. This very large cavern with many structures, which appeared to be buildings carved out of the rock, left them gazing speechless.

Three levels were immediately visible in this immense cavern. The river was the lowest and appeared to be running directly through the middle, but it also appeared to be a structured water course with smooth, perfectly engineered edges directing the water on a prescribed course that gently meandered through the cavern and veered to the one side to continue through the tunnel outlet at the far end.

From the river level it stepped up to another flat level where no structures existed. The walls of this level were again perfectly engineered to look like a flood-way. There were steps literally carved into the rock leading down to the lower river level. Yet again, there was a third level which was also lacking any structures but did have debris from the river lying in organised stacks.

Everyone was speechless but thinking the same things, how did these levels come to be carved so intricately?

What was the purpose?

They slowly approached what appeared to be a central pavilion which was very large and stood sentinel over the whole area. The entrance was very wide with ornate doors made from many timber poles held fast to large posts with hinges intricately carved to represent hands supporting each door. Two carved figures of naked-breasted maidens with long, flowing hair were standing sentinel, one each side of the steps. The lower section of the carved figures became a part of the timber and faded into the base.

"Wow," someone said. "They look like they should be on the front of the old sailing boats in the pirate days."

The group stepped very slowly in awe of this underground city as they slowly surveyed everything. They walked up the

8

twenty-five steps leading to the large central pavilion and were very aware of the fact that not one soul had been seen or heard.

They didn't even feel the presence of another person or creature.

"This is very weird; this has been locked down from the outside! Who wants to open it?" someone mumbled.

After a long silence, Dean stepped up to the door.

"OK, slowly, we don't know what's on the other side so I'll do this while you all stand aside, no sense in all of us coming head to head with whatever might be there."

He lifted one pole and then the other, and gripped the handle of one door and slowly pulled it open and waited. Again, only silence greeted them, the intense silence that only comes with being underground.

One slow step at a time, they entered the huge room that confronted them. The floor was solid rock and the whole room was glowing brightly like it was the middle of the day. Again, a single ray of light from somewhere was being reflected onto many very shiny surfaces which were obviously strategically placed to result in incredible light. The group finally relaxed and started to chatter in amazement as they ran around exploring this wonderful place.

They came to the conclusion that this was a central living area used for preparing food and possibly the central social hub of a group or civilisation. Basic furniture such as tables and stools were carved into the existing rock of the cavern. Walls and what appeared to be shelving was made from timber washed smooth, a legacy of many years in the water. Large mounds of different seaweeds were stacked in piles with shells and fish bones and other unknown items.

A huge central rock had been carved to make a large open oven similar to what they all knew as a pizza oven. It had ashes and blackened cooking objects inside the large belly.

They walked back outside the pavilion and began to explore the other constructions which were obviously for individual groups, maybe families' sleeping quarters, but again, found not a living soul.

The dwellings took advantage of the existing rock to use as walls or benches and other walls and bedding was constructed using timber, seaweeds, and a rough cloth made from vegetation of some kind.

Everything here was very impersonal with only basic requirements. There were no decorations to give clues about the inhabitants of the place. One wall near the river had many planks of timber hanging one above the other. Each piece of timber had a name on it.

"These must be the name plates from boats," said Joel.

"Yes, if only they could talk."

The group were puzzled by the pristine condition of everything, but still, not a sign of a living being.

They found a few simple but strong structures made from poles with cloth hanging between, which could possibly be used for carrying produce from place to place. Dean immediately saw the potential of using them to bring the injured folk who were left behind in the tunnels back to this point. He organised groups of four to take the stretchers and head back upstream in the tunnel.

The remaining people took it upon themselves to do a full reconnaissance of the area with the plan of finding food and a central comfortable place for anyone who may be injured.

They found nets made from vegetation strung across one part of the river. It was torn on one side allowing the river to flow freely but catching clusters of debris in the intact part of the net.

An overhead swinging bridge with a very well-constructed rope ladder leading up to it was found against one end of the cavernous tunnel. As they ventured over it to the other side of the cavern, they discovered a passage-way leading to another large cavern, which appeared to be a storage area full of debris. They guessed the debris had been delivered by the river and deliberately caught in the nets.

10

Debris from broken boats, fish bones of all sizes, birds feathers and skeletons, buoys, life jackets, and many things not recognisable. Everything had been sorted into stacks.

The sound of the rescue crew coming back to the cavern, brought everyone running back to assist with the injured and comfort those who had realised their family members and companions were not amongst the rescued.

The darkness in the tunnels, made it impossible to bring back the unconscious and dead. Only those who could call out and be tracked by voice could be rescued. They could only go back each day and call for any more conscious people.

The strength of the reflected light coming into the cavern started to fade and they realised that its source was the sun being reflected from the surface and sunset was approaching. They then realised that the light inside the tunnel would depend on the strength of the sun outside and knew that they needed to find somewhere to sleep before the light totally faded. They were surprised by how quickly total darkness engulfed the cavern when the reflected light disappeared.

The first night's sleeping arrangements were disorganized as everyone found somewhere to sleep only by using their hands to feel their way around.

The temperature in the tunnels appeared to be a constant, comfortable level so the need for bed covers was not a concern at this time.

It was during these hours of darkness that discussions about survival were conducted. Everyone agreed that at first light next day, they would divide into groups and select an area of the tunnel to explore and note anything which could be used to assist with their journey or an extended stay. There were many questions put forward relating to food and water supply.

At the first ray of light next day, everyone gathered into their groups and proceeded to explore and map their new temporary residence.

11

Caves were discovered which appeared to have been carved into the solid rock walls within the tunnel. No-one was prepared for what they found in these caves.

One was a storage place for whatever could be retrieved from the flowing river as it passed through the tunnel. The debris from the river was obviously retrieved, sorted into stacks, and eventually stored here.

Large stacks of boat steering wheels, rudders, buoys, life jackets, and fishing traps from ocean trawlers. Many rolls of sail cloth in a myriad of colors, fishing nets with cork floats still intact and bundles of knotted fishing lines.

There were pieces of timber in many shapes and sizes, glass, and metal strips from broken boats that had been washed into the tunnels and broken up as they were tossed against the tunnel walls and over the falls.

There were stacks of clothing and bags, shoes and belts, kitchen utensils, and a multitude of rolls of ropes in different colors and sizes.

Many colored foam seat cushions and remnants of mattress stuffing and kapok.

Polystyrene boxes, plastic containers, and petrol cans.

There were collections of sea sponges and shells, feathers and fish skeletons, and sadly, human bones and hair.

Another ante cave was full of timber, drift-wood from the sea, and tree trunks and roots ripped from their ground and delivered to the tunnels in storms.

A section for coconut fiber and whole coconuts, many strange pieces of foliage with seeds intact, and dehydrated whole fruits, some of which were identifiable but many that were not.

Mountains of seaweeds of all kinds were stacked in another cave; the smell was overpowering but quite wholesome in a smelly sort of way.

A cave found further away from the main area was the biggest surprise. Inside, human bodies were enclosed in beautifully decorated bags with only their faces showing. They appeared to

12

be perfectly preserved, lacking only the full-cheeked appearance of a living being. Shells and stones were woven and threaded into decorative hairpieces hanging down the sides of the faces.

The survivors immediately noticed a difference among these dead people. Some looked quite modern but others appeared to be from another time or place. In fact, it looked like four or five different civilizations, cultures, or eras were represented here.

The further the group looked, the more questions presented themselves.

A few of the older, less agile people stayed in the main area and searched through the main pavilion hoping to source food for immediate consumption, as hunger was becoming an urgent consideration.

They were not disappointed.

Stores of seeds, nuts, and dehydrated strips of fruits and vegetables were soon discovered in a large collection of racks behind the open oven.

In the same area, the stone floor had a round, smooth hollow about as round as a baby's bath but much deeper. Again, it appeared to have been handmade: it was not a natural formation.

Someone suggested that it might be a grinding apparatus like the one many indigenous people use to make flour. They immediately looked about for something which may have been used as the pounding instrument. Nothing was recognized but they all agreed that it would be easy enough to find something to use.

In one corner of this pavilion, a large hole had been carved into the rock and it was full of water. On one end, water was slowly spilling over the edge into a small drain which went all the way down to the river. The water appeared to come from a spring high up in the wall of the cavern and was caught in the bath. It was fresh, clean, cold, and continuously flowing. The water would be filtered through the rocks and sand before reaching them so they felt very confident about it being free of any

13

contamination from radiation or poisons deposited by the wars. And besides, what choice did they have?

High up on another level they saw vines hanging over the edge. A series of steps had been carved into the wall leading directly to the area. On closer scrutiny of what appeared to be a garden, they found that it extended a long way back into the cavern. It was indeed a garden which was full of neglected, overgrown vegetables of some sort which had reverted back to a self-sufficient eco-system. The whole area here was illuminated very brightly by the deliberately guided light from above.

As they stood and looked, the light rays moved slowly from one highly polished surface to another, ensuring constant light to the garden.

The engineering was a feat to behold!

As they walked through the garden, it was impossible to tell how long it had been there as it was overgrown and wild with vines intertwining and dead, damp vegetation knee-deep on the ground. A source of a constant water supply to the garden was found as small constant dripping sounds were heard and found to be the seeping of water through the walls.

A woman called Aida quickly claimed the garden as her responsibility and began to search through the miniature jungle for recognizable plants. She recognized many different types of potato, yam, and turnip-like tubers with serrated leaves. Amongst the vines she found a sort of cucumber, large beans - larger than she had ever seen—hanging from the heights, with dried gourds and seed pods ripe and ready to explode. She was very excited, rushing from one area to the next not believing what her eyes presented. There were tomato plants, corn, papaya fruits, and many fruits that she had never seen before.

As she stepped on the vegetation, aromatic herbs and plants released the wonderful smells as their oils were released by the crushing under-foot.

She ran excitedly yelling as she approached the community.

14

"We'll be OK," she yelled. "It's amazing, the vegetables up there, the light, it's unbelievable!" She fell to her knees crying. The discovery had given her hope in a hopeless situation and now her fears and sorrows for her missing family members were releasing. She sobbed as others joined her in the mixed emotions of grief and happiness which everyone had been keeping to themselves.

They were constantly thinking about the possibility of radiation or poison emitted by the weapons, and every night in the darkness the sounds of people weeping was a common occurrence as thoughts of home, families, and their unknown future filled their minds.

They now felt reassured about food and water, but there was an underlying uneasiness about the whole situation. It was too easy; everything they needed to survive was here.

They could be forgiven for thinking that it was a deliberate plan. But how could it be? The wars were real and had been anticipated for many years!

The ocean delivered them here without human intervention.

After discussing the improbabilities of something like this existing and then the improbabilities of them being delivered here, they concluded that they were just damned lucky to have found this place; they could easily have been killed or washed through this place!

They agreed that they had come across the residence of a current or past race of people or civilization and were very thankful for it.

Realizing that they could be here for some time, they began the process of cleaning debris out of the remains of the net which was strung across the river. They were not really sure why they were compelled to do this but it gave them something to do.

Many things were found and recognized as items from their boats were caught in the nets including a few bodies; one was a child of four months, which caused immense grief to the young woman named Liz who recognized her precious first-born.

However, others believed that she was lucky to know the fate of her child. Many others could only hope that their missing children were spared the fate of living and finding themselves alone and fearful in the darkness of the tunnels.

Following the example of previous occupants, they collected and stored everything in the caves. However, Liz refused to deliver her daughter's body to the cave of corpses and instead took her to her bed.

The net had considerable damage and they discussed the possibility of repairing it by replicating the materials and method.

Lighting the first fire in the cavern was close to being a ceremony. Everyone gathered around and watched as the fire was started using indigenous methods by the friction of wood against wood to create a small flame in a nest of soft coconut fibre found near the large oven.

The first small fire brought tears to the eyes of some; it created a soul to the cavern, a central place of comfort. Everyone watched as the smoke slowly formed a slim stream and found its way to an exit hole in the top of the cavern where the rays of light also entered the cavern. The engineering feats of the cavern continued to amaze!

They stopped questioning and just accepted each new discovery and admired those before them who had created this refuge.

Although time meant nothing to these folk, they felt a need to record the days as they passed by. They began to carve a notch into the wall of the kitchen area for each day that passed.

Each day a group of people scouted back upstream in the tunnel to call and listen for more survivors. Over five days, four more individuals were discovered after having regained consciousness and being thus able to answer calls in the darkness.

An area was designated to act as a hospital and recovery area. Unfortunately, no one in the surviving groups had any medical

16

training so everyone was called upon to offer assistance and advice to care for the injured.

Broken bones were strapped into splints using wood selected from the wood cave and strapped with fine ropes from another previously found storage area. Open wounds were padded with seaweeds and clay scraped from the side of the cavern, and it didn't take long for the self-proclaimed healers to realise that whatever they did appeared to work. The injured healed very quickly and not one instance of infection occurred. While giving themselves credit for their new-found skills, they started to question their extremely good results.

At the next meal time, each person who had any injuries ranging from scratches and bruises to sprains and dislocations was asked to describe the healing process. Each person had a similar story. Initially, they all had thought the injury was significant but after a period of a few days they had assumed that maybe their injury was not as bad as they had first thought due to the quick healing time.

Their thoughts turned to the very well-preserved dead bodies in the cave on the storage side of the river.

Now they started to take notice of other strange things such as their food. No food appeared to develop mould, it just dehydrated.

They decided to keep a daily vigil on the body of a woman which was retrieved from the river as it was seen floating into the main cavern area. It was taken to the opposite side of the cavern and put into the cave where the other bodies had been discovered. They were thinking that it might dehydrate without going through the decomposing process.

After six weeks, a decision was made to stop checking upstream for survivors and they set about thinking about the future.

Everyone agreed that they were very fortunate to have been thrown into their current situation, which appeared to be capable of sustaining them all for a long time if not indefinitely. There was still a lot of doubt about their safety, however, due to

17

the fact that this was a sustainable environment with no obvious deterioration. This led them to think that sooner or later the rightful occupants might return and claim their home back. If this was imminent, what would be their approach?

Would they be friendly or defensive?

There did not appear to be any personal items in the main compound which could mean that the previous occupants had abandoned the cavern system and taken all personal effects with the intent of never coming back. There were no signs of any aggression or attack on the compound so they had to agree that it was a willing abandonment.

A decision was made that if they did return, the survivors had to be submissive and avoid any negative confrontation. If all negotiations failed then they would have to leave.

Due to this decision, a plan was conceived to send out scouting groups further downstream to seek out possible escape routes or eventually a way out of the system sometime in the future.

A plan was devised to set up packs of supplies for these scouts.

They would set off downstream and walk for as long as half the food would last then come back to the compound. This would ensure that they would at least have food to get them home again and the information gathered would be discussed.

After the first expedition, which lasted two weeks before the scouts returned, it was obvious that the task was going to be a long and challenging one. They returned with no enlightening news apart from that it was very dark and treacherous and they really had no idea about how far they had travelled. The lack of light made it impossible to gauge hours passed, so the time recorded in the main pavilion was the only way to measure that they had been way for two weeks. Distance was not measurable.

When they returned, the light in the cavern caused havoc on their eyes and one person was emotionally distraught. The perpetual darkness and uncertainty about their future became very real and unsettling on the nerves.

18

A map of sorts noting perceived ideas about obstacles encountered was created using charcoal and paint made from vegetable dyes onto cloth.

Again, this was guesswork in an unmeasurable timeframe.

The next group would need to take more food with the intent to travel further with the knowledge that fresh-water was constantly found seeping through the stone walls throughout the tunnels, making the carriage of water not necessary. This in itself would make the weight lighter, enabling more food to be taken and longer distances possible.

The next scout party included Dean and a group of companions—Tom, Michael, and Les, who had arrived on the same boat.

They said their goodbyes, anticipating a long time away, hopefully to return with good news.

The predictions about the dead body retrieved from the river appeared to be true. After four weeks in the cavern, no decomposition had happened. It was dehydrating extremely quickly and was preserved very well like the other bodies found earlier. This made it hard to determine how long the others had been there, as they all appeared to be at the same stage of preservation. Their clothing and decoration was the only difference between them, and without any written historical record it would be impossible to put an age or era on them. A person with archaeological knowledge in the group would have been helpful, but unfortunately this was not the case. This just added another unsolved question.

As they all settled in to a new way of living, having no idea at all about what the future might hold for them, everyone took it upon themselves to take on a role within the group which suited their particular skills.

Aida had already taken responsibility for the garden and had decided that she would not interfere with the ecosystem which had developed. She resisted the temptation to clean up and remove what she thought was rubbish. She took on a purely gatherer role and noted every day the different fruits and plants that

19

she discovered. This information was given to those who liked to cook and had taken on the chef role. She was delighted to find many plants that she knew and could not believe that plants such as aloe vera, burdock, nettles, and many varieties of mints and culinary herbs could thrive in these conditions.

The bladderwrack was aplenty as the tunnels delivered it from the seas. Tea was made every day utilising it as a defence against any radiation that they may have been exposed to.

The plants that she could not identify were dried, and Aida experimented using herself to note what effect the plants had on her. She first used teas as a skin wash, if it caused irritation the plant was put aside. If no irritation formed on the skin, she tasted with a drop on her tongue. She noted tastes and effects such as astringent and saliva promoting. If the tongue test was successful, she swallowed a few drops, which led to more drops, and then recorded the effect on her emotions, physical reactions, and if it was pleasing to taste. She asked her companions to take notice of her demeanour and alert her if she seemed to be reacting or behaving differently in any way.

If no ill effect was experienced by her, she asked for volunteers to undergo the same testing and noted the comments.

After many months, Aida had created a supply of plants for specific uses, both culinary and medicinal.

Now that they had some structure in their life, everyone became more relaxed and started communicating and socialising to get to know more about each other, trying to put their losses and regrets behind them.

The realisation that the ratio of men to women was about ten to four began to cause a few problems as the natural instincts began to emerge. The traumas that they had to suffer, favoured physical strength, thus the survival of more men was expected.

The men became restless with the prospect of never having the opportunity to have a partner. This restlessness was replaced with competitive traits as they started challenging group decisions

20

and others were forced to take a side, which caused opposing groups to form.

An older man named Arthur became very concerned to see this happening and decided to call a gathering to discuss what was happening.

Amidst a very tense atmosphere, Arthur called for everyone to put all negatives aside and give discussion a chance. He asked for everyone who had something to say, be given the opportunity to talk without interruption or retribution.

Silence descended upon them as no one wanted to be the first to complain.

Arthur started it off by pointing out the obvious good fortune that had befallen them by avoiding the fate of being killed or severely maimed if they had not taken to the sea.

A woman called Molly then found the courage to speak out.

"Yes, we are fortunate, but at night time when I think of my family and friends I left behind, I wish I was not here," she said. "Sometimes I wish I was dead, it would be easier than not knowing how they are and wondering if they suffered."

Another woman agreed. "I feel the same, Molly, but then I think of where we are. It's not real in here," she said. "I don't feel connected to that outside anymore, nothing here is familiar to me, and I keep thinking that I will wake up and I'll be home again and nothing had happened. It sort of makes it easier, do know what I mean?"

"Mm, it is like that," another answered. "It's like our emotions have been put on hold, let's hope we don't all release it at the same time, hey?"

"That could be messy," stated Aida as she giggled nervously.

Arthur then broached the subject of aggression and grouping, which was causing problems and had the potential to bring them undone.

"Come on, let's get to the nitty gritty and talk about it," he said. "Jake, what's your take on this? Talk to us, man."

21

"OK, but remember we can't run away from each other here if we don't get on with each other and you don't like what I say." He hesitated. "I'm a single man; I set out with everyone else with a boat-load of mates. Only six of us made it to here. We appreciate the grief and losses everyone is bearing right now, but we need to have an idea about where we go from here, you know?"

Another young man called Ron added, "Look, let's not beat around the bush here, but we can see that there are not many single females here."

Annie, a young woman who had lost her partner, interrupted him. "How can you be so shallow in a situation like this. All you guys are thinking about is your appendages!"

"Hey, I'm a man! That's just how it is!" answered Ron.

Aida noticed people getting up to leave the gathering.

"Stop, everyone!" she called. "Look at us; haven't we learnt anything from all of this?"

Everyone stopped and looked at each other.

Aida continued, "Here we are, our future is uncertain and we are arguing already. This is what brought us here!" She begged, "Remember how we came to be here!"

Again Arthur picked up the thread of conversation. "That's a good point. Arguing on a larger scale has brought about all of this."

Silence once again descended upon them as they all realised what was happening.

No one made eye contact. Jake finally broke the silence. "I think we need to nominate a leader." He paused. "Well maybe not a leader in that sense but we need some sort of order…"

He stopped talking and shrugged his shoulders, realising that he was promoting government. "Damn it!" he yelled. "We need something, but I agree we don't want to replicate what we left. OK?" he said impatiently. "If we have a leader as such, he or she will become a target for aggression and competition." He paused then added, "Maybe, hell, I don't know how we're going to do this!"

22

"I reckon we've made a good start here," added Arthur. "Everyone needs to tell what they're thinking like these guys have. It makes us think, and I may be wrong but I suspect that all of us know what we don't want."

"Yes, a bunch of bureaucrats making decisions for everyone else," someone said.

"Yeah, we need to do it better this time around," another person added.

"Well," a third person said, "we did something right by getting ourselves here, hope we don't blow it."

They agreed to call it a day but encouraged discussion and spontaneous gatherings to try to get everyone to have some input into their future.

As the weeks grew into months, they sorted themselves into compatible groups but made a concerted effort not to be reclusive as they still had central communal food and cooking areas. Daily chores such as reaping, sorting and storing debris from the nets, collecting food from the gardens, and laying out the excess to dry were taken on by those who gained some pleasure out of it.

Others took it upon themselves to care for those who had lost all their families or friends. Solitary children seemed to fit into a group very easily and were given enough space to have private moments when they needed to cry or just to sit silent.

The cavern was large enough to form a village-like atmosphere whereby anyone could walk along the pathways on one side of the river, cross over a swinging bridge to the other side, and return to their starting point in between meal sessions. Every day small changes were noticeable as everyone cared for their local space and maintained structures for sleeping and adding personal touches to their individual areas.

Many opportunities were provided in the main pavilion especially at meal times, for everyone to talk about their experiences and feelings about a new community structure.

As yet, no need for a leader or general hierarchy was mentioned and it was looking like none would be. Disagreements were quickly resolved as they ended up being positive things reminding them of the disharmony and non-compromising attitudes that led to their demise.

The second scouting group returned after eight weeks and they brought back no news of an exit to the tunnel and stated that they never saw any light.

The constant darkness had made them quite lethargic and unmotivated and they were happy to sleep and not mix with others for many days.

At the next discussion session, Dean suggested that he and five or six of the young men who were becoming increasingly restless should form the next group to go further down the tunnels than the last group. The younger men were very keen to join him and began preparing immediately. They planned to take as much food as they could carry and planned to push themselves as hard as they could.

None of this group had family or a partner to leave behind.

The day they left was full of different emotions such as anticipation, excitement, and also hesitation as everyone gathered to bid them farewell. As they disappeared into the tunnel, everyone was speechless and set their hearts on news about an exit would be forthcoming

As the sight of the fire in the cooking and dining hall made everyone feel safe and comfortable, a small group who had claimed the far end of the cavern as their home decided to build a stone hearth and light a fire with the hope of becoming more independent and lightening the burden on the main hall by cooking for themselves and creating comfort through the warmth of the fire.

They carefully constructed a hearth, collected debris from the firewood cave, and ceremonially began to create sparks by

24

friction. They cheered when the first small flame grew to fill the hearth with a glowing fire.

Everyone throughout the cavern cheered and laughed as the glow of the fire at the other end of the cavern added a new dimension to their enclosed home.

They stacked larger pieces of wood onto it and the flames leaped into the air as smoke swirled to the rooftop.

Their excitement quickly turned to fear as the smoke, having nowhere to escape, slowly crept across the roof and began filling the cavern. The grey blanket of smoke was slowly descending upon them and panic overcame them as the people in the higher areas of the cavern became overwhelmed by the smoke. They began coughing and gasping for air as they worked their way down to the lower areas.

In their effort to extinguish the fire, they caused more smoke by smothering the flames: the smoldering wood kept creating more smoke until it was completely extinguished.

The only smoke-free air was now on the lower levels near the river.

Everyone had gathered there and the silence was broken only by quiet sobbing and coughing.

It was night time so the lack of any light compelled them to stay where they were until morning offered some light to show them exactly what they had to deal with.

The morning light was dulled by the smoke, but it was possible to see that the area of the cavern where the kitchen and dining hall was had nearly cleared. Smoke was still seen forming a stream as it traveled to the hole where the light entered the cavern.

They sighed in relief and chatted as they climbed back to the kitchen area to get comfort from food.

They agreed not to light the main cooking fire for at least a day so that they did not add to the smoke problem.

The group who started the fire the day before began walking back to their abode but were stopped in their tracks when they saw that their end of the cavern had trapped a large amount of smoke which was still hovering close to the roof. It appeared that the cavern roof was considerably higher at that end and the smoke had nowhere to go. The pristine air in the cavern was now contaminated by the smell of smoke that hung over them.

Just two weeks after Dean and the boys had left, faint noises were heard which may have been aboveground. They wondered if the wars were still pounding the earth with extremely violent weapons. They felt uneasy and sad that the earth might be still taking a serious beating. The sounds were like dull thumping noises followed by grinding sounds. Everyone was feeling a bit nervous, worrying about a cave-in.

They talked about their worries with each other looking for reassurance that all would OK. They came to the conclusion this place had been here for a very long time and maybe many generations of people had lived here. Due to these facts, they settled down a little, believing that this place had survived so long and possibly many earth movements and they should be very safe here. It was a long day listening to the noises but they finally subsided and everyone felt much safer. As evening fell, they all looked forward to a good night's sleep.

However, during the dark hours, everyone was woken by the sounds of water rushing violently through the cavern. The noises were accompanied by large knocking sounds like heavy objects being tossed around by the waters.

No one moved. It was pointless with no light.

People were heard screaming in their beds.

They were the screams of fear of the unknown.

Fear of impending death.

After many hours of the same the knocking sounds stopped and the rushing water sounds lessened to a steady, smooth flowing sound of calm waters again.

No one spoke a word. The silence once again became intense as they lay awake, waiting for the first light to see the expected damage.

26

As the first ray of light illuminated the cave, they emerged and climbed cautiously out of their beds and crept to the edge of the river.

If the cavern and everything in it surprised them when they first discovered it, the sight before them now totally shocked them!

There, floating on the river, were many small and larger white objects of differing shapes.

"Icebergs, bloody icebergs!" stated Annie.

Icebergs, some the size of a large family car, were being carried through the cavern with the waters.

No one spoke a word.

What could they say?

"For crying out loud," exclaimed Aida.

They all sat and watched the curious pantomime.

"Look at that! The river is flowing in the opposite direction; the icebergs are going upstream, the river is running backwards!"

"Yes, funny, I didn't notice till you mentioned it."

Others joined in, "What do you think is happening? Anyone have any ideas."

"How can it go in reverse, the water has to go somewhere?"

"This is getting creepy," wailed Aida.

As they stood there watching in disbelief, the level of the water was lowering and the flow was slowing down until it eventually stopped.

"Look, it's starting to flow the other way again."

The icebergs had broken the nets across the river as they crashed through the tunnel system and they now began to float back down the river very slowly. Two larger ones seemed to be caught on something as they appeared to be very still.

Icebergs had a larger mass below the water line so the likelihood of getting caught on something underwater was very possible in here.

Someone ventured down to the edge of the water, reached out to touch one of the icebergs, and whispered, "This is ridiculous."

27

"Taking a guess, I'd say we are under the Andean Mountains of Ecuador or Peru. Maybe there was an avalanche or the bombing of the wars possibly broke off parts of a glacier and it was forced into the river. Our river," Will said.

"Must be a bloody big river out there?"

"Yes, maybe a frozen dam or lake of water was broken and the excess water and ice back-flowed up the river to here," suggested Will.

"Well, we now know that the river definitely surfaces somewhere…eventually."

A few gasped and looked at each other in horror.

In all the excitement of their morning surprise, everyone had forgotten about the group who had gone downstream to find a way out.

"Oh. God! What about the scout party?"

"They've been gone thirty-three days now. We just have to hope they had warning and a place to shelter," said Will.

"Maybe they are out?"

As they began to clean up once more and were pulling the remains of the nets out of the river, they found a large fish trapped in the nets, still alive. Everyone gathered round cheering in anticipation of having fresh meat for dinner—their first for many months.

It was a large fish with a pinkish color and its scales changed colors of blues, greens, and yellows as it moved about. It had a large flat head with yellow and black eyes. Its mouth was moving open and shut, gasping from lack of water as it was retrieved and dragged flapping in resistance onto the stone embankment.

Someone brought a long sharp piece of driftwood and started to hit the fish on the head. The fish was tough and defied death, kept on writhing about as it was pounded with the piece of wood.

Blood started running from its head as it continued moving about. The blood flowed down the embankment and collected in a small pool before overflowing and running into the water, turning it red.

28

A final blow killed it.

Nerves in the fish kept it twitching for a few moments more as blood continued to run from its head.

The cheering had stopped. Most people had never witnessed the slaughter of their food and were shocked by the killing of a creature trapped and unable to resist.

No one wanted to be the one to take the knife and cut into the flesh of the fish.

After a tense moment, Arthur spoke. "What have we done?"

"Reverting back to our old ways, that's what," said Molly. "Killing! When there is an abundance of food without killing defenseless creatures."

Arthur then moved toward the lifeless body, knelt down onto his knees and lifted the body and lowered it into the river. He stood up and opened his hands to show blood on his hands. He sighed and walked away. Some followed him while others sat on the embankment and watched the fish float off down into the tunnels.

No one ate that night. Their appetite had gone.

Nothing was mentioned about the incident again.

It was now four months since Dean and the boys had left to follow the river and guessing on their demise was the main topic of discussion. The general consensus was that they were killed by the iceberg flood but this was disputed by some. Their reasoning was that the river had flowed backwards and if the boys were caught in it, then their bodies would have been carried back to them with the icebergs.

It was during one of these discussions that the air became still and an eerie mood descended upon them as a gush of wind began blowing through the cave. The gush became stronger and delivered sounds like people whistling and moaning.

Suddenly, the wind turned into a vicious, menacing force accompanied by louder whistling and screaming as it forced its way into small crevices and holes as it entered and passed through with incredible power. Everyone ran for protection in the central hall of stone. It was coming from the ocean side from where they all arrived and blew through to exit through the tunnel where the river flowed. The force of the wind increased and became very violent as it swirled around the cavern, causing havoc by blowing down any structure which did not have a base of stone. Personal items were swept into the river and lost.

The sounds created by the winds travelling through the tunnels and forced through small exit holes were like wailing women.

As suddenly as the winds entered the cavern, they passed through and calm was restored.

However, the wind could still be heard as it made its way further down the tunnel and culminated with a terrifying sound many miles further. The screaming sound penetrated all through the tunnel and back to the cavern. It was a sound like a siren screaming at a very high pitch.

Then it was quiet.

Once again they had to clean up and rebuild sleeping huts. The only dwellings not affected by the winds were the original huts that were there when they entered the cavern. The previous residents had found a way to live with the forces of nature. Every time something happened here in the cavern, it was a very strong reminder that they were totally at the mercy of Mother Nature. They had to find ways to yield to her and redesign structures that offered least resistance to anything that she desired to throw at them.

Some decided to not rebuild, to live in an open arrangement instead. The darkness at night offered privacy so walls were not really necessary. The positive result of the winds was that all the accumulated smoke in the higher areas of the cavern had been blown out.

Once again, Mother Nature delivered a blow and followed it with a positive.

30

Discussions were many during the day as they tried to figure out the geography that would cause such dramatic reactions to the environment of their new domain.

The conclusions were that the river had forked, maybe where they crashed over a waterfall on their journey from the sea. Maybe it branched off at that point. This would explain why more survivors or bodies were not found after they were all thrown into the tunnels from the sea.

They could have been swept away into the other fork.

It would also explain the water from the night before going in the opposite direction. If there was a fork, the extra water could have been diverted into it, causing it to continue flowing; once the excess was dispersed, the river could revert back to its set path.

They were thankful that the waters had somewhere to go wherever it was. The other option was for the cavern to fill up with water and they would surely all have perished.

They also found that anything which was left on any of the lower levels near the river had been washed away with the flooding. This was a lesson to be remembered.

It was times such as these that thoughts turned to survival aboveground. Their knowledge of nuclear energy was minimal; however, most of them had done some research before setting off in their boats. They knew enough to give them confidence in the decision to stay underground for a long period of time. Reports gathered before the first blast was fired indicated that the planned long-term continuous blasts would possibly cause global fallout, and the targets would indicate that every country on the planet would receive direct hits on major cities and industrial plants. Some smaller countries would possibly be totally obliterated.

In the event of not knowing what happened directly above them at ground level, everyone agreed that staying underground for as long as possible would ensure survival.

This was confirmed one day as cries of despair were heard coming from the upstream end of the tunnel.

31

Everyone ran to the entrance of the cavern as the voices came closer. The waters eventually delivered four people, three men and one woman, on the remains of a boat hull. They flowed into the nets where ropes were thrown to them and dragged to the solid ground.

Two of the men had severe burns to their faces and hands and their hair was melted into lumps. They were taken straight to the upper area of the cavern to the area designated for the unwell. Aida harvested flesh from the aloe vera, poultices were placed over their burns, and the leaves of various plants, mints, kelp, and nettles were crushed and placed into hot water for ingestion.

One male and the female were traumatized and continued to cry and tremble until they were settled into the pavilion and comforted by the residents.

After many hours, they began to talk of their experiences aboveground.

They spoke of also taking to the sea but not until hopelessness had descended upon them after witnessing unharnessed destruction and death caused by continual bombing and cross-retaliation by the four major political countries. As they set to sea, they took aboard the two men who had received burns from being in direct exposure to a blast. They had been mesmerized by the sight of the forming of the mushrooming blasts which left them no time to take cover in a shelter nearby.

They told of massive amounts of water being vaporized by blasts over the sea. This caused heavy clouding and smog effects as the water particles collected and slowly descended, carrying radioactive particles down upon them.

They told of cities totally obliterated by direct overhead hits, buildings vaporized, and the dust being sucked up into the atmosphere, causing temporary darkness.

They told of small pockets of buildings and parks still standing as a result of being in voids on the extreme outer edge of blasts.

32

The woman, whose name was Amy, was sobbing as she described animals innocently going about their day unaware of what was about to happen to them. Of families locking themselves in their homes, listening to music and continuing with their daily routines knowing what the outcome would be but trying to keep the truth from their children, hoping that their fate would confront them after they had all gone to bed. They prayed for direct overhead hits to prevent prolonged suffering of their children.

She told of saying final farewells to her family members and of the panic and hysteria which was followed by calm acceptance by most people after the realization that there was nowhere to escape to.

She was heartbroken by not being able to convince her two sisters to accompany her and her fiancé Ben in their eighteen-foot launch and attempt survival at sea.

Ben was exhausted and only spoke a few words as he lay next to her and let her do the talking. He stated only his concern that they were more than likely contaminated by radiation and expected sickness and maybe death to overcome them.

A large pot of bladderwrack was brewing in the oven and fed to the four newcomers, knowing that it might be too late to prevent radiation sickness but in the hope of protecting them from increased damage. The bladderwrack was made into a tea and mixed with nettles and the bark from a vine with thorns shaped like claws. Aida had found it to be very effective for most toxic illnesses.

The news brought by Amy and Ben was devastating for everyone and confirmed the decision that they had to stay underground for many months or even years.

The silence was broken by Aida. "Don't be disheartened, Amy, ending up here maybe the best result for you," she said. "Amazing things seem to happen here."

Jake walked away and muttered, "More men, just what we need."

33

"I told you, Jake, you should have gone with Dean and the boys," said Aida. "You're just a misery to everyone here."

"They're probably dead too," answered Jake.

Aida shook her head and slapped her forehead. "Jeez, Jake!" she exclaimed.

Joel and James had been sitting for many a day with the dead, trying to learn more about them, noting differences between their appearances and clothing trying to get some answers. They decided that the dead had many things to tell if they could only work it out.

Joel noticed that a few of them had cords wrapped around their waists. Attached to these cords were many more strings and cords of varying thicknesses and lengths. These hanging pieces had many knots on them and some of the knots had pieces of colored string entwined through them. He removed a complete assembly from each of three bodies and laid them out on the floor so that he could have a better look at them.

Each waist cord was made of three lengths of sail cloth plaited together. On this cord there were many lengths of strings tied a finger's width apart from each other. They were similar, however, Joel noticed differences between them. Two of them had the same number of strings hanging from the waist cord but there were more knots on the older person's cord than that of the younger man in the same clothing.

The third cord, however, was quite different. It belonged to a person with quite different facial features and was much taller than the others. His cord had fewer strings hanging from it and the number of knots was much less, but it had more colors entwined in the knots. Day after day Joel and James went to study the cords to try to get some understanding about them.

Eventually they came to the conclusion that they were a record of time.

34

The two similar cords appeared to have one string dedicated to the age of the person. He assumed this because the last string on the cord of the older man had seventy-two knots on it and the same string on the cord of the younger man had thirty-four knots. Despite the dehydrated condition of the corpses, the age differences were still quite obvious.

The other strings on these two were similar and Joel decided that his reasoning made sense. His conclusions were that one string had six knots which could have represented days. The next string had three, this could have been weeks. The next string had eleven, maybe months.

The last knot was a bit of a puzzle as they both had fourteen knots but each knot was separated by a colored piece of string.

The third person's cord was quite different as it only had four strings.

Joel guessed that this one did not record weeks, only days between full moons maybe, and did not record his age.

The common denominator on all ties was a string with fourteen knots.

They returned the cords to the corpses but their curiosities were now running at full speed. James suggested getting help to gently move all the corpses to check if they had waist cords and compare the differences.

The following day they returned to the corpse cave with Liz, the mother of the dead child, and a young girl named Abby to assist. Together they moved each corpse and put aside those with waist cords. Amongst the one hundred and thirty-two corpses, Joel counted fifty-eight waist cords with knotted strings attached.

They all followed variations of the same scenario of what appeared to be recordings of days, weeks, months, years, and ages of the individuals.

The one common string was a string with fourteen knots, which Joel thought was the total number of years spent in the tunnels.

"Why is it fourteen years? Why not ten years or twenty?"

"That's not the only similarity," stated Liz. "There's their strange appearance too."

"So what is this telling us, there has to be a lesson for us here?"Joel said.

They stood silently, thinking.

"OK," said James, "let's call it a day and come back tomorrow to put them back in their places."

They turned to walk away but Joel hesitated and looked back at the corpses.

"What happens after fourteen years?" he mumbled, then turned to follow the others back to the dinner hall.

The following day, they returned to the corpse cave and Joel asked that each body be checked for obvious wounds or broken bones. This was done by removing the wraps on each corpse and looking for stains which might be blood, then running their hands over their limbs to detect any change in the bone structure.

None were found.

"OK," said Joel. "What killed them, any suggestions?"

They all shook their heads.

"Bit of a worry, isn't it?" stated Abby, who was getting restless with all the talk about dead people. "I'm going back you guys; I've had enough of this."

Liz and Joel were busy with the mystery of the bodies and waved a hand to Abby.

"If we stay in here longer than twelve years, we've got to consider leaving, I reckon," concluded Liz.

"You could be right," James said.

"What about radiation outside?" said Joel.

"We might have to risk it unless we can figure out what happens in here after fourteen years!" said Liz.

"Fourteen years is when this happens," James said as he waved his hand to the corpses. "Something might start happening sooner than fourteen years, this is the result."

They stayed in the corpse cave for a few hours more returning the cords to the corpses and thought and occasionally commented about the secret held by the corpses.

They finally agreed that they would not share their thoughts and conclusions with the rest of the tribe to avoid hysteria and fear of the future. They also agreed to be alert to any changes in the cavern as the months passed by, even though they had no idea what to look for.

"Where's Abby?" asked Aida when Joel, James, and Liz returned to the central cavern.

"She came back earlier, she got spooked with all the bodies," answered James.

"I'm here!" interrupted Abby.

"Where have you been?" James demanded.

"Just exploring," she said.

From that day on, Joel spent his days making his own waist cord and wore it constantly. Each morning upon waking he would record the new day and on the eighth day he would undo the knots and add one more knot to the weekly string. At the end of the fourth week he would undo those knots and add one more knot to the monthly string. These would then be undone after the end of twelve knots and added to the annual string. This way, at any time Joel could see how many years, months, weeks, and days he had been in the cavern.

He also translated the carved notches on the kitchen wall to knots on his waist cord.

James had noticed that Abby would disappear for a while each day, usually after their meal upon rising. He had asked her many times where she went but Abby always dismissed him with "Just around."

One morning as soon as the light arrived once more, James decided to keep an eye on her with the view to follow.

37

He watched her from a distance as she quietly walked to the rope bridge, crossed over the river and casually paused and looked over her shoulder every minute or so. When she reached the other side of the river, James quickly climbed up the ladder and rushed to the other side in time to see Abby disappear into the darkness of a minor tunnel close to the entrance to the large storage tunnels.

He hesitated when he saw how dark it was, but continued, knowing that Abby had entered here a few moments before.

He had only walked in darkness for maybe fifty paces when he saw a faint glow of light ahead. He slowed down and approached cautiously when he heard Abby singing softly to the tinkle of a musical instrument.

"Abby!" he called.

"Ah!" she screamed. "What are you doing?"

"That's what I am asking you? What's this?" James said as he gestured towards her.

Abby jumped to her feet. "Look what I found!" she said. "It's like a storage room for music instruments. I think this is a sort of xylophone and there's lots of other stuff."

The cave was lined with many instruments, most of which were made from wood but he saw a large white piano and many guitars, drums, whistles, and flutes, and many instruments that looked like they belonged in an orchestra.

"Whoa!" added James. "Did you bring the light?"

"Yes, it wasn't easy. I had to bring fiber and sticks and get it lighted in the dark but it gets easier."

"You want to be careful, Abby; the cave will fill with smoke like the big cavern."

"No, it's OK. See, the smoke is being sucked further that way, like this tunnel goes on somewhere."

"Mm, well, what are you going to do now?" asked James.

"I wanted to keep this to myself for a little while, but now I guess I will have to tell everyone," she said. "I wanted to learn a tune and just come out playing it as a surprise for everyone."

38

"So, can you play a tune?"

"Yes. Not too good, but OK."

"All right then, let's surprise them now," said James.

Abby sat quiet without answering him.

James smiled and said, "OK, you want to keep to your plan, don't you?"

"Yes, do you mind?"

"Nah, I'll go and act normal for a while. You come when you are ready."

Abby smiled and nodded her head in thanks.

It was moments before the evening meal was being served in the main pavilion that someone heard the melodic sounds of a small wind instrument.

James smiled.

"What's that?" Arthur said.

Everyone stopped what they were doing and watched as Abby slowly emerged from the tunnel on the other side of the river. She had made herself a long flowing garment using sail cloth and had tied many strings with stones and shells attached to it. Her long golden curls of hair were braided and intertwined with colored strings and shells, similar to the corpses.

As she approached the edge of the river, the flute music she was playing delighted and mesmerized everyone. They had not heard music for many months and the enclosed space in the cavern amplified the sounds.

No one said a word until she finished her tune. Abby laughed and said, "Da dar!" as she curtsied to everyone.

Many people cheered and clapped as others ran to greet her as she crossed the bridge.

"Where did you get that?"

"Where did you find the dress, it's beautiful," said another.

"Abby, tell them what you found," said James.

Abby laughed and continued playing the flute as she walked towards the main pavilion with everyone following her as if she were the Pied Piper.

39

"I found a treasure cave," she said. "It's a treasure of many beautiful musical instruments. There is even a big piano in there!"

"Where? Can you take us there?" said Arthur.

"I'll show you all tomorrow, it's getting dark now and it's even darker in there. We can take fire torches tomorrow," answered Abby.

Meal time that night was full of talk about the instruments and those with any musical talent gathered together around Abby to ask about their favorite. No one raised the subject about the origin of the instruments, how they came to be there. They had come to accept all the strangeness about the cavern and tunnel systems.

The discovery of the music cave lifted the morale and changed the whole atmosphere in the cavern as every day the sounds of music bonded everyone with singing and dancing.

Every person with musical talent found an instrument to suit their skills, and it did not take long before a group was formed. The music improved every day.

In anticipation of a move to the outside, they all agreed that they would not take the instruments with them but try to replicate the instruments using materials gathered from the river since their arrival. They did not want to take anything from the original stores.

As the weeks passed, many flutes were made using bamboo and hollow steel rods found in the storage caves.

Guitars were proving to be difficult only because the tools needed to work the timber were not available, but after many hours of slow chipping and grinding with stone instruments, the timber exposed its beautiful grains and required shapes.

Different-sized steel wires from the wrecked boats were retrieved to use for the strings of the guitars, but they anticipated many hours of experimenting to get the correct notes from them.

40

Hollow logs of many sizes and shapes were used to make drums. The time passed quickly with music and song now a major part of each day.

Fourteen weeks after leaving, Dean returned from the journey to find a way out of the tunnels alone.

He was greeted initially with great cheers but this changed after a few moments when his condition was realized. His face was lacking color and he had lost a lot of weight. He had difficulty talking due to extreme fatigue.

"Let the man rest," called out Aida. "He will fill us in when he's stronger."

"It's OK, Aida," stated Dean. "You need to know that we found the entrance."

Screams of delight abounded and everyone hugged each other.

He said that they had finally reached the entrance or exit of the tunnels but did not register much of what he saw as he turned to return immediately. He did this so that an accurate time of travel to the exit could be measured by the amount of days that had passed since leaving the group in the cavern. Due to the tunnels being in total darkness, the passing of time was only gauged by the amount of rest periods.

This would give the whole group a solid time frame to organize food if they planned to abandon the cavern in the future.

He told them that the boys chose to stay outside and set up a base camp somewhere near the entrance and survey the surroundings for resources.

Dean had not noticed any destruction but he did notice that the outside atmosphere had an eerie overcast appearance and was a little concerned about the boys if the overcast was in fact a result of some kind of nuclear fallout or contamination of some sort.

Dean did not recommend an exit at this time.

41

As the years passed by, the community had settled down and the days seemed to sort themselves out without too much hassle. Everyone had taken a role that suited their interests and capabilities. There was no room for lazy souls who wanted to let others cater to their needs. Being a closed society with nowhere to hide, these people were easily recognized and their lack of input was very conspicuous and was rewarded with the same—no food or consideration by the others. This appeared to be a peaceful way to resolve lazy issues as the person concerned would soon feel on the outer fringe of the community and pull themselves into line in order to be fed and included in activities.

However, there was an instance where a lazy one stole food from the kitchen. It was decided that if anyone stole from others, then others would go to the guilty person's abode and take whatever they wanted to compensate for the stolen goods.

As personal items were created by the individual, having it confiscated sent a strong message to the guilty person and they experienced the same pain that they inflicted.

The realization that even though they knew what type of society they wanted to be, human nature was proving to be a major element of disruption.

Many babies were born to both existing couples and new relationships, and no one was surprised when the births proved to be easy with no complications.

It was twelve years after their fortunate deliverance to the caverns that Tom and Micheal suddenly returned from the outside.

They looked very fit and healthy and were full of vitality.

They looked so good, in fact, that they had to describe details of the original entry to the cavern to convince everyone that they were indeed who they professed to be.

Tom and Micheal, however, were shocked to see their friends. Muscle atrophy and dehydration had given their skin a sagging, thin, and yellowish appearance.

They took Dean aside and asked him what had happened.

"What do you mean?" asked Dean.

Tom and Micheal looked at each other.

"Dean, sorry, mate, but you all look awful, you've deteriorated immensely."

Dean stared at them, not understanding.

He turned and walked away to sit on a shelf overlooking the river.

Tom and Micheal followed and sat beside him.

"Haven't you noticed changes?" Tom asked.

"You know, I have noticed that no one has an opinion anymore," said Dean. "We don't have discussions anymore, seems like there is nothing to say. I thought it was because we know each other too well now and we seem to be happy here."

After a moments silence Micheal said, "Is it happiness or complacency, you know, a sort of decline in mental attitude?" He took a step back fearing that his words may have disturbed him.

Dean stood up and looked at both of the boys. He then proceeded to walk slowly around the compound looking at their environment and his companions with a different point of view. He tried hard to remember what it looked like a few years ago.

Why haven't I noticed this before? thought Dean. Tom and Micheal were right. Faces had become hollow and empty— started looking like the corpses. He then acknowledged that they had lost their vitality and discussions on leaving the tunnels had ceased many years ago.

They had stopped creating new ways to use the food, so cleaning the nets became less frequent. One net was never put back into the river. Sorting happened less often and debris was permanently stacked on the edge of the river and not allocated to storage areas.

He couldn't remember the last time they had played music, sang songs, or danced.

He turned around and walked quickly back to Tom and Micheal. "How could this have happened?" he asked nervously. "We are dying without being aware of it!"

"Like the frog in boiling water," laughed Micheal. Tom nudged him to be quiet.

"Lucky we came back then, isn't it; it's not too late to get everyone out."

Dean stood silently, then added, "You're right, but how do we motivate them, I would never have noticed the change in us if you guys had not shown me."

"We'll talk to them," said Tom. "We made a difference to you so hopefully we can do the same to them. Come on, let's get things moving."

The sound of the bell ringing from the central compound startled everyone. They had not heard it for years and everyone became agitated but made their way towards the compound anyway.

"Hi, everyone, remember us?" said Tom.

If they did remember them, no one responded.

Dean stepped forward and said, "We're in a bad way, folks, you may not think so but...believe me; we need to get out of here. Look at me next to these guys. How do I look?"

A few people huddled together and whispered to themselves and covered their eyes, not wanting to be confronted.

"Look at me!" shouted Dean. "Please, look at what we have become; we have neglected ourselves, look at us!"

Suddenly Dean had an idea. He picked up a drum and began beating it as he sang a song that he knew used to bring joy to everyone.

Tom joined in clapping his hands and then Dean tried to sing but missed words as he tried to remember.

The first reaction was intimidation and fear as the tribe clutched each other and held their hands over their ears, hiding their faces.

Tom, Micheal, and Dean kept on singing and beating the drums until finally someone showed some interest and stood up and uncovered himself. Then a hint of a smile came over his face.

44

It became contagious as startled looks of recognition became smiles, and some even began clapping their hands.

At last, Dean knew that he had their attention and raised his hand to silence Tom and Micheal.

Dean's eyes became slightly weepy as he said, "Remember now?" He paused. "We need to get out of here; Tom and Micheal will take us out."

The mood had lifted but Dean could see that he still had a hard time in front of him.

He continued to try to talk them into leaving. Like him, they didn't appear to have noticed that their physical condition had declined and their mental attitude was still complacency.

In an attempt to get them motivated, he took them to the cave of the corpses and made them look at the corpses and themselves. The resemblance was remarkable and could not be denied that something was happening to them and they had not noticed.

Tom and Micheal stayed in the central compound where they collected many fresh fruits and vegetables from the gardens and began cooking a large meal. They used many aromatic herbs and seeds and let the food cook in open pots to encourage the smells to drift through the cavern.

As the crowd slowly returned from the corpse cave, Tom and Micheal continued singing as they stirred the food in an attempt to keep them stimulated and attentive. It appeared to have a positive effect on them. They began to chat amongst themselves and some began to arrange eating vessels and tools on the large stone benches.

Dean knew there was a turnaround when Aida began singing with the boys and added more roots to the large pot of food.

As the light was beginning to fade, Dean reinforced the idea of leaving and asked them all to anticipate leaving in a matter of days.

The change in confidence the following morning was unbelievable. Although everyone was nervous, there was also excitement in the air.

45

Tom and Micheal had breakfast prepared and plans were made for their exodus while enjoying the food.

After their hunger was quenched and discussions had given many a positive lift, Liz stood up with her dead baby's corpse in her arms and stated, "I am not leaving. I want to stay here with my daughter. I can't leave her here."

After a long silence, Micheal said, "Bring her with you, we can make a small sack to put her in and you can carry her on your back."

The woman smiled. "Can I?"

"She belongs to you; it's not for us to make that decision."

"Then, she is coming with me."

To leave the tunnels, they had to do a lot of preparation and planning.

Tom was worried that it would take a minimum of fifty days to reach the entrance of the tunnel, and food for this many people would be impossible to manage for that time.

"We need to plan for twenty-five days," he told Micheal and Dean. "We need to make food drops halfway out to feed us for the last half."

"I thought about that but I really don't think we can delay these people for that long," said Dean. "We've got to get them moving as soon as possible or they'll slip back into the stagnant mindset." He paused. "I know, because every day I have to focus on you two to keep myself motivated."

"Everyone will have to collect and carry their own supplies then."

"Mm...What if we measure by handfuls what an average person eats tomorrow then we take fifty times that much for each person and put it aside," said Tom. "We'll be able to see how much food it is and see how heavy it is."

"OK, sounds good," said Dean.

46

Dean explained the importance of the need to note quantities of food to everyone as they prepared the evening meal using only dried food and no cooking. They realized very quickly that fifty meals of dried food were going to be very heavy for many of the people to carry.

"This is only one meal each day," said Arthur.

"We can't take any more, Arthur."

"Yes, we have had it pretty good here. We've never had to worry about food."

"Yes, and the bags will get lighter each day."

"We will need the strong to carry some of the food for the weaker ones."

"The men of course!" said Jake.

"Not you, Jake," said Aida sarcastically. "He said 'the strong.'"

The decision was made to leave the compound in a week's time. However, a group of twenty-four people decided not to go.

"We are happy here, we have everything we need," one person said.

"I agree, why risk our lives following Tom and Micheal?" another added defensively.

This made Micheal very sad as he knew that they would slowly deteriorate further and join the fate of the cave's corpses. The closed environment of the tunnels that appeared to be a utopia had ended up imprisoning their minds, offering no exit door.

The pristine environment offered no challenges or obstacles. It was a lesson about human nature, which needed the stimulation of the unknown and unpredictability.

In the evening, those who chose to follow Tom and Micheal to the outside were busy making cloth bags to carry their food through the tunnel. It was recommended to have a long strap to hang over the shoulder and head to leave hands free for climbing if necessary.

At least one week was required to collect and prepare enough food for everyone and it also gave enough time for everyone to think about and prepare mentally for their journey.

Water was not an issue as the river was fresh and became more pristine as they got closer to the entrance.

Finally, the day arrived for them to begin their journey.

They all tied a length of rope around their waists, leaving a length about an arm's length long hanging free at the back. It was agreed that anyone who needed to could hold onto this length of rope attached to the person in front of them. This would offer reassurance and guidance in the dark journey to the outside. It would be easy to let go if the person in front fell or if two hands were required to climb over obstacles, but it wasn't long enough to be a hindrance to the carrier.

They said tearful goodbyes to those staying in the cavern and made last efforts to persuade them to join them.

The journey through the tunnel was frightening in the dark, and talk was encouraged to reassure each other. They traveled like this for many days in total darkness. It was impossible to gauge how many days due not only to the continuous darkness but also the many rest breaks they had to have as hysteria overcame a few and weariness demanded time for sleep. Most people were not eating much as they were not sure how long the food had to last them.

It was many days after they had begun this journey that someone up front indicated that light was ahead. Excited chatter began and they felt the air change to quite a chilly temperature.

Dean said, "It's too soon to be the entrance, I am sure it is too soon."

"Looks like you're wrong, Dean. There's definitely light ahead!" someone called.

They pushed on towards the light and eventually came across another large cavern with a large waterfall dropping in from a gaping hole above, washing over the rocks on the opposite side of the tunnel to join the river in its rush downstream. They could not see the sky but the hole was large enough to allow some light to reach the tunnel.

As their eyes became more accustomed to the surroundings, they noticed that the light was reflecting off large white masses sitting on rocks and ledges up in the hole.

"Ice?" asked Annie.

"Wow, we must be under a mountain!" Jake said.

"Yeah! A bloody big one too. It has to be huge to have snow on it!" said Annie.

"That explains our icebergs," said Jake.

"Doesn't explain how they got to our end," said Annie.

"Well, there could've been a storm up there that caused a breakaway; if there was more water coming through there than the river could cope with it could've ended up down here and back flowed up there," he said, pointing to the direction where they had come from.

"Smart arse!" Annie said under her breath.

"Oh! The old Annie is coming back!" said Aida.

Dean was puzzled by how he had bypassed this section. He remembered passing through many places with water flowing but they were in darkness. He then realized that if he had passed through these places at night time, he would not have known. This got him thinking about how many more places that were possibly habitable like their home back in the bowels of the tunnel.

He pondered on the unlikelihood of the timing of their arrival there. If it had been night time, would they have passed right through it? Would their fate have been different?

He felt very hopeful then that others may have found refuge in other caves if they had been fortunate enough to pass through them when the sun offered some light at the right time.

"This might be a good place to have good long rest," he said. "Do we agree?"

"I'd like to continue, just get out of here," said Jake.

"Me too," said Annie. "I'm getting edgy and feeling uncertain about ever getting out of here."

49

"I reckon we should go back to what we know, we were very comfortable and happy," said another.

"Happy? I guess we were but I think it was acceptance of a situation that had no alternative." Dean paused. "Yes, we were happy, weren't we?"

The others sat down mumbling. "Yes, why put ourselves through new obstacles when we know we don't need to. We have everything we need back there," said Annie.

"Not everything," muttered Aida.

"What do you mean?" snapped Annie.

Aida slowly turned to face Annie. "We didn't have a reason to get up in the morning."

Silence engulfed the group as everyone was torn between what they knew and the unknown.

Dean knew he had to tread lightly or there would be a major turnaround on their pushing forward.

"Look, I've been out and believe me, please, it is beautiful out there. Every day is different; it's a feast for the eyes and senses! I suggest that we push forward now and keep it open to going back if you think it's too much. What do you say; we can always go back if we don't like it."

Dean waited for someone to take the initiative and suggest heading forward. He looked at Aida, pleading with his eyes for her to get it going.

Aida could see deep concern in Dean's eyes. She remembered what he said about their appearances when he first returned and knew deep down in her heart that they had lost their zest for life. She looked around to the others who were sitting with eyes to the ground. *Yes,* she thought, *the tunnels were sucking the life out of us.*

She stood up and said, "I'm all for moving ahead, right now while we have the will to make our own decisions." She lifted her small bag over her head and settled it on her hip and stepped over the legs of people on the ground. "Come on, let's go," she said.

50

After a few tense moments that felt like hours to Dean, everyone followed Aida's example and rose to their feet.

Dean sighed with relief. It was then that he realized that no one could or would make a decision in their current demeanor so he decided not to ask for their opinions again until they reached the outside and had become accustomed the new environment. Hopefully, they would regain their zest for life and be able to communicate independently.

It was on the thirtieth day that the sounds of many feet stepping on wet ground were interrupted by a woman's screams of despair.

"My baby has gone, where is she, she's gone!" wailed Liz. "Please, has anyone picked her up?"

"What happened, Liz?" called Arthur.

"She's was here in my sack on my back, now she's gone," Liz said, crying. "We have to go back to find her."

"Liz, please listen. It is dark, we would not find her. She may have fallen into the river. Please, Liz!"

Liz fell to the ground and started feeling the ground all around her as she screamed hysterically. "No, I can't leave her!"

She continued to run her hands over the ground in the darkness and to everyone's delight she found her.

"Here, she's here. My baby, I thought I had lost you."

The sound of something falling into the river was followed by Liz's scream. "No, no. I dropped her. Please help me get her out of the water," she begged.

"Liz, the water is running very fast. Liz, she's gone. Let her go," Amy said.

The sound of Liz plunging into the river devastated everyone. She did not make a sound. She was gone in an instant.

No one commented. The long line of travelers in the tunnel turned in silence and continued walking. The long ordeal in the darkness had taken its toll on everyone and they had no emotions left to react to the tragic loss of Liz.

"How many days do you estimate we have to go, Tom?" asked Micheal, wanting to change the subject.

"I'm guessing ten, we are more than halfway," answered Tom.

As they continued their race against time, a familiar faint wailing became louder. Sometimes they would not hear it for many days but when it began again, it seemed to go on for hours, piercing the darkness and putting fear into the hearts of many. Some women cried, "It's Liz, she needs help!"

"It's the wind," Said Michael.

"We come all this way to get killed by something, great," said Jake.

"If something wanted to harm us, it's had plenty of opportunity before now," Annie said.

"It's the wind, I'm telling you," said Micheal. "I know. I've been here, heard it before!"

"OK, so how close are we then, seeing as you've been here before?" asked Jake.

"I didn't want to excite everyone yet, but maybe three days," Micheal said.

Those who heard Michael's answer reacted with happy screams and passed the information down the line. The tunnel became full of excited chatter.

"You better be right, mate," said Tom quietly.

"I hope so too," laughed Micheal.

Fortunately for Micheal, two days later a faint glow of light in the distance became brighter and gusts of air carried new smells into the tunnel. The slow walking became quicker and chatter became more animated as they tried to guess what was ahead.

The entrance was a revelation to many but the source of fear to others. The glare of natural sunlight on their eyes was unbearable and they had to turn away. A decision was made to retreat back into the tunnel and slowly expose them to the daylight. They headed back into the tunnel and set up camp at a distance where they could see the entrance at about two hundred steps away. Many wanted to return to the security

52

and comfort of their cavern, but Arthur placed himself on the narrow path leading back into the tunnels preventing anyone from passing. He guessed that after a day or two outside they would not regret the move. As the sun was setting, a few ventured back to the entrance. As darkness followed the last light up the valley outside, they emerged from the tunnel to stand in the open.

They stood for many hours watching the sunlight disappear. As the darkness enveloped the planet, others ventured outside, where they sat for many hours in the darkness taking in the sounds of the open air and gazing at the stars. The waters disappeared into the darkness below. The dark of the night prevented them from seeing how deep it was and what was beyond the cliff on the opposite side of the ravine. Not knowing what tomorrow had to offer, they decided that a good night's sleep was in order right now.

The following morning, when the fear had dissipated and excitement was aplenty, everyone jostled for a good position at the entrance of the tunnel to see what was presented to them.

They stood silent in awe of the sight in front of them. They appeared to be on a high ledge looking down into a deep valley where the waters were running very fast over rocks. A curtain of mist was being blown down upon them from a thundering sound of water falling from a great height above them.

Overhanging greenery was being tossed back and forwards as the waters scrambled over the rocks, finding a pathway downstream.

"Look there," someone said as he pointed to movement in the shrubbery. "A bird...no, many birds, look!"

Everyone watched as many small birds flitted in and out the shrubbery, scooping up small flying insects in their beaks making snapping sounds. They watched as the birds maneuvered between the shrubs and skimmed across the turbulent waters in pursuit of their prey. They seemed to know if another bird had sighted an insect as only one bird would pursue one insect; there was no squabbling. They changed direction with one flick of a wing and gained altitude with a quick flick of both.

Simple pleasures that the people once took for granted were now moments to stop and absorb. Children who were born in the caverns stared at the endless space and colors in front of them, finding it difficult to understand.

They wrapped their arms around the legs of their parents in fear of the feathered creatures they had never seen before.

The months following the first exit from the caves and tunnels were filled with discovering many new things and reconnecting with old memories of the outside. They made a temporary home in the ravine under the shelter of the overhanging cliffs. It gave them some comfort and familiarity having the rock walls and river close to them.

As the weeks passed by they were confronted with new challenges which were mostly related to their health. The pristine environment in the caverns had given them no reason to take precautions or care regarding their physical condition.

Sun burnt skin soon became a major issue, and Aida was occupied most days testing new plants and clays to use for these new ailments. Stomach problems were common as new plants and foods were found to be edible and consumed in large quantities. Wounds did not heal as quickly, and many of the group found themselves incapacitated for days after contracting lung ailments.

They soon found a new respect for their environment when they realized that the environment would now be their unpredictable dictator and they had to learn very quickly to be flexible and adapt to each day as it presented different challenges.

However, it did not take long before a new confidence was gained. Many of the refugees began exploring further from the camp each day, and talk about moving on began to be the topic each evening as everyone gathered around the central fire.

They all agreed to stay together as a group but would support anyone who wanted to go their own way at any time.

54

The restless young men were first to leave. They decided that they would be better off roaming as nomads rather than staying with the tribe with no prospect of having a mate.

Dean and Joel went with them but returned after seven days. They told of climbing a very large mountain and seeing an endless view of more mountains covered in snow: stretching as far the eye could see. They told of many large, woolly animals roaming high in the mountains and other animals such as a large yellow cat. A black bear with white patches on its face, many small birds, and a large black and white bird which moved over the mountains without moving its wings.

Encouraged by the prospect of seeing many animals and birds that they had never seen before, the group decided to venture out and begin a nomad life. Accidental loss of lives became more prevalent as they were confronted with challenges such as crossing large rivers and deep ravines. They learnt very quickly that the feelings of immortality in the cavern, were now replaced with vulnerability.

The sharing of information relating to survival skills, food and plant medicine was now made a priority. They learnt to watch and listen to the environment, the animals, birds, and insects and learnt a new way of living in partnership with the earth.

Pachakuti ... then history began again

Hundreds of years later, the surviving humans had slowly adapted to a hostile atmosphere and increased the species to small tribes scattered across the land. The deformities and illnesses inflicted by the wars were few and far between as the years of generations had overcome their heritage.

The tribes learnt to survive in their new environment and used the knowledge gained in their lives before their fortunate arrival in the tunnels to attempt to build a future based on preservation of their environment.

As the originals grew old and passed away, their descendants adopted the traditions laid down by their elders. Some moved away from the tribe and formed their own societies.

One such tribe dwelt in a mountainous land fed by streams of freshwater from the snow-capped mountains.

Their philosophy of life was one of gratefulness and gratitude to the earth for supporting and feeding them; they believed waste was an offence against the earth itself. Each day was one of striving to fulfil the physical needs of the tribe and as each decade passed it became easier by managing the harvesting of the fruits of the land and never staying in one place for more than two years. They had learnt that the earth needed time to recover from the constant habitation of humans.

They remembered the stories told by their ancestors: stories of the hard times and were very aware of the fickle nature of man and the destructive power of ambition. They were an intelligent people and taught each generation the knowledge which would reward them most. They learnt the magnetic forces of the planet and indeed the universe by studying each day with its own unique set of vibrations and planetary lineage. They studied every plant in their path and treasured them for the gifts of food, medicine, warmth, clothing, and shelter that they provided. Their dwellings were conical structures based upon an ancient indigenous race of people from a great northern country. Heavy poles of timber were leant up against each other to form a large, hollow circle, and then covered with smaller poles, grasses, and mud, which made them surprisingly weather resistant and very strong.

As the years passed by and people were venturing far beyond the village, more information relating to the previous existence of the earth was being found as they crossed old sites in unexpected places and discovered time capsules buried under stone beacons. These capsules yielded much incredible information confirming the need to resist the lure of mechanical inventions and changing the ways of nature.

However, it was during the travelling far and beyond that they learnt of other tribes, some of which were developing aggressive traits and were pursuing the excitement of plundering nearby tribes for easy provisions. It was for this reason that the precise location of village sites was never discussed openly; neither were the size of a village and the availability of food and shelter. Contact with other tribes was not pursued, but sightings and locations were noted by the elders, who chose not to share this information with others.

The oldest people held the most honoured and revered position in the tribe. The accumulated knowledge and experiences

58

of these people were considered tribal treasures and were drawn upon for daily decision making.

One such person in a remote village was a woman with wisdom way beyond that of anyone before her. It was said that the earth had delivered the gift of ancient knowledge and energetic powers to her during her encapsulation in a frozen glacier.

She was only eighteen years of age at the time and had slipped and fallen into a deep glacier. Her survival was described as a miracle by some and as unfortunate to others who believed that the physical deformities inflicted upon her by the moving ice would be impossible for a person to bear.

The moving glacier delivered her frozen body from the mountains as the spring warmth melted the ice in the lower sections. A group of food gatherers spotted her blazing red hair in the melting ice of the glacier thinking it was a frozen animal, whose bones they could utilise to make useful items. As they chipped at the ice, they realised that they were looking at a grossly deformed human body, which they gently retrieved and placed on higher ground. They proceeded back to the village site with the intention of returning a few days later when the body would have defrosted and a passing ceremony for the body could be conducted.

Upon their return, they were astounded to see that the body had not begun the process of decomposing—the person was alive and the remains of cloth on the body had slipped away, revealing a broken female form.

They formed a human stretcher by joining arms under the body and carried it back to the village. The elders took her aside and cared for her with the expectation that complete recovery would not be attained. As the women washed her down, the full extent of her injuries inflicted by the movement of the glacial ice soon became more obvious.

Her face was distorted in such a way that her nose was flattened and pushed to the right side so that it appeared to be under her right eye. This in turn had dragged her mouth up on the left so that her mouth had a perpetual smile. Her skin was scarred and rough, but a small section of her face which included her eyes had been spared and appeared to be smooth, young skin as soft as silk. Her remaining patch of hair, which was as red as the setting sun, hung from the right side of her head in various lengths almost as if it had been chopped off in clumps.

One of her legs appeared to be considerably stunted in growth and thicker but otherwise not damaged. She was missing three fingers on one hand and the nails of the remaining finger and thumb had been pushed back to the first joint. Most of her abdomen was scarred, and lumps of calcified bone, which indicated a legacy of broken bones, were obvious under the skin.

The healing process was long and painful for the woman and her screams of agony pierced the air night after night. After three long weeks of slipping in and out of consciousness and never opening her eyes, the screams subsided, and she slipped into a deep sleep. Everyone in the village took turns sitting with the small, fragile frame of a woman and dripping fluids into her mouth.

It was at this time that the oldest person in the village, a man named Tsulib who was a descendant of originals from the caverns, Aida and Jake, made the decision to contact a tribe of women referred to as the Misha, who were renowned for the powers of healing. Tsulib was reluctant to do this as he knew very well that there would eventually be a price to pay and the price would be great.

No one had ever seen the home of the Misha, and indeed it had been said that they may have been nomads moving with the winds. Only a few had seen them and then only a glimpse of movement in the forests and always under the veil of darkness. However, they always answered the call for help, which was transmitted by the burning of the grey ghost weed commonly called blue sage. Thus, as darkness enveloped the day, a fire was lit and as the flames died down, a bundle of grey ghost was placed upon

60

the coals and left to smoulder as everyone continued with their chores and retreated to bed.

The dawn was broken by anxious screams declaring that the ice woman has gone.

And so it was: the Misha had answered the call and tears flowed silently down the cheeks of many as they wished their mysterious guest strength and courage in her time of healing.

Yondalin

Tsulib was quite concerned about his son Yondalin's apparent lack of interest in leaving his wild adventurous youth behind and choosing a life partner. He was a young dynamic man who was raised without his mother, who died when he was a child. His dark hair and eyes combined with his brown skin was a constant reminder to Tsulib of the beauty of his wife. Yondalin was tall with a solid build like his father, and his courage and zest for life was contagious. He was very aware and a little embarrassed by his affect on the young women who adored him.

A young woman by the name of Sinai held a special place in her heart for Yondalin and had denied the attentions of others in the hope of becoming a permanent partner to him. Yondalin knew of her affections for him and felt unhappy that he could not return the same.

Yondalin filled his days with improving his skills on the back of his close friend and companion, a horse named Hepsibarb.

She was a beautiful animal who had grown with Yondalin from the time he was a boy. She had grown very close and protective of Yondalin, almost like a mother who never left his side and would come between him and any danger. Together they were one mind, anticipating each other's thoughts and understanding each other's body language. Words were not needed between these two souls. She was a magnificent creature of many hands. Her color was a golden chestnut which glowed in the sunlight, and her mane was long and flowing in a color like the rising sun. She was equally as proud of her beauty and power, just like Yondalin. No matter where Yondalin went, even a distance of twenty paces, she followed alongside him and constantly kept in physical contact by gently touching his arm. She instinctively knew how he was feeling and what he wanted to do and willingly offered her back to him to share in games of racing with the wind.

The Misha

The Misha were a product of the great wars which ravaged the bodies of a group of traditional land owners. The toxic fall-out resulted in the rearranging of their DNA helix's, which settled down after many generations of painful evolution to the current status. They were a female race, very pale of skin with a golden hue about them. Their skin appeared to melt into the atmosphere without a clear defining line to separate them from their surroundings. Their hair of the same color was literally alive, independently swirling and caressing their shoulders like a veil even as they stood still. They were very similar in appearance, their pretty faces without blemishes or distinguishing features. When they spoke, their voices were slightly louder than a whisper but each word was very precise and clear. Their need for food was very minimal as they could draw the majority of their nutrition and water from the atmosphere through their skin.

The clothing of the Misha was made from very fine threads of yellow tones made from the silk of silk worms and webs of the spider, making them soft and flowing, moving with the slightest breath of wind.

The perception of the Misha was that of femininity, gentleness, and fragility. The underlying truth was much different as these women had the ability to reproduce themselves without a partner but only in the face of extinction.

This was a result of changes to their DNA which caused the addition of a Bdelloid Rotifers organ that located itself just on top of the left kidney.

This organ could release partner chromosomes, causing the creation of a genotype.

This made them totally independent, not requiring other people, not needing another person's attention for survival of the race.

They lived by practical, uncompromising conventions which did not allow for emotional intervention.

Their relationship with the earth was mystical. Their accumulated knowledge of the medicinal values of all plants made them a sought-after race in times of illness. They were very willing to assist with physical and mental disturbances with the body but were not negotiable with if betrayed. Swift retribution was delivered without debate or compassion.

Each month at the time of the full moon, the Misha were re-energized by ceremony and celebration. This was their most powerful and playful time and not a time for others to communicate with them or ask for favors.

The Misha still had a compassionate side to them, however; they would not hesitate to nurture sick or injured creatures, including humans. However, if the injury or illness was such that a satisfactory recovery allowing complete integration with their life could not be achieved, then a gentle merciful application of a fatal herbal decoction would be administered without hesitation or consultation.

Their mode of travel was by using the magnetic grids of the planet. The energy of these grids had been severely disrupted and amplified by the wars, making them extremely powerful and capable of stopping passage through them in some places. The Misha had learnt how to ride these power grids to enable them to travel long distances in a few seconds.

66

Training to use these grids was very hard and many Misha were lost, never to be seen again by not learning to dismount correctly. Training was always done on a one-on-one basis with an experienced flyer strapped together tandem style. The grids moved at extremely rapid pace, so fast that the Misha could move from one place to another virtually unseen. It took many years to perfect the mounting and dismounting of one of these grids.

Kettiajya

No one knew where she came from or where she went for months on end without sighting.

Kettiajya had always been a loner, happy to be free from all the trappings of relationships and obligations. There were rumours that she was a child of the rivers and returned to the rivers when in need of revitalisation. It was said that she headed north to a place where two rivers joined and disappeared into the waters at a place close to a waterfall which fell from the heavens. From this place Kettiajya's mentor and guardian was in full view, framed by the high valley walls. Veronica was a beautiful mountain capped with snow. She changed moods with every hour of the day. She had always been there for Kettiajya to comfort and soothe her and was ever ready to answer her calls.

Kettiajya was content to roam with her sole and constant companion—her horse, Paterson, a magnificent ebony-coloured stallion. It was rumoured that he had rescued her from a flooded river after she had been ejected from caverns below the rivers and washed downstream into the rapids when she was very young. He entered the river and put his body in her path as she was washed down the rapids, offering her his mane to grasp, and dragging her out of the water. He laid next to her, giving the warmth of his body to comfort her in her distress. They wandered the mountains together and the bond between them grew. She learnt to ride on his back and let him carry her to new places, but they never let themselves be seen by other inhabitants of the mountains until a time when she became ill.

Paterson knew of the healing powers of the Misha, who always assisted with sick animals who crossed their paths, and carried the delirious Kettiajya to them. He watched and stayed close as they took her to a sweat lodge and began to infuse the inside with steam and aromatic plants and fed her concoctions of plants. After many days Kettiajya finally recovered, and she befriended the Misha who allowed her to mingle, watch, learn their ways, and join in the full moon traditions of the tribe. She became adept at the use and knowledge of the plants by assisting with the healing of people brought into the domain for special treatments. One such person was the ice woman from the tribe of Tsulib. Kettiajya built up a strong friendship with this strange woman during her long road of healing and repair and came to know that she brought many mysteries from the glacier. When it was time for the glacier woman to leave, the Misha presented her with a basketful of odd pieces of cloth and plant materials.

"You'll need something to wear, woman, make yourself something from this," said the Misha as she dropped the basket at her feet.

Kettiajya watched as the ice woman lifted pieces from the basket.

"And what am I supposed to do with this?" mumbled the glacier woman. "There's nothing here large enough to make anything!"

"Will you let me?" asked Kettiajya as she reached for the basket.

"You a magician are you, mm?"

Kettiajya laughed. "No, but I think I can make something pretty special just for you from all of this."

"Please yourself. I have to wear something."

70

Kettiajya took each piece out of the basket and arranged them into colour, size, and textures. She then walked into the cloud forest and picked a handful of long thorns from a palm tree. Using one thorn, she punctured the thicker end of the other thorns to make a hole. She then went into the valley below the cloud forest and, pulled reeds from the river's edge. She took two flat stones. She dragged the reeds between them, forcing the soft tissue to be squeezed out from the tough tubular reed. She then pulled the husk of the remaining reed apart, making long, fine lengths of husk.

As she found her way back to the Misha camp, Kettiajya threaded the thin lengths of husk through the hole in the palm thorns, ready to commence her task of making a garment for the glacier woman.

She sat for many a day and night stitching the pieces together, being mindful that the ice woman's body was very deformed and any clothing could severely impair her movement.

When the robe was completed, Kettiajya entered the lodge of the ice woman and offered it to her and asked her to put it on. She knew the ice woman well enough to know that she would find something wrong with it.

She was correct.

As they both sat on the ground while Kettiajya made the requested adjustments to the robe, Kettiajya dared to ask the ice woman about her memories of her time before the glacier accident.

"I don't think it was an accident," she said.

"What?" cried Kettiajya.

"I was pushed by someone."

"Why would someone want to get rid of you?"

For the first time since knowing her, Kettiajya had a glimpse of a softer side of this ice woman as she dropped her head and turned away. She was silent for a long time and Kettiajya gave her the space to recover.

71

"I was in love," she said. "Can you believe that, I was in love with a beautiful man who loved me too?" She laughed like she couldn't believe it herself. "Yes," she continued. "His mother and my mother had an ongoing mutual hatred for each other and I am sure his mother arranged for me to disappear."

"What do you remember about that day?"

"I was digging a plant on the edge of the glacier high in the mountains and I felt someone push me. I remember falling but that is all."

Kettiajya put her arm around the woman's shoulders.

"He was beautiful," she continued. "I heard his song!"

"His song?" asked Kettiajya.

"Everyone, every animal, every plant has a song in their heart, Kettiajya. A special song. It is a song which no one else will hear unless you choose someone very special with whom you want to share it. When this happens, the message you want to impart will be felt. Children learn their mother's song within the womb but quickly forget it once the challenge of survival outside the womb begins. As the child grows older, he yearns for the song which he instinctively knows exists but remembers not from where it comes."

Kettiajya stared at the ice woman and after a long pause said, "You know, I think I knew that, but I did not know that I knew until you spoke the words."

The ice woman sat, silent, relieved that she could finally talk about the incident with someone.

"We all know much more, Kettiajya; we just need a trigger to awaken the memory. There is so much to be reminded of."

"I understand now that you have said it," said Kettiajya. "Thank you for saying the words."

"Yes, well," said the ice woman impatiently, a little embarrassed that she had exposed her vulnerability to Kettiajya. "Enough of that, I have to go."

"Go where?"

"Just go," she answered. "Tell the Misha thanks from me." And without another word she was gone. Kettiajya watched her

72

disappear in a cloud of multiple colours, her robe swishing from side to side as she moved down into the valley towards the river. Kettiajya smiled and felt honoured with the trust that the ice woman had placed in her. As she finally lost sight of the ice woman, Kettiajya also felt the need to move on.

Kettiajya never stayed for long periods with the Misha, and such was the nature of the Misha that they were never curious about her destinations. After becoming accustomed to being alone and giving up her search for some answers to her existence, Kettiajya settled into a nomadic life, roaming the mountains and following the rivers to see where they took her. She encountered many small, scattered tribes and would spend days at a time observing them and learning their daily routines and rituals of living. She saw the conflicts between individuals, she saw the fun and games they had, the celebrations when new life was brought forth and the sorrows when death of a tribe member occurred. Still, she was never tempted to join any group or approach them for companionship. Her intimate connection with the earth, the plants, and the animals was enough to nourish and stimulate her. It was on a journey such as this that Kettiajya and Paterson came upon a tribe nestled high above a river between two large mountains. They settled in to do their favorite pastime, which was observing different tribes and their daily rituals.

Kettiajya dozed off in the warm sun and didn't notice Paterson wandering closer to the tribe where a few horses were grazing.

He was exchanging calls with a magnificent golden chestnut lady horse that had a long flowing golden mane. As he approached her, she walked towards him and greeted him with a cheeky nip on his neck. It was love at first sight for both of them.

Yondalin was heading back to the tribe from the river and saw his horse with a beautiful ebony stallion. He was tall and proud and obviously taken with Hepsibarb. He climbed up onto a large mound and sat watching them with a smile on his face.

So, he thought. *Hepsibarb was not the iron lady I thought she was.* She had always shunned the attentions of the opposite sex and he was concerned that he had humanized her to the point that she wouldn't recognize herself as belonging to the tribe of horses. He watched as she followed the stallion halfway up the mountain where they stopped, and the stallion showed her a delicious clump of clover which they shared.

Kettiajya was woken by the snorting of the two horses. She slowly raised herself to sit and watch them.

"I like your choice, Paterson!" she said quietly. "She is very beautiful."

The mare was startled at the sound of Kettiajya's voice and quickly raised her front legs as she jumped backwards. Paterson snorted and moved to her side and nuzzled against her neck reassuring her that Kettiajya was his friend. The mare settled down again and resumed eating.

Yondalin wondered what had startled his precious friend but was happy to see the stallion looking after her.

He did not see Kettiajya, who was concealed well behind the plants.

Paterson and his lady wandered over the mountainside together for a few hours, sharing grasses and seeds, and eventually found themselves on the perimeter of the campsite.

Yondalin took the opportunity to approach them but Paterson was reluctant to go any closer. The mare walked back to him and butted her head against his as if to say, don't be shy. Yondalin understood his hesitation and stopped moving towards him. He stood admiring this very impressive horse whose coat was like polished ebony, and who stood very tall and proud.

Kettiajya stood to see where Paterson had gone. As she looked down to the campsite, she saw him with the mare but a man had joined them. She panicked for a second, hoping that the man was not trying to secure him. She recognized Paterson's demeanor and realized that he was in complete control of the

74

situation and was relieved when he tossed his head and turned to trot back up the hillside.

The mare turned to follow him but stopped, changing her mind.

Yondalin walked to her and put his arms around her neck. "Don't worry, Hepsi, he'll be back sometime. I can guarantee it," he said with a knowing smile on his face.

Kettiajya stayed out of sight and Paterson went to her shaking his head up and down and snorting. She giggled, stroking his mane.

"You cheeky devil, I suppose we'll have to hang around this area for a while now, will we?"

Paterson snorted and thumped his front foot on the ground in excitement and quickly turned and galloped at full speed over the ridge willing her to follow him, which she did.

They stayed in the area for many days before slowly putting more distance between the camp and them. Paterson, however, would disappear each day at sunset and not return until just before sunrise.

Kettiajya was hoping that he would eventually choose to follow her again and resume their nomadic life. She was not happy to stay long here. She had seen other tribes slowly extending their journeys to these distant lands, which had always been inhabited by only a few tribes who were very scattered and had never become aware of any other tribes. She sensed that if they were to meet, there could possibly be times of unrest as she had seen before.

After many weeks, Kettiajya decided to begin moving on without Paterson. Her heart was very heavy when she said goodbye to Paterson at sunset as he headed off on his daily visit to his lady. She wanted him to go with her but she knew that like her, he was free to do whatever he wanted to do. Paterson stood and watched as she gathered her few belongings and began walking in the opposite direction. He ran to her and nuzzled against her arm and whinnied.

"When you are ready, mate," she said as she wrapped her arms around his neck. "You'll find me easy enough."

Yondalin was happy to see the large ebony stallion every night knowing that Hepsibarb was very likely to be in foal. He didn't worry about this as he thought that the stallion could possibly stay permanently as he had mixed with the other local horses and had allowed Yondalin to get close enough to stroke him. As Hepsibarb's pregnancy grew longer, Yondalin was hoping that the black stallion might offer him his back. He was delighted to notice that after many days, the stallion did not disappear at dawn; he stayed all day with Hepsibarb. He did not look totally at ease being there all day and constantly galloped to the top of the mountain and looked to the south.

Yondalin felt that he was torn between staying and leaving.

You have another love, don't you? Yondalin thought.

As the days passed by, Hepsibarb was beginning to get agitated and moody and behaving badly toward the stallion, nipping and biting him if he approached her. Yondalin's heart became heavy as he realized that the stallion was being driven away by Hepsibarb and realized that it confirmed his thoughts that she was indeed pregnant.

One morning after rising from bed, Yondalin approached the horses as they grazed nearby and saw the stallion receive a savage bite from Hepsibarb, leaving a bloody wound. He trotted off toward the river with his tail held high and galloped away out of sight.

Yondalin walked over to Hepsibarb. "No use for him anymore, is that it?"

Hepsibarb ignored him and continued to graze.

Kettiajya was lying awake looking at the stars when she heard the familiar rhythmic sound of Paterson's trot approaching. She jumped to her feet and ran along the ridge toward the sound, which increased to a gallop as Paterson sensed Kettiajya's

76

presence. When she saw him she lunged forward and wrapped her arms around his neck, crying with happiness.

"Paterson, boy," she whispered. "I've been lost without you. I'll never leave you again."

She began to sing to him as she clapped her hands and danced around him, compelling him to respond by turning in circles in sync with Kettiajya.

The following morning, Kettiajya noticed many bite marks on Paterson's neck and rump and concluded that he had been dismissed by the mare. When she touched the bite on his neck, Paterson twitched and pushed her hand away with his head. She led him to the banks of the river and searched for a clay patch. She used her hands to dig until she found clay the color of the palms of her hands, a soft, pale, rose colour with a sticky consistency. She took a handful and with Paterson's permission, packed it over his wound and picked two large leaves off a plant of comfrey and stuck it onto the clay, completely covering the wound.

She stood with Paterson with her hands on the poultice until it dried out enough to form a crust that gripped onto his hair.

"There you are, my boy, it'll feel much better in a day or two and you will know when to remove it."

Many moons after the incident with Hepsibarb and the stallion, Yondalin was certain that Hepsibarb was indeed with foal. He was happy for her but a little sad for himself.

He thought that once she was a mother, he would no longer be the centre of Hepsibarb's life.

77

Return of the Ice Woman

As the evening sun began to meet with the horizon, the sound of children's excited screams became louder as they drew closer. The words "Nuembla, animal nuembla, animal nuembla!" were shouted as they ran into the protection of the camp. Parents ran to their children in anticipation of an imminent danger, knowing that the word *nuembla* indicated an unknown factor which must be assumed as dangerous until otherwise decided.

Tsulib quickly approached the children and asked for more information about the nuembla.

"Something was following us, Tsulib! It was an animal thing, half walking on two legs and bouncing along very fast. It was just there! Quick, run and hide!"

The children were gathered quickly and moved to the central area as everyone gathered in preparation for the nuembla. As they waited, they heard unfamiliar sounds of an animal moving. One heavy thump was followed by two quicker, softer thumps which became slower as it grew close to the perimeter of the cleared camp area.

Then it stopped! The silence was heavy and weighed upon everyone's hearts as they waited for a glimpse of their unknown opponent.

Everyone's eyes were glued to the spot where a slight rustling noise accompanied by a sound like something dragging was approaching.

A glimpse of a shape and many colours slowly began to emerge from the trees enveloped by the subdued light of dusk.

Suddenly, the form of the nuembla moved very slowly into the open compound and stopped in a spot where the last rays of the setting sun shone through the open spaces of the trees.

Quiet astonishment overcame all present as they took in the being which had presented itself to them.

Here was a form similar to them but the multi-coloured clothing draped over it camouflaged the true shape. Only the face and hands were visible under the hooded robe. The hands were very visible and displayed grotesquely misaligned features on the face framed by very long, shining clusters of brilliant red hair which appeared to be planted randomly on its head.

As Yondalin stared, he smiled as he recognised the woman whom the children referred to as Icemon, the ice woman who was rescued from the glacier and taken by the Misha.

He slowly moved towards her.

Tsulib grabbed his arm to stop him but Yondalin gently removed his father's grip and smiled at him, indicating that it was not a threat. As he approached the woman, she stood firm and only her eyes moved as she watched him approach.

He stood an arm's length from her, offered his hand to her, and said, "Welcome back, Ice Woman.'

She responded by reaching out, exposing a hand which was grossly disfigured, and returning the firm hold. They stood looking at each other for quite a while and then the ice woman drew Yondalin closer to her and wrapped both arms around him. Yondalin was consumed by a feeling of deep comfort and reconciliation by this woman but could not understand why. He pulled away, taking her hand, and stood next to her facing the gathered people.

"Don't be afraid," he said. "This is our friend from the glacier."

80

Silence once again descended upon the group and was broken by Tsulib, who started humming a welcome tune and clapping to the beat. Everyone joined in and Yondalin noticed a tear slowly formed in the ice woman's eyes.

When the singing stopped, the ice woman approached Tsulib and spoke for the first time in controlled and very clearly pronounced words. Her voice was that of a young woman, which appeared to be out of place with the figure she presented.

"Thank you, Tsulib…"

The gathering cheered upon hearing her words and rushed towards her, eager to ask many questions.

Yondalin interrupted. "Please be patient. Tomorrow we will talk, tonight is for celebration."

"Thank you, Yondalin…You are just like I thought you would be."

Yondalin hesitated before saying, "You know my name?"

They stood looking at each other in silence until the ice woman smiled and squeezed his hand. "Come, show me the way."

Suddenly, the moment was broken by a violent gust of air moving through the compound. It stopped as quickly as it started.

Tsulib knew it was the Misha returning their patient and he acknowledged them with a handful of blue sage plant thrown on the fire, knowing that they would return one day to demand reimbursement.

As the days went by, the ice woman became less of a curiosity to everyone and the children had asked all their curious questions and taken her to the place where they had found her in the glacier. She asked to be left alone at that place and not to be disturbed no matter how long she was there.

Hours drifted into days but she was left alone with a silent guard watching over her from a distance.

Finally after five days, she joined the village, none the worse for her ordeal.

She asked Tsulib for time to talk to him and the other elders of the tribe.

81

This was organised for two days' time when everyone could be present.

Tsulib was a little anxious, as he had suspected this woman was sent to them for a reason.

When all the elders were gathered and settled into the large round lodge, Tsulib invited the ice woman to speak and asked everyone else to be silent until she had indicated that she had finished delivering her words.

Her talk was about choices.

She discussed the history of the earth and how many races of people over the history of the planet had made the same mistakes over and over again. She spoke of the caves and tunnels which were often talked about by the elders, who had been told by their elders. She told them that they did exist but only a few knew where they were.

She told how they were living museums, holding much information about previous civilisations from all over the world and how they had all repeated the same mistakes by concentrating on what they called progress which led to greed, unhappiness, disrespect for their fellow beings, and stubbornness. The eventual outcome for all these different eras was the same: death and destruction not only to the races of humans but to all creatures and the earth itself.

The message she brought from the glacier was a message of hope for the current civilisations.

She warned of uprisings against tribes such as theirs by other tribes already on the path of greed and dominance. They should be considering how they would handle an attack upon them.

The elders tried to interrupt her talk but Tsulib called for respect.

She continued to say that it would take a special person to be able to talk to all the restless nomad tribes and ask them to consider the possibilities of leading peaceful, happy lives.

"Tsulib," she said, "your son is not that person. However, he needs to father a child in total love and that child will be the special one."

Tsulib laughed. "That may take a lifetime. He is a restless soul, not willing to think about such things," he said. "Please forgive me for interrupting you, continue."

"I have seen a very large war of tribes and, Tsulib, I am sorry but you need to know that your son will be killed in it."

Tsulib drew a deep sharp breath and looked shocked by the ice woman's words.

"Before this war, your son will impregnate a woman whom he will love more than life itself. He will never meet his child."

Tsulib rose to his feet and left the gathering without saying a word.

The remaining people sat silent.

"I will never speak of this again to any of you, but please heed my warnings and be alert to other tribes. Try to learn more about them so that you will not be surprised by any actions. This tribe has a real chance to change the perpetual cycle of self-destruction by the human race." She paused. "I am done."

As the months passed by, many discussions were had by groups and families about the words spoken by Icemon. Most people decided that they were not under any immediate threat and happily put any thoughts of aggressive confrontations out of their minds.

Icemon settled into the tribe but disappeared from time to time for many weeks and sometimes months. She never discussed her journeys with anyone and the tribe grew to accept her comings and goings without fearing for her safety. They were always excited to see her return with new seeds and herbs and stories of magnificent birds and animals that she had seen.

A Cruel Lesson

A group of four juveniles collected themselves some food, added it to their kutcha bags, and set off for a four-day journey of discovery into the mountains to the north. They were three males, Antonio, Peter, and Steven, plus one female called Taisha. They had all grown up together and had been drawn together by their common bond in their love of exploring new places and bringing news of strange fruits and grasses that they found on their journeys.

Together they were a classical example of the strong, vibrant youth of the tribe. Tradition called for the females to grow their hair long and adorn it with beautiful clusters of seed husks and nuts, bound together with strings made from many grasses dyed with vegetable and clay resins. These clusters were woven and plaid throughout the head of hair and met on each side of the face under the ears. The men chose to keep their hair shorter but still below the shoulders and tied back into a single tassel at the back, bound with long strips of cloth with an overlay of their traditional family colors.

Their clothing was similar: a simple tunic and drawstring long pants with variations only in the fit of the tunic. They each wore a wrap around the waist over the tunic. These wraps were each a work of art created by the older members of the tribe, who wove family histories into them. Each member of the family was represented by a symbol, chosen by the individual when they were ready.

Some were ready to choose a symbol at a very young age, others not until adulthood. The wraps were worn with pride every day, not kept for celebration events only.

Their current ages added a new dimension to their friendships as they were beginning to appreciate the opposite gender and the affect they had on each other.

The childhood aversion was changing to a subconscious longing to be near each other. Such was the relationship between Antonio and Taisha as they subconsciously chose to sit close to each other at meal times and coincidentally chose the same events and excursions to participate in.

Peter and Steven had noticed the change in their friends but had not been courageous enough to discuss the matter with them.

After bidding their families farewell, they decided to follow the ridges of the mountains; at every change of direction, they placed an arrangement of five stones to guide them into the correct direction on their return trip. Four stones were placed in a row across the path they were taking. The fifth stone was placed offside to the four between the second and third stones indicating the direction from where they had come and to where they must head to find home. They were experienced travelers and had excellent skills in reading the environment, the animals, and birds, all of which offered signs and symbols of the terrain and any imminent danger. The mountains offered them comfort and protection through their naked feet. The night skies offered reassurance and a cross-reference in their mapping skills.

On the third day, they woke early to a beautiful clear day. The sunshine was warm on their backs so they decided to walk further north until noon before heading back home, knowing that their families would not worry about them if they returned only one day later than originally planned.

86

As they approached the peak of a mountain, sounds of people laughing and talking were heard. They quickened their steps with the excitement of seeing new people. They had heard that there were other tribes but had never encountered any.

Antonio and Taisha broke into a run down the slope to the temporary camp of these strangers, but Peter and Steven took their time picking their way down the rocky slope. As they came closer, many people ran towards them, which made Antonio and Taisha scream in delight and call out greetings to them.

They were shocked when the approaching people grabbed them and forcefully dragged them into the camp. Peter and Steven stopped in their tracks and stood staring at the rough treatment being dealt out to their beloved companions. They watched as Taisha was dragged into a large abode and followed by many men. Antonio tried to run toward her but was struck down. As he tried to get up and force himself into the abode, he was struck again and fell to the ground.

He didn't move.

Peter and Steven ran down to the compound calling their friends but were also met with aggression. They both received fatal blows.

One day later, after relentless abuse from her captors, Taisha awoke in blinding pain. Her eyes were so swollen from the beatings that she could not see clearly, but she heard a voice close by.

"Wake up, are you all right?" it whispered. Taisha could not answer; her mouth was stuck with crusted blood, and she could only acknowledge with a sound.

"You must try to get on your feet," the voice said. "They will return soon, you must get up. I will help you but you must get on your feet."

Taisha tried to move but the pain wracked all through her body and she cried, tearing her lips apart and causing fresh bleeding.

87

She slowly turned her head to look towards the voice and saw a man similar to the men who had abused her kneeling at the rear of the abode where a hole was torn in the wall.

"Please, you must get up," he pleaded. "I will help you to the top of the track where you came from but that is all."

"My friends…" she groaned.

"They are dead," the stranger interrupted.

Taisha began crying.

"Shush, please, girl, they have not finished with you yet. Come, take my arms, you must go now or you will suffer more before you die here."

She found strength from somewhere and rolled onto her stomach and then pushed herself onto her hands and knees. Her helper then lifted her to her feet and started shuffling her towards the hole in the wall. She winced in agony as every step created pain shooting through her whole body. She reached down for her kutcha bag and was reassured to feel that it was still strung around her shoulders.

"Stop," she pleaded. "Please…my friends?"

"What the…" he answered impatiently.

"Please, I need their bags."

"What's wrong with you, girl?" he answered angrily. "Do you understand what is happening here? I will be killed if I am found here. Now come on or I will leave you to your fate."

He moved to the doorway and saw that the others were still eating and laughing at the fireplace. He noticed the body of one of her companions just outside the door and reached out and tore the bag from his body. He turned to face Taisha and reached out and grabbed her tunic at the neckline. Taisha froze with fear and her eyes reflected the horror she felt in anticipation of more abuse. The man stared at her for what appeared to be forever, then he forced the bag down the front of Taisha's tunic. She winced in pain.

"There, that's all I can do. Now: come or stay? This is the last time I will ask."

88

She nodded her head, tears running down her face.

He half-supported, half-dragged Taisha up the track to the top of the ridge and sat her on the ground where he left her.

"Goodbye, girl...good luck...sorry for what they did."

"Hmm...thank you," she cried.

He stood for a moment watching her before running back down the slope, hoping she would find her way home, wherever that might be.

Taisha climbed to her feet and began shuffling along the ridge towards the south, but the pain in her legs and stomach was so intense that she had to stop every thirty or so steps and rest. She found shrubs or rocks to lie behind out of site.

Drifting in and out of consciousness, she reached inside her tunic and dragged out the bag which her helper had put there and cried to see that it was Antonio's. She caressed the design that recorded his life, knowing that his fate would be added to the bag one day. It gave her strength to carry on, feeling that Antonio was with her and needing his bag to be returned to his mother.

Taisha did not know how long she had been walking, crawling, and dragging herself towards home; her throat was dry from thirst and her head was spinning when she finally collapsed.

She fell unconscious and her body rolled down the steep slope, stopping only when she hit an outcrop of dry, woody shrubs and stones. She regained consciousness as the pain of woody stems pushed into her flesh.

She opened her eyes to see a large bird hovering over her; it was an ugly bird with a white fluffy collar around its neck and a very large wingspan that seemed to hold it suspended above her forever. As she watched it, it lowered itself down against the thermals and settled down on the shrubbery next to Taisha and turned its head sideways to get a good look at her. It then raised its wings to form a shelter over Taisha, who closed her eyes again and drifted into unconsciousness.

89

When the group didn't come home the evening that they were expected, no one worried too much. They often extended their journeys for an extra day; but after the second day had passed and still no sign of them, anxiety crept into their hearts.

This was a concern considering the constant rain and winds which had been consistent all day and would possibly continue throughout the night. Their parents stood vigilantly all through the long, stormy night, hoping they had found shelter somewhere and would return home at sunrise.

As sunlight crept over the mountains, groups set off in all directions in search of their children.

One of Antonio's friends took six others and headed off to the north, knowing the track well as they had traveled many times with Antonio and knew the course he would take. They found directional stones indicating the direction that the group had taken. At sunset with still no sign of their friends, they decided to make camp and commence the following morning.

Before dawn, they packed their bags and waited for the very first light. They talked to each other, offering assurance that they would all be found, and pondered on why they had not returned yet. An injury would have slowed them down and they were excellent food gatherers so the rest of the tribespeople were clinging onto the hope they were OK.

After two hours of walking and following the stones, their hearts missed a beat when they saw beads scattered on the track in front of them. They scooped them up and recognized the yellow and orange colors and patterns of Taisha. They scanned the area further down the track and went back to the place where the beads were found and stood running their eyes around the area.

They saw a very large bird hovering above them. As they gazed at it, it glided down to the rim of the mountain where they were standing, dipped over the edge in front of them, floated

90

with the downdraft, and came to a halt at a group of small shrubs and landed.

The boys followed the bird with their eyes and gasped in fear when they saw Taisha wrapped around the shrubs, hanging precariously on the very steep slope that led straight down to the river in the valley.

Without thinking the boys threw themselves down the slope and began sliding towards Taisha. In their haste they started a slide of stones and rubble as they fell, causing more rubble to fall on her. One of the boys fell down past Taisha and kept sliding out of sight. The others managed to stop themselves and sat looking at Taisha, who was still many meters below them.

"We need to climb back up top and rethink this," one of them said.

"Agreed, come on, guys, we're not helping Taisha here."

They slowly found their way to the track on the top of the ridge and took a better look at the situation.

They finally agreed upon tying their tunics together to form a long single length to wrap around Taisha when they reached her to make getting her to the top easier, dead or alive. They then proceeded to move down the ridge on their hands and feet backwards until they reached Taisha.

They removed all the rubble off her and positioned themselves around her to prevent her sliding further down the ridge.

They were very distressed to see her battered body; dry, crusted blood covered more than half her body. They gently supported her face, crying out her name.

It was when they turned her onto her back that they realized she was still alive.

They noticed Antonio's bag on Taisha and fear engulfed them.

"Something bad has happened to them," Mal said. "We've got to get Taisha back quickly."

They poured water from a gourd hanging from their waist cord onto the bottom of their tunic and tried to wipe blood from

Taisha's face with no success. They then put the wet cloth into her mouth and dripped more water into it.

They were delighted when Taisha opened her mouth and began sucking the cloth. She moaned and her eyes flickered. The boys called her name and offered comfort by holding her close. She responded violently and screamed.

"Taisha, it's me, Mal. Taisha you're OK, you're going home," he pleaded.

"Please stay still, we are in a dangerous position," cried another.

Taisha calmed down and squinted though her swollen eyes, looking at each of them. Her body went limp and she began to sob.

They carefully wrapped the tied tunics around her under her arms and tied the other end around the waist of another who sat with Taisha in front of him. The others then dragged them both up the slope to the top of the ridge. They laid her down and reassessed the situation.

They called the name of Will, who had fallen down the slope and were very surprised and happy when they heard him whistle back to them. They knew that he would follow the river downstream and eventually find his way home from there if he was not injured.

The boys decided that no matter how distressed Taisha was, they had to get her home, so they took turns supporting and carrying her for a day and a half.

They stopped only for small rests as Taisha appeared to be getting weaker every hour. They again used the tied tunics to carry her. Two boys tied the tunic length around their shoulders and sat Taisha between them and supported her with their arms.

They stopped when darkness enveloped them and lay with Taisha between them in an attempt to keep her warm. They untied the tunics and put them on themselves to keep themselves warm. Taisha slept erratically and woke from time to time

92

frightened and panicked until the boys reassured and comforted her.

The boys singing familiar tunes seemed to calm her down and also gave the boys confidence that all would be well as they thought of Will.

Before dawn as the darkness waned, they again tied their tunics to form a single length and lifted Taisha onto the makeshift support and headed into the rising sun towards home.

Everyone at the village was very tense. It had been seven days since they had seen Antonio, Taisha, Peter, and Steven, and all the search teams had returned except the boys. There was no sign of them.

"I can hear whistling," someone shouted. "Listen, it's coming from the north."

Then someone heard Mal calling from a distance. Everyone immediately ran toward the voices and screamed in delight to see the boys. The delight was soon replaced with dismay as they recognized the broken form of Taisha being carried by the boys.

As they entered the village, the sight of the battered Taisha caused immediate distress. She was taken to her mother's abode, where she was greeted with immense distraught. She was followed into her mother's hut by many women eager to assist. They tried to cut her clothing from her but were forced to stop as Taisha reacted violently and screamed. They gave her a concoction of passiflora and maracuja which finally caused her to drift off into a light sleep. The women then tried to bathe her without removing her clothes. They were extremely distressed when they realized the extent and cause of her injuries.

It was mostly severe bruising and cuts all down her legs. Dried blood was caked on her upper thighs all the way to her knees, and Taisha winced and resisted any touch in that area. Her eyes and mouth were swollen and bloodstained, and her fingernails were full of a mixture of blood, skin, and dirt, indicting a desperate

93

fight offered by Taisha. Her wrists and ankles were purple from the burns of a restraining device. Her hair was knotted and mud-caked, and her scalp was bare in sections where whole clumps of hair had been torn from her head.

The women fed her concoctions drip by drip to rehydrate her.

The families of Antonio, Peter, and Steven were frantic, asking the whereabouts of their children.

They were quickly told that Taisha had not spoken a word but assumed the worst fate for their sons.

Two days later Taisha opened her eyes, and her mother saw fear in her eyes as Taisha drew her knees up to her chest and held them with her arms. She moved to the edge of the hut and sat shaking and unresponsive. She clenched Antonio's bag close to her and could not be separated from it. Her mother approached the elders and suggested that the Misha might be her only chance for recovery.

They advised that time would heal and that they had used the Misha before and they did not want the debt to the Misha to be too great to pay. She begged them to call the Misha but received the same response.

Taisha's mother waited until darkness. When everyone had retired for the night, she quietly walked into the forest and collected a handful of grey ghost herb and dropped it onto the dying coals of the fire and climbed back into her hut where her child was lying. She sat cross-legged on the ground watching as Taisha lay, her body convulsing in response to her silent, restrained sobbing.

She did not have to wait long before the doorway was blown aside, and within seconds, her daughter was gone with the Misha. She lay down in the space left by Taisha, feeling the warmth of the bedding where she was lying just moments before. She covered herself with her robe and cried a mother's grief for not being able to help her child in her greatest time of need.

94

Taisha was swept into the grids with her Misha pilot and arrived at the Misha domain within seconds, not long enough for her to be further traumatised. Upon arrival, Taisha was carried by four Misha to a place on the outer edge of the settlement where young, flexible saplings had been drawn and tied together to meet at a central point over a cleared area.

All the branches on the perimeter of this area were drawn into the central point in this way to create a skeleton of a structure which would support many more branches, straw, and mud to form an enclosed dome with a small entrance.

Preparations had already begun for a healing sweat lodge. Rocks had been laid into a shallow hole and a fire was burning furiously on top of them, causing the rocks to glow red with the intense heat.

The Misha were gathering to assist and witness the ceremony. Some younger Misha had never witnessed a mending ceremony before and were chatting excitedly amongst themselves as they waited for the rocks to reach their required heat. They all gathered to look at Taisha and tried to touch her as she lay curled up on the ground; they would tell others that they had touched a wounded one before mending.

Leader Misha arrived and they immediately behaved. They asked if they could come into the lodge and learn. Leader Misha looked at each of them and chose one.

"You only," she said as she pointed to the one second from the right. "Come in, sit in the west."

The rocks were then moved one at a time into a hole in the dome after being rolled onto a flat slab of wooden poles covered in smaller pebbles. This was then dragged into the dome and the red-hot stone was rolled into a shallow hole. Each rock was treated in this manner until the hole in the lodge was full to the top with red, glowing rocks.

The neophyte Misha was as excited as a Misha could be as she scrambled into the lodge and sat cross-legged in the westerly side, eagerly awaiting the beginning of the ceremony. She felt very privileged and would boast about it when she told her friends who were not permitted.

Taisha was carried inside the dome and laid in a north-south position by four Misha who then sat, two at her head and two at her feet. A handful of grey ghost herbs and a ladle of water were thrown upon the red stones, creating an aromatic mist to fill the dome.

Taisha did not object to anything that was happening to her; she had lost all inclination to struggle or try to oppose, she was defeated physically, emotionally, and spiritually. She lay with her eyes closed, her body limp and unresponsive.

The leader Misha then entered the dome and sat on the ground next to Taisha.

She sat a pot of water onto the rocks, and as it heated up, she began to call for plants by name.

"Caapi!"

"Cielo!"

"Toe!"

The four assistant Misha reached into their kutcha bags and dropped the herbs into the pot.

Many hours passed by with chanting and nurturing the rocks to keep the pot of herbs brewing and bubbling to a form a constant froth of bubbles on the top of the brew.

"Cascabel!" called leader Misha. She was answered with the addition of another herb into the brew and a ladle full of honey was added when leader Misha nodded to the neophyte Misha.

Taisha was then pulled by her underarms to a sitting position with her back against leader Misha, onto leader Misha's lap with her buttocks fitting firmly into the cavity formed by leader Misha having her legs crossed. Leader Misha then put her arms under the arms of Taisha, resulting in a well-supported sitting position for her.

Leader Misha then called for a cup of liquid from the pot of water and plants and held it with two hands in front of Taisha and slowly handfed her the tea.

96

"Another," she called.

After the second cup of liquid was consumed, Taisha began vomiting.

This did not stop the tea being fed to her, however. She continued vomiting and emptying her bowels after each cup was fed to her. Her vomit covered her legs and down the front of her clothing and face, but the Misha did not appear to be affected by it.

"What is all that coming out of her, leader?" asked the neophyte.

"Quiet," demanded leader Misha as she reached into a small pocket inside her robes and withdrew a small handful of jurubeba and gervao leaves and handed them to the neophyte, who excitedly dropped them into the brew.

This brew was fed to Taisha; it appeared to stop the vomiting, and she became unconscious.

They laid her back down and proceeded to undress her. Clothing that was stuck to her body with dried blood had to be soaked in the warm plant brew to release its grip on her skin. Then they began cleaning all the vomit, excreta, blood, and dirt from her body.

A different pot was put on the hot rocks, and resin of sangre de grado with balsam and andiroba, a large piece of beeswax, and a pot of thick, sweet, yellow fruit pulp were added to it. The consistency became thick and paste-like as it was stirred and all the Misha put their hands into it and took cupped handfuls. They then began covering Taisha's body in the substance and gently wiped and massaged it into her skin, leaving it in a thick layer all over her naked body.

For hours they massaged the paste in a relay from the top of her body to her toes.

The Misha rocked in unison, moving the paste up and down Taisha's body in waves, one picking up the motion where the other left off at the end of her arms' reach.

Many more Misha congregated outside the lodge throughout the night, chanting beautiful melodies.

Taisha was in a semiconscious state of ecstasy. She could see every cell in her body being rocked back and forth and the plant cells being absorbed into her system, putting on a display, showing every cell in her body how to get back into accord with each other. She saw colours dancing in rhythmic unison up and down a double helix formation and surging forward and then back, like an ocean tide sucking debris from every cell of her body. Her physical body was purged of all grossness as her stomach and bowels ejected it.

Taisha felt like every cell in her body was being invited to accompany a plant cell in a dance of harmony. She resisted for a while, but then she was swept up in the beautiful melody of perfect unison as the plant cells taught her how to release the damage and trauma and restore the equilibrium.

They danced and regained balance for hours.

Dried plant resin and ladles of water were continuously thrown into the rocks, keeping an aromatic mist throughout the lodge as the leader Misha continued to massage Taisha's body, concentrating on her wounds. She made a poultice of canagre, nispero, and honey and placed it into Taisha's most private parts.

They sat with Taisha in the lodge all through the night, keeping the aromatic mist thick and comforting. Other Misha were continuously replacing the rocks inside the lodge with more rocks which were kept glowing outside with fire burning on top of them.

As dawn approached, leader Misha called for more plants.

"Picao preto."

"Epazote," she called.

Again the helper Misha reached into their kutcha bags and placed them into a clean pot of water.

Cloth was then placed into the pot and each of them took the plant-soaked cloths and began to wipe Taisha's body clean of the paste.

98

Leader Misha removed the poultice.

She soaked Taisha's hair with the brew and combed it, removing all traces of paste and debris.

A fresh pot of water was handed in from outside and more herbs were called for.

"Damiana."

"Mulungu!"

A set of clothing was brought into the lodge and offered to leader Misha, and they all assisted in dressing Taisha in the beautiful Misha robes of golden silk and web. They were multi-layered in varying lengths and colours of golden hues.

A helper Misha combed Taisha's hair and rolled it over hot stones to form long, gentle curls.

Leader Misha then pulled Taisha back onto her lap into the upright supported position and asked for cups of the new brew to be handed to her.

She fed them to Taisha, who was beginning to respond.

Everyone sat quietly, watching Taisha as she slowly recovered.

She lifted her head slowly, opened her eyes, and looked around her strange environment and smiled. She ran her hands over her bare arms and then her face and took a handful of her hair and twisted her fingers around a long curl, looked down shyly, and said softly; "Thank you…thank you…" and tears flowed from her eyes.

Leader Misha then reached inside her robes and took out a long strand of blue threaded stones with a five-sided plaque hanging from it. The plaque was made from a strange shiny material intricately carved into five sections with many symbols of animal, bird, and plant origin in a spiral design.

She held it in front of Taisha and placed it over her head and gently centred it on her chest. Taisha reached down and placed her hand upon it.

Taisha did not remember all that had happened to her here, but she did remember what had happened to her before coming here. She felt that it was all OK now. She knew and would always remember that she had suffered tremendously, but the Misha had cleared her from it and it would never trouble her again.

She lifted herself from leader Misha's lap as everyone slowly raised themselves to their feet.

Taisha turned to face leader Misha.

She looked into her eyes and noticed something.

Was that a tear in a Misha eye? she thought. *Can't be, they don't have the same feelings as us.*

Leader Misha then reached over to take the medallion hanging from Taisha's neck in her hand and said, "This will protect you for the rest of your life. If your safety is ever compromised, show this and you will not be harmed. Don't worry about losing it, it can never be taken from you or lost. Remember also, that you will never be the same," she said. "Your body now sings to a different tune, I'm certain you will not miss any part of your previous being."

Taisha stood up and looked down at her clothing, smiled, and ran her hands over the fine woven cloth as the doorway to the lodge was lifted. She shuffled outside.

Leader Misha followed her and the Misha outside the lodge parted to form a pathway to a pilot Misha.

Taisha stopped and turned to face the leader Misha, who waved her hand to her, bidding her farewell.

"Go," leader Misha said as she put her open palm of her hand to her heart, clapped her hands together and intertwined the fingers, then simultaneously pointed her two digital fingers at Taisha. Taisha instinctively did the same to leader Misha, who smiled, knowing that the ceremony was indeed successful.

As Taisha reached the pilot Misha, she was swept up and taken into the grid.

She found herself on the banks of the river which she recognised and knew that she was only a half a day's walk to her home. She knelt beside the river and saw her reflection in the water.

100

She smiled. "I'm going to be OK," she whispered as she jumped to her feet and swung around, ready to head off towards home.

She was startled to see a girl standing there.

Kettiajya she was a pretty girl, with long, wavy, fair hair with a reddish tinge in it. She was fair-skinned, tall and slim with a long tunic and a heavy garment of some sort draped over her shoulders.

Her eyes were dark and penetrating but softened when she smiled.

"You were delivered to me, Taisha," she said. "I will take you home, it will give you a chance to get used to the person you now are."

She offered her arms to Taisha, who did not hesitate to step into her embrace.

Kettiajya invited Taisha to sit for a while beside the river and offered her food from her sack.

Taisha began to talk about the event that led to her Misha encounter. Kettiajya let her talk uninterrupted while holding her hand as she listened.

"Why did they do that to me, do you know?" asked Taisha.

"Shorthairs! That's what they do."

"But why?"

"Well, it's like that bird up there cruising the thermals," said Kettiajya. "They do it because they can."

Taisha looked up to the bird. She jumped to her feet and yelled, "That's my bird!" she called excitedly. "That bird protected me from the sun when I was injured. I'm going to add it to my kutcha bag."

Kettiajya turned and smiled at Taisha then embraced her as she said, "It's good to find a totem, Taisha, but it's better when the totem finds you. Come on then, we must get you back to your mother, she must be very concerned about you."

Kettiajya left Taisha at the top of the ridge overlooking the camp and watched as she made her way down into the forest perimeter.

101

Taisha hesitated before walking into the cleared area of the camp then slowly walked toward her mother's hut, but stopped when she saw her mother appear at the door. Her mother was astounded by the transformation in her daughter. She looked beautiful in Misha robes, and her face glowed with self-confidence and pride.

Others in the camp called out, alerting everyone to the arrival of Taisha back home.

Tsulib came to see her and was also astounded by the change in her.

Taisha's mother approached him and said, "Whatever the price, Tsulib, it has to be worth it don't you think?" she asked. "My daughter has returned."

Tsulib looked at Taisha.

"I think you have more than your daughter back...much more," he said as he walked away.

As the days passed by, Taisha approached the parents of Antonio, Peter, and Steven to try to give them some comfort in knowing that their children were put to death very quickly.

She offered Antonio's bag to his mother and confessed the love she had felt for him.

Taisha waited for a moment when all the elders were gathered together and approached them.

Her heart was very heavy and she had many questions for the elders. She had a clear memory of what was done to her, but the Misha had done something to her to enable her to know but have it filed away in place within her where it could never harm her. However, she needed answers to be able to move on.

The elders sat quietly, not knowing what to say to each other and feeling like they had no answers for the unspoken questions that they all had. They knew that they needed to reassess their lifestyles.

Taisha entered the lodge and sat at a nominated place facing the twenty-nine elders.

102

She sat quietly composing herself rearranging her hair and settling her kutcha bag on her lap. She then placed one hand on each knee, lifted her head, and looked at each elder one at a time from the left to her right.

Tsulib began. "Taisha, we are here for you," he said quietly. "We will not speak until you ask a question."

"I need to tell you everything that happened to me, Antonio, Peter, and Steven," she said.

"That is not necessary…"

"Oh, but it is necessary," Taisha interrupted loudly. "You need to know everything, and you *will* listen," she said firmly. "All of you will listen," she repeated.

The elders moved uncomfortably in their seats and nervously nodded their heads.

She told of the atrocities committed upon her and her three companions.

"There is a message for us in all of this," she said. "I now realise that we have been very lucky to live so long in our simple, peaceful lives without interaction or conflict with other tribes."

She continued as she gripped her kutcha bag for comfort.

"I have been curious about the way all of you have related to me since my return. At first I thought you did not care, but I now know that none of us have been exposed to brutality before so you don't know how to respond to it…or to me. This incident has stolen our innocence and changed our hearts. The lesson is that we can no longer avoid taking on a defensive and maybe an aggressive attitude or we may be all destroyed."

The elders sat quietly, not knowing what to say to each other.

A few of the elders leaned towards each other to whisper but Taisha raised her hand to stop them.

"I need to know if any of you knew about people such as these who would do things such as this to other people. I feel that the boys and I were betrayed by our lack of knowing. Why didn't we know? Why weren't we warned of what other people might do to us? We ran into their camp expecting to be greeted as we would

103

greet others. Antonio…" she cried as she took a big breath and said, "Antonio would be alive today if…we had known. Now, I am caught between Misha and what I was before." She sat silently for many minutes before continuing.

"It is a good thing; I would not survive any other way. Now I ask you all, please try to explain to me why my friends died like that and why I was treated as I was."

Tsulib began. "Yes, Taisha, we knew there were people like that but many generations ago as told by our grandparents. We have never come across other people before and this is a whole new scenario for us."

He continued, "We are all very confused, not only by what happened but also because we really don't know how to handle this. We don't know how to feel, Taisha!"

Silence again fell upon them.

"We were all taught to be equal, no person was dominant over another," Taisha said.

"But now…I feel like I will always be different and others look at me and talk to me differently," she said. "Even you all here, do I embarrass you? You don't look at me the same as before anymore!"

Another elder stood up, walked over to Taisha, put her arms around her, and stood to face the elders.

"We need to stand up and take full responsibility for this tragedy," the elder said. "We as educators and carers have let our young ones down bitterly. We have neglected them by leading them to believe that life has always been how it was before this. We chose not to educate our children with knowledge of life before the tunnels. Sure, we thought we were protecting them… but in fact we have abused them." Tears flowed down her cheeks as she knelt beside Taisha and held her tight. "Oh, Taisha, I am so sorry, I don't know what to do."

Taisha stood up. "Educate us!" she yelled. "Tell us the truth, tell us the history. Please, I beg of you!" she cried. "Please, don't

104

let the boy's death be for nothing!" Taisha then walked quickly out of the lodge and retreated to her hut.

The elders then made the decision to gather everyone and begin educating them about everything they knew of the past.

Days passed by as anyone who wanted to talk was given the opportunity.

The mood was sombre as life before the tunnels was disclosed and many left the lodge sad and longing for the discussions to finish. Others were happy to know the truth.

Their lives had changed forever.

The Shorthairs

A decision was made to familiarize themselves with the potential enemy. A small group of three men, Jude, Chris, and Trevor, volunteered to track back to the place where the boys and Taisha were taken, with the intention of observing the people and learning as much as possible about them. They traveled lightly, with only their robes for the cold and sleeping and minimum food.

The master of fitness gave the boys a quick lesson on the exercise patterns that had been a part of their everyday routine for all their lives. The difference this time was information on how to change the patterns to inflict fatal blows should they have the need to defend themselves. The lesson learnt from Taisha's experience told them that if contact was made, then they would need to know how to survive, even if this meant inflicting fatal wounds on their aggressors. They were shocked to learn how easy it would be to turn their exercise routine into deadly blows, enough to kill a man, and they doubted their courage to inflict such a blow.

"How did you learn such things?" they asked the instructor.

"From my father. Like all the information we have, it is passed onto each generation as needed," he answered.

They were prepared to stay away for many weeks if necessary so a return time was not discussed. This was a new experience for all the tribe and was anticipated with a mixture of excitement and fear. After many discussions, it was agreed that should any conflict arise, one of them must try to get back to the tribe with any information, even if this meant leaving others who could be in extreme danger. This was a large expectation considering their life education and conflict-free upbringing.

They bid their farewells with confidence in the fact that they would return safely in due time, as the intent was to observe only.

After three days of steady walking, they heard the sounds of other people. It was in line with the information that Taisha was able to give them regarding the location of the tribe that she had confronted.

They decided to move off the ridge and down into the shelter of the cloud forest until sunset, when they would move closer and get their first look at the tribe.

As they found their way into the cloud forest, they came upon bones of different sizes and shapes scattered around randomly. Amongst the bones were old food scraps and clothing remnants. They soon realized that they had encountered a place where the tribe dumped items which they did not use any more.

The bones particularly bothered the men, as they only ever saw bones if they came across a dead animal or bird and the bones were taken to make useful items.

"Why are there so many bones?"

No-one answered.

They looked around and slowly walked through the debris.

They stood speechless.

They moved on through the bones when Jude suddenly stopped and gasped, staring at the ground where a bundle of items were. The others joined him and stood in shock as they saw what was there.

"It's the boys," Jude said. "They dumped the boys here like rubbish."

They dropped to their knees and touched the remains of their mates, sobbing silently in disbelief. Their tears dripped

108

onto the ground as they reached out to touch the remains of each of the three boys.

"We've got to get them home," Chris cried.

Jude answered, "No, we can't disturb them yet, we have a job to do—and besides, if we disturb them it'll alert them to us."

"But we can't just leave them, look at them," Chris wailed.

"No, Chris, Jude is right. We'll take them home soon but we must find out what these people are about," said Trevor.

They sat silently with their friends until the darkness of the night enveloped them. Unfamiliar smells drifted from the tribe down to the cloud forest and noises were becoming louder as the night settled in.

Without speaking a word, the young men prepared themselves for their night vigil and began the slow cautious walk back up the mountain towards the camp of the tribe. They agreed not to speak a word to each other once they arrived to a good vantage point looking over the campsite.

An outcrop of rocks and vegetation just over the ridge of the rise offered a perfect place to settle into, with excellent views of the whole camp.

The mood was solemn as they thought about their friends' remains. Their bodies had begun to decompose but their facial features and hair were still recognizable. Two of the bodies had blood on the neck and shoulder areas, but Antonio had severe damage and multiple bloodied areas which indicated that he had put up a fight to his last breath. Their clothing was intact but dirtied with dry blood and dirt. Insects had begun to invade the decaying bodies.

The boys absorbed every detail about the camp and the occupants. The camp did not look like it had been there very long, as vegetation had been removed still lay about the dwellings. The whole camp was a group of sixteen dome-shaped dwellings which were different sizes. They appeared to be covered in animal skins that had been thrown over the frames and tied down with a form of rope.

109

A large fire was burning to one side of the camp; the boys looked at each other in disbelief when they recognized the shape of an animal strung out over the flames.

"That explains the bones," they thought.

There appeared to be eighty or ninety males in the camp, leaving the men to wonder why there were no women. The strange men were dressed in long skirts with short-cropped vests made from a mix of animal skins and cloth. Wide lengths of cloth were wrapped around their waists, forming a thick support from which a multitude of items were hanging. These items were varied in shape and size. Some were small wooden handles with large round and pointed shapes tied to one end. Others were long, narrow wooden items with sharp, pointed ends; all had loops of string on one end holding the item onto the waist wrap. The same type of wrap was around their wrists but had solid shapes protruding on the outside edge.

Their hair was all the same length, very short and in unruly curly clumps. Around their necks they wore a loose but wide, thick circle of cloth or skin; some had this drawn up over the back of their heads, leaving the front part to hang around the neck. Their feet were bare with strings tied around their ankles.

As the night grew darker, the occupants of the tribe appeared to get very loud and jovial and some staggered and fell, but the others did not seem to notice or care about their companions' demise. As they tore pieces of flesh off the animal on the fire, they devoured it with much gusto and drank an unusually large quantity of liquids from large individual gourds. These gourds were refilled constantly from large bladders hanging from the abodes.

The noise became increasingly louder and men began fighting each other to the ground, which appeared to be a fun exercise though many ended up with bleeding mouths and eyes, unable to get themselves back onto their feet.

Eventually, the camp became quieter as many men fell asleep where they sat or lay with injuries. Others staggered back to their

110

dome huts, and silence descended upon the mountain. Smoke still swirled around the camp and drifted together with unfamiliar smells up to the boys as the air moved around the mountains with the moving clouds and mists.

The boys signaled to each other to meet back at the cloud forest where the three boys' remains were.

"What do you think was happening to them?" asked Chris. "Are they sick?"

"I don't know, they were too happy to be sick," Jude said.

"They're big," Chris said.

They were silent. They did not have the words to describe how they were feeling. Disbelief and confusion was overwhelming them.

"They eat animals! Can you believe that?" asked Chris.

"Maybe that's why they are big," Trevor mused.

"Wonder if they eat people," said Chris.

The other boys quickly looked at him and stared.

"Well, just wondering," he said. "If they eat animals…maybe."

There was silence.

"What do we do now?" Chris asked.

"We've got to go back and lay low, watch them tomorrow. See what they do in a day," Trevor stated.

They went back to their secluded place overlooking the campsite and rested.

Before dawn, they woke and prepared for a day's observation.

They were surprised that no one had appeared, and that the men lying in the open where they'd fallen the night before had not moved by midmorning.

The boys were getting uneasy and kept looking around, thinking that the men must have left their camp during the night. They were worried that they might be seen if anyone came to the camp from their direction.

Eventually, movement was seen as men slowly appeared from their huts; as they walked past the men on the ground, they kicked them to wake them. This provoked a few fights and dust

111

began rising from the camp. Men began ripping flesh from the animal that was left on the fire the night before, and it was eaten as they walked about and rekindled the fire.

One man took a red, glowing piece of wood from the fire and handed it to another and sat on the ground. The man with the red-hot stick then proceeded to run the stick closely all over the seated man's head, burning his hair and then rubbing the ash off with his other hand.

Chris couldn't believe what he was seeing and shook his head as he looked across to the other boys.

The men then swapped positions and the stick was used to singe the hair of the second man. This explained the similar short hair on all members of this tribe.

The boys stayed for two days mentally noting details of clothing, activities, and their interactions with each other, which were aggressively friendly.

Before they headed back to camp, they went back to collect the remains of the three boys. However when they saw the corpses again, they realized that it was an impossible task, so they decided to cover them with stones without making it look too much like a grave. They assumed that the shorthairs would move on in the future and the families of the boys could return and bid them farewell. They took the kutcha bags and a tuft of hair from the boys for their mothers, and began their return journey to the camp of Tsulib.

Kettiajya Meets the Tribe

One day during one of Icemon's roaming journeys, she came upon Kettiajya and Paterson.

"Icemon! Over here!" said Kettiajya. "What are you doing way out here?"

"Reconnecting, just reconnecting," answered Icemon as she approached them. "How did you know it was me?"

"You have a distinctive walk—thump, drag, and hop. Thump, drag, and hop. Thump, drag, and hop." She laughed as she jumped to her feet and began emulating Icemon's walk. "You could never sneak up on anyone."

Icemon laughed with Kettiajya and joined in with the rhythm.

They sat on a ledge overlooking the river below, admiring and assimilating with the mountains as they changed color and temperament, the sun moving behind the peaks. They watched the large woolly animals trekking home one behind the other in their march along the worn tracks that wrapped around the ridges of the mountains.

Once the sun had disappeared, the line between shadow and light moved quickly up the mountainside, which was reluctant to release the last ray of sunlight. As darkness emerged, one by one stars appeared and covered the dark sky with a soft, glowing, relentless chatter that was irresistible to the nocturnal creatures.

Icemon and Kettiajya sat silently in awe of the opera presented to them every day and night. Words were not necessary between these two kindred souls. They had both spent time with the Misha learning many mysteries and they both had chosen a solitary, nomadic life.

Kettiajya offered her food sack to Icemon, who took it and reached in to retrieve a handful of seeds, nuts, and dried vegetables. She then took her own food sack and took a piece of flat bread and offered it to Kettiajya.

"Where did you get this?" asked Kettiajya.

"The camp of Tsulib, about eleven days' walk from here. It's a bit dry now and needs to be eaten, take another piece."

"You spend a lot of time there these days, Icemon."

"Yes, they are a good bunch, but I worry about their future with all the other tribes coming down these ways."

"I've seen the other tribes, bit nasty aren't they?"

"Yes, if they confront Tsulib's tribe and others like Tsulib's, I'm afraid they will suffer greatly."

"Can you warn them?"

"I tried."

"But?

"They don't want to get involved, but they don't realize that they won't have a choice."

They sat silently again and watched Paterson trying to find a comfortable place to rest for the night.

They laughed as he impatiently changed his mind three or four times.

"What do you see for them, Icemon," said Kettiajya. "Anything?"

"Yes, I have told them what I see, but...you know, Kettiajya, they just don't want to know!"

"Can you tell me what you see for them?"

"Mm," said Icemon. After a long pause she said, "There will be a period of running away for the Tsulib tribe, but a time will

114

come when they will have to confront the aggressive tribes or perish. Tsulib's only son will die in the fight."

"Will the tribe survive?"

"I don't know that much; however, the son of Tsulib will father a child who will have many answers in generations to come."

They both were silent as they continued to pick at their food and drink water from their gourd.

"This is sad, Icemon," said Kettiajya. "I think the tribe you speak of is the one where a beautiful chestnut horse lives, whom Paterson spent some time with."

"Yes, there is a horse such as you describe, and they have spoken of an impressive black stallion that stayed there for quite some time. I thought of Paterson but they said he was not with a human."

Kettiajya smiled. "So, Icemon, is she in foal?"

"I don't know that, dear girl! Why are you concerned?"

"Paterson could be a father soon and tribal conflict could jeopardize mother and the baby."

"If that is so, then many moons must pass yet before the birth. How many moons ago was he there?"

"Eight."

"Not long to go." Icemon continued, "Why don't you come and see her, I'm heading back that way."

Kettiajya didn't answer.

"They're a good tribe of people, you'd like them," Icemon insisted.

"I'll come back with you, Icemon, but only to see Paterson's lady. You know I'm not into people."

Icemon turned her face to look at Paterson and smiled as she nodded her head.

"She's a beautiful creature, I'm sure you'll love her."

"I hope she's more receptive to him," said Kettiajya as she nodded her head in Paterson's direction. "She gave him a few nasty bites last time, left scars on his neck."

115

The following day they all headed off in the direction of Tsulib's camp, which was about eleven days away. After three days, Icemon wanted to leave the river route and go over the mountains to get to the camp in five days.

"You go that way, Icemon, but I'm in no hurry. We'll continue this way and meet you there later."

"No, I'll come with you," said Icemon, laughing. "I know you won't come if you don't go with me."

Kettiajya giggled, "Oh, I'll be there. I want to meet the lady love and besides, she needs to know that she has another place to go if things get bad at the camp."

As they climbed up to the last ridge that would overlook the camp, Icemon stumbled and sat on the ground.

"Bugger!" she said.

"You OK?" asked Kettiajya.

"Yes, just tripped," answered Icemon as she used her sticks to get to her feet. She took a few steps and fell again.

"Hurt my good foot, can you help?"

Kettiajya stood, looking at her on the ground. She whistled for Paterson.

"Hey Paterson, how do feel about carrying Icemon to the camp?" she said in a pleading voice. "Please? You can take her all the way to your lady?"

Paterson had been a little anxious over the last day as he sensed that they were heading back to the golden mare. He snorted and trotted off, leaving them behind.

"Well, I guess that was a no," Kettiajya said. She helped Icemon to her feet and prepared to help her walk.

They didn't get very far when Paterson appeared again and rubbed his head against Icemon and leaned against her.

"Yes?" she asked.

Once Icemon was comfortable on his back, Paterson headed back up to the ridge with his cargo. He stood at the top of the ridge, looked down to the camp, quickly found the chestnut with his eyes, and shuffled his feet nervously.

116

Icemon smiled, knowing that Kettiajya would not leave Paterson for very long and would soon join her in the camp.

The chestnut noticed them and left the group to slowly walk towards them. Paterson was hesitant to start the descent to meet her, not knowing what his reception would be like.

"Let's go, Paterson, I can't walk," said Icemon. "I need your help here!"

He proceeded slowly, one step at a time, watching for a sign from the chestnut. As they slowly grew closer, the chestnut's pace increased to a gallop as her demeanor changed to excitement. Paterson responded by trotting faster in anticipation of meeting again with the chestnut, sensing that she had forgiven him for whatever it was that upset her.

In his excitement Paterson had forgotten that he had a passenger who was tossed about on his back. Icemon screamed, as her gnarled legs did not have the ability to grip his back, and both were tossed from side to side and her buttocks were bashed against his back as she was bounced around. She wrapped her arms around his neck as she screamed his name.

Yondalin ran to the camp perimeter as he heard the screams of a woman and horses galloping. He saw Hepsibarb charging up the mountain slope. He looked in the direction to the top of the mountain where she was headed and saw the black stallion coming to join her. Then he saw that the stallion had a rider. He panicked and began to run to assist but stopped when he recognized the rider as Icemon.

"What...?"

Both horses slowed quickly as they approached each other, causing Icemon to fall off.

Yondalin rushed to her and grabbed her arm and began shaking her, willing her to move.

"I'm OK," yelled Icemon. "I'm OK now, bugger off!" she said as she pulled herself up and began brushing herself free of debris.

"Thanks, Paterson!" she shouted sarcastically.

117

Yondalin was smiling and nodding his head. He shifted his attention to the horses. *Stubborn old woman!* he thought.

"So, Icemon, what's with the stallion? Do you know him?"

"No I do not!" she answered reluctantly. "He is her companion," she said as she waved her hand back towards the ridge without looking.

"Who do you mean, Icemon?"

Icemon turned and pointed then said nothing as she realized that Kettiajya was not with them.

"You'll see soon enough, she wants to meet Hepsibarb so she'll show up sooner or later."

Yondalin wanted to pursue the subject but felt the time was not right as Icemon's pride had taken a beating by falling off the stallion in front of the whole camp.

He reluctantly left Icemon to get herself down the mountain to the campsite and went to greet the stallion.

"Well now, you are a mystery aren't you?" he said as he approached Paterson. "You're going to be a dad, did you know? Look at this," he said as he stroked Hepsibarb's belly. "Another two moons maybe."

Yondalin followed as both horses began to walk down to the campsite but he stopped many times and stared back to the ridge, wondering what Icemon was talking about.

Icemon had not been back to the campsite for many months so it was decided that a feast was in order. The central fire was lit and everyone busied themselves with food preparation and the musicians began beating out music, prompting songs to be sung.

Preparing the food was as big a part of celebrations as eating it. Many different foods were brought together and everyone assisted.

The customary community gourd of soup had many more grains and vegetables added to it to make a thick stew.

Potatoes and corn were abundant in the area and, combined with the leaves of a variety of plants, made a very filling and tasty meal. Flat, grainy breads were made from crushed seeds, and

118

whole yams were buried in the ground close to the fire to be retrieved later and eaten with pastes made from crushed very ripe fruits.

After the food was consumed, many took the opportunity to question Icemon about her recent journey.

She willingly shared the sights she had seen. She told them of the different birds and creatures she had seen and drew laughter as she tried to emulate the noises of some of them. She told of a land she had seen from the distance. She had followed a river which led her to the edge of the mountains.

"Do you mean that the mountains stop?" Taisha asked.

"Yes. That's what it looked like, although I didn't follow the river any further when it began to flow down and disappear forever."

"What was it like?" Yondalin asked.

"It looked like the mountains stopped and the river disappeared into a forest, but not like the forests we see here in the clouds." She continued, "The forests seemed to go on forever as far as the eye could see and all that was visible was treetops so thick together that nothing else could be seen. The river disappeared into mists even though the day was not cloudy; the mists seemed to rise from the forests."

Someone in the group giggled and said, "I think she imagined it, sounds a bit strange to me."

"I have seen the same," an unfamiliar voice interrupted. "It does exist."

Everyone turned around to look for the source of the voice.

Not a sound was made as they focused on the figure of young woman standing very still and obviously feeling anxious about interrupting the conversation.

"Ah, Kettiajya!" said Icemon as she indicted a seat next to her. "Come into the light, dear girl, and meet the tribe of Tsulib."

Kettiajya felt extremely nervous as she found her way between others and sat at Icemon's side.

119

"I would like you all to meet Kettiajya, Paterson's companion," said Icemon. "Oh, Paterson is the black stallion who befriended Hepsibarb a while ago."

Icemon's eyes did a quick flick around the fire and mischievously smiled when she saw the looks of astonishment on the faces. She loved to shock people. "She'll be my guest for a while," she added.

After an awkward pause, Tsulib was first to speak by querying how long she planned to stay.

Kettiajya answered quietly, "I wanted to meet Paterson's lady love and then I'll be gone. Thank you."

"And where will you be gone to?" asked Tsulib. "Where is the campsite of your people?"

"I don't belong to a tribe," she said. "I prefer to travel alone."

"How long have you been alone?"

"For as long as I remember; it's just been Paterson and me."

Many sounds of wonder followed by muffled chattering began to filter through the group. Kettiajya felt uncomfortable and began rearranging her robe to cover as much of herself as possible as she felt all eyes upon her.

Yondalin had not spoken a word since he heard her voice, and his eyes had not left her since she walked into view. His close friend, Carlos had nudged his arm many times since she had sat next to Icemon waiting for a response, but Yondalin was frozen and speechless.

"I apologize for all the questions Ketti...Sorry, how do you say your name?"

"Kettiajya," she answered and smiled for the first time. "Please do not apologize; you have the right to know who I am."

"Ah, Kettiajya, did you meet Icemon on your traveling?"

"No, I have known Icemon for many years. I met her at the Misha during her healing. I believe you claimed her from the glacier higher up the mountains."

Tsulib looked to the ground and sighed. "So you have attachments to the Misha?"

120

"I know them well; they also helped me some time ago. Paterson took me there when I was very ill," she said. "I am permitted to visit them…" She began to speak but stopped when she detected negative feelings from Tsulib. She knew that the Misha were not liked by everyone and sensed that Tsulib was suspicious of her relationship with them.

"I will be on my way tomorrow," she quickly added. "I thank you for your friendship…I will leave as soon as I have met the chestnut mare with the golden mane. Thank you…"

Tsulib smiled and nodded his head. He liked the girl but also had an uneasy feeling about her.

"The chestnut you speak of is the companion of my son Yondalin," he said as he indicated to him. "He will show you the mare at first light before she goes to graze."

Kettiajya looked to the person whom Tsulib indicated. She saw a young man who did not acknowledge her; he kept his gaze focused on the ground in front of him.

"I would appreciate that, Tsulib. Thank you, Yondalin," she said in a determined voice, challenging Yondalin to acknowledge her.

Yondalin slowly lifted his head and looked directly into her eyes and nodded his head.

They both looked at each other for a brief moment before Yondalin stood and left the group.

Kettiajya smiled nervously and looked forward to leaving the tribe the following day. She felt reassured that living alone was a good thing.

Yondalin rose early the following day and began walking towards Icemon's hut to meet Kettiajya when he heard the sound of a horse galloping. He scanned the mountains surrounding the campsite and saw Kettiajya approaching on the back of Paterson. She was a very good rider, he thought.

Yondalin stood watching as Paterson slowed down and trotted towards him. Kettiajya had decided that she would not stay

121

any longer than it would take to meet the mare as she felt that the tribe was not sure of her intentions.

She threw one leg over Paterson and slipped off his back before he had stopped and walked towards Yondalin.

"Good morning, Yondalin," she said, "sleep well?"

"Of course," he answered, knowing that he was not being truthful. He had lain awake all night with images of Kettiajya on his mind. He stared at her, mesmerized by her, and felt very intimidated by his own feelings and not knowing what to do. He turned and began walking away from her.

"Come on then, you want to meet Hepsibarb?" he said impatiently and not understanding why he was being rude towards Kettiajya.

"Thanks, that's why I'm here," she said firmly. "Then I'll leave you in peace."

Yondalin stopped and turned to face her with the intention of apologizing for his attitude but the words did not happen. Kettiajya stopped in anticipation of some conversation but it did not come. They stood silently looking at each other until Kettiajya smiled and turned to whistle for Paterson. She looked back at Yondalin, who had appeared more relaxed and smiled at her before he waved his hand towards the valley. "There," he said. "Hepsibarb likes the river in the mornings, she'll be there."

Kettiajya smiled and nodded her head as she followed him on the steep decline into the valley.

Paterson emerged from the valley in answer to Kettiajya's whistle and trotted to greet her.

"Is everything OK, Paterson? Is she in a better mood now?" asked Kettiajya.

"What's that about?" asked Yondalin.

"She gave him a nasty bite last time he was here."

"I'm sure he's tough enough to take it."

"Being tough has nothing to do with it," stated Kettiajya. "It was nasty. It drew blood!"

122

Yondalin stopped and looked at her. "What do you want me to do about it?" he asked angrily.

They stood silently before Yondalin added, "They seem to be over it now, so..." he stopped and shrugged his shoulders.

Silence again consumed them.

Kettiajya broke the uncomfortable silence. "Just take me to meet Hepsibarb, OK? Don't want to take any more of your precious time," she said loudly as she waved her hand forward. "Go on!"

Kettiajya was feeling confused by the response she was getting from Yondalin. *What's his problem?* she thought.

Hepsibarb had heard them approaching and had come to meet them. Kettiajya quickly forgot about Yondalin and his attitude when she saw Hepsibarb walking towards them. She was very heavily in foal and appeared to be very healthy and content. She walked straight up to Yondalin, who wrapped his arms around her neck and stroked her forehead before running his hand down the length of her body, pausing on her extended stomach.

Kettiajya watched and felt the special bond between the man and the horse.

She wondered what she had said or done to make him dislike her. *Maybe I haven't had enough contact with other people,* she thought. *I don't know how to communicate properly. It's a shame; he has very nice eyes and a smile to die for. Careful, Kettiajya, he doesn't like you so forget it.*

Yondalin indicated with his hand for Kettiajya to approach.

"This is Hepsibarb," he said affectionately, "my friend and companion."

Kettiajya reached out and stroked her neck.

"She's more beautiful than I imagined," she said looking at him directly in the eyes. "I've seen her briefly before today but pregnancy suits her." She held Hepsibarb's face in her hands and looked into her eyes.

123

"She likes you," said Yondalin, returning her gaze. He watched her as she communicated with Hepsibarb. She was talking very softly to her as she stroked and caressed her face and neck.

Yondalin sat on the ground and gave Kettiajya private time with Hepsibarb, but it also gave him a chance to collect his senses.

He noticed the sun on her hair making it turn different shades of gold and reds as she moved. Her clothing was simple with many different coloured stones and feathers entwined around the neck and sleeve ends. The same patterns were on the pouch hanging around her shoulders. He was angry with himself for responding to her this way and could not understand why. He desperately wanted to talk to her, there were many questions he wanted to ask her and did not want her to leave.

Kettiajya felt the urge to linger longer. She felt comfortable in the quiet of the situation. She stole glances of Yondalin as she walked around Hepsibarb, stroking her stomach and offering comforting words to her.

"Well, Hepsibarb, you are a great lady aren't you? Pity about your friend over there," she said, nodding towards Yondalin. "Is he always like this or is it just me?"

She kissed Hepsibarb on the forehead and whispered, "Good luck, girl, we'll see you again sometime, hey?"

Yondalin stood as Kettiajya left Hepsibarb and walked towards him.

"Thank you, Yondalin," said Kettiajya as she stretched out her open palm to him.

Yondalin reciprocated and placed his open palm on hers and wanted to say something...anything, but once again he froze. Kettiajya smiled when she realized that they had been holding hands for a long time without speaking. Yondalin immediately dropped her hand and started walking back to camp with Kettiajya following. Before reaching the camp Yondalin found the courage to stop and turn to face her. "Look, sorry for the behavior," he said. "Don't know what that was about, I am not usually so unfriendly."

124

"OK, I thought it was my attitude that upset you."

Yondalin smiled, "Never."

Kettiajya's stomach knotted up as Yondalin's smile twisted her whole life around.

"You're not leaving tonight, are you?"

"No, tomorrow," said Kettiajya nervously.

"Good," answered Yondalin as he turned to resume the walk back to camp in silence.

Kettiajya stood watching him walk away from her and didn't start following him until he looked over his shoulder while offering his hand and said, "Coming?"

Without a word, she quickly caught up to Yondalin and took his hand and let him guide her up the narrow track. She had to admit to herself that it felt good, very good.

As they approached the camp perimeter, she quickly released her hand from Yondalin's, causing him to stop and turn to look at her. He understood her action and smiled as he took a step closer to her and reached out and pulled a tassel hanging from her hair. The tassel fell off in his hand and, without apologizing, he pushed it into the top of his tunic and reached out and brushed his hand against Kettiajya's cheek before running towards the camp.

Tsulib was not surprised when Yondalin requested music after the evening meal. His happiness had not gone unnoticed, neither had the source of his happiness.

This did not concern Tsulib, who constantly thought of Icemon's prophecy relating to his son because he knew that Kettiajya was a free soul and would not be able to commit to tribal life.

The music was energetic with the drums leading the beat. The dancing matched the music's every rhythm that dictated steps and changes as the groups moved, forever entwining.

Yondalin took every advantage of Kettiajya's inability to dance by nominating himself to teach her on the perimeter of the groups.

125

They laughed as they stepped on each other and pushed into each other's bodies as Kettiajya stepped in the wrong direction or misunderstood the instruction.

When the groups insisted upon them joining in, Yondalin always jumped the queue to be close to Kettiajya, who did not mind at all.

As the music came to an end and everyone sat around the fire, Kettiajya thought about what was happening. "This is nice," she thought. "But what if Icemon's prophecy is right?"

As the people slowly wandered off to their huts, Yondalin moved to sit close to Kettiajya and took her hand in his. Yondalin's close friend Carlos left them alone and joined the musicians, who were sitting in a group practicing new tunes.

Yondalin turned to Kettiajya and said, "I want you to stay here, Kettiajya, don't go!"

"I can't stay," she answered.

"Why can't you?"

"I can't stay in one place, I have to keep moving," said Kettiajya as she thought to herself, *but I could with you.*

"I will come with you," answered Yondalin.

A tear found its way down Kettiajya's face and Yondalin wiped it with his hand.

"Why the tears, Kettiajya?"

"Please, Yondalin, please try to understand. I can't do this."

She stood to her feet and looked down at Yondalin, she stooped and kissed him on the forehead and whistled for Paterson, who appeared within seconds.

Despair engulfed Yondalin as he watched her walk away from him. She seemed to be far too willing to leave without even a look back. With a gentle nudge, she commanded her horse to carry her away into the twilight. Yondalin walked slowly to the edge of the area and followed the sound of her horse with his eyes.

It was only at this time that Carlos realised how much his treasured friend needed this woman and his heart reached out

126

to him. He walked to him and touched him on the shoulder in an attempt to comfort him.

Realizing his despair, Carlos ran back to the compound and directed the music team to pick up their drums and start pounding out a strong, rhythmic beat in an attempt to draw Yondalin back to the comfort of the group. The beat slowly built up intensity and the chanting automatically picked up the beat as Carlos directed them to continue as he watched Yondalin for a response.

However, Yondalin moved further to the edge of the compound to a vantage point, willing Kettiajya to return to him. The drums continued to pound out the rhythm and Carlos turned suddenly to his troupe of musicians as the sound appeared to be subsiding even though the drums were still being pounded. As the sound of the drums subsided, a new sound became apparent. Carlos started to walk towards Yondalin when he realised that the vibration was being directed from him. When he approached Yondalin and looked at his face he realised that the song was the song of Yondalin.

His arms were crossed on his chest and his eyes searched the forest as his song penetrated the stillness.

His song was a song of total surrender, offering his soul and deep unconditional love to Kettiajya. A tear escaped from his eyes as his fist clasped against his heart and reached out, offering his song to the direction where he last saw Kettiajya.

The song subsided too quickly. Carlos ran back to his troupe and commanded them to commence. "Play the same as before!" he yelled. "Whatever it was, do it again!"

"But what happened to the sound, Carlos?"

Carlos shrugged his shoulders and said, "Just play the music."

The drums frantically started to build up the rhythm again as Carlos watched Yondalin for a response.

Again, as the pounding gained momentum, the sound was muted as Yondalin's song took over stronger and engulfed the night, penetrating the forest. It was picked up by the breeze and carried to Kettiajya.

127

Kettiajya felt relieved that she had been able to turn away from Yondalin and get back to her nomadic life with Paterson. She leant over and hugged him as he gained pace, whisking Kettiajya through the forest, disturbing birds, forcing them to rise into the air in flocks, screeching their annoyance as they tried to settle in for the night.

As she put distance between them and the compound, Kettiajya looked over her shoulder as she felt that they were not alone.

Paterson started behaving badly and tried to slow down as Kettiajya tried to force him on, but he was too strong and pulled up to a sudden halt, rose onto his rear legs, and whinnied loudly.

Kettiajya let his mane go and they both stood silently, looking curiously back down into the valley.

The impulse to stop was overbearing, and like a soft breeze, a song was heard. This song was hauntingly beautiful, sad and happy all in one; she could not turn away from the message it brought to her.

It was a message of unconditional love and a bearing of innermost emotions, words never spoken before.

An image of Yondalin's eyes came into her mind. She smiled when she saw his naked soul offering her his total being, and she realized that he was possibly the only person on earth who could create a need within her for something more, something she had never known.

Her emotions became overwhelming when she realised the implications of such a need and the sacrifices which would need to be made if she listened to her heart and soul at this time.

"No! No!" she screamed, "I will not listen to your song, your destiny is not mine!"

She nudged Paterson with her heels and took a firm grip on his mane as she ordered him to take her away from this place. Paterson was not happy with the decision but obliged anyway, carrying her high above the valley and across the ridge.

128

Yondalin continued offering his song until he saw the silhouette of Kettiajya disappear over the ridge high above the valley.

Emotionally exhausted, Kettiajya slowly turned to Paterson and whispered, "Just you and me, Paterson, it was a big ask, I understand."

For many days after the experience, Kettiajya felt restless and unsettled. She tried to put Yondalin and his song out of her mind by pushing Paterson to his limits under the guise of playing games, but Paterson felt the insincerity in her games. She walked for hours following the rivers and found her way back to her home and the comfort of Veronica, her beloved minder. She squatted on the rocks with her arms wrapped around her knees gazing into the waters.

"What do I do, Paterson?" she said. "Can Icemon be wrong?"

Paterson nudged her, nearly pushing her into the water. She laughed and caught her balance as she jumped into the shallow edges of the river and sat waist-deep, flicking water back to Paterson.

In frustration, she jumped to her feet and dived into the water, coming up on the other side and climbing up onto the cliff above. Paterson watched her and waited, knowing that she would return and he could not follow.

She climbed up the steep treacherous cliffs to the very heights of the waterfall as she had done many times before. She stood above the valley looking down to Paterson, who was a small figure at the base of the long, descending fall of waters.

Then she slowly pulled herself across the rocks to the centre of the river inches from the edge of the falls.

She called out loud as she faced Veronica. "Veronica, please guide me!" she cried. "Help me make the right decision!"

She turned and slipped herself into the current of the waters and yelled joyfully as she dived into the falling waters. Paterson tossed his head restlessly as he watched her coming down in the waters and moved to the place where she had emerged many times before.

She screamed in exhilaration as she emerged through the foaming mists caused by the falling waters crashing into the large pool of water at the base, and settled back onto the rocks near Paterson, who gave her a nudge of delight.

As she relaxed and laid back into the water and closed her eyes she heard a sound, a tune from within.

It was familiar, comforting sound that she felt she had always known but never heard. She jumped up to her feet, wet clothes clinging to her body, and started humming the tune as she danced, swinging her hips and strutting around Paterson, who turned with her as she circled him humming the tune. Together they danced and laughed. It felt good but it also felt that it was a lonely song that was incomplete. She smiled; she knew it was a song to be offered and to whom it was offered.

She put her arms around Paterson's neck. "Our lives are about to change big time, boy. I need to do this. Do you understand, your life will also change?"

Paterson nestled his head into her neck and snorted.

"Thank you," she whispered.

She went into her dwelling and dried herself and began selecting a special piece of clothing. For the first time in her life, she was dressing with someone else in mind, not just comfort. She decided upon a long winter robe but left the long-sleeved under-tunic off, leaving her arms and neck exposed. She never imagined that those long winter days spent decorating her robes with feathers, stones, and plant dyes would be for any other purpose than to occupy the cold days. The hem was jagged and each peak had intricate details of coloured stones and feathers woven into the cloth and replicated around the neckline. It had long, loose strings hanging from many places. These strings had coloured stones wrapped tightly at uneven intervals and feathers attached to the ends of each length. She loved how she felt with it on and decorated her long mane of hair to match with the same trimmings. She looked at Paterson, who was patiently waiting and watching her strange behaviour.

130

Kettiajya walked to the entrance of her abode in her glorious robes and stood silently, gazing out into her valley and watching the waters fall from the cliffs down into the river. She faced Veronica and put her hand onto her heart, clasped her hands in front of her, and pointed both digit fingers towards Veronica. A gust of wind passed by, lifting her hair and causing the decorations to make sounds as they clicked against each other. Kettiajya smiled shyly.

"Yes, the time is now, Paterson," she said, then sprang up onto his back.

They started their slow but deliberate walk, following the river for an hour and then crossing it to change direction where it divided. They looked a magnificent pair with Kettiajya's robe and hair decorated and her bare legs hanging over Paterson's shiny ebony coat.

As they began the long climb up the mountain which led to the camp of Tsulib, Kettiajya slipped off Paterson and walked with him to the peak. There, she looked down upon the village and watched the changing colours of the earth as once again the sun line began its daily slide up the mountains to bid farewell. Paterson nudged her, encouraging her to keep moving as the sun was setting.

The village had settled into another evening sitting around the large fire in the middle of the compound, and one by one, the people wandered off to their huts. Carlos stayed with Yondalin as he knew he was still pining for Kettiajya after she had denied his song many weeks ago. They sat quietly watching the flames in the fire and occasionally rearranging the logs.

Carlos tried to make conversation but Yondalin was not responding, just staring into the flames.

Carlos silently rose, placed his hand on Yondalin's shoulder, and walked away into the dark.

131

Yondalin was sitting, elbows on his knees and hands clasped in front of him.

He lifted his head to watch the flames in the fire as they rose and was startled when he thought he heard a song coming from afar. He checked himself and dismissed the sounds as a figment of his imagination.

He impatiently poked the fire once more and stood up, watching the sparks rise into the sky.

As his eyes lowered back to the flames, the song became louder; it was a beautiful, slow-moving tune with a song that was breaking his heart the longer it went.

He looked back to the flames.

He thought he was hallucinating when he saw the outline of Kettiajya through the flames standing on the other side of the fire. She was smiling. Her hair was hanging loose over her shoulders, glowing in the fire light, and her body was gently moving in tune with the song. She was a sight to behold with beautiful adornments on her clothing and hair and her exposed arms reflecting the golden hues of the fire. Her smile was soft and giving.

He now understood the song; it was her song and it was for him. He slowly walked around the fire and approached her, offering her his hand, which she accepted without hesitation. Her song was now pounding very loud in his heart and mind.

No words were necessary as they stood looking and smiling at each other before Yondalin pulled her towards him and put his arms around her. The embrace changed to a slow moving dance to the rhythm of the song that they were both engulfed by.

Without a word spoken, Yondalin guided her to his hut. Both were happy that no one else had been there to witness their very private moment.

Icemon turned in her bed, smiled, and closed her eyes.

The following morning, the sight of the black stallion outside Yondalin's hut drew enormous excitement from the tribe.

Yondalin and Kettiajya were awoken by the sounds of whispering and shuffling of feet as everyone gathered around the entrance to Yondalin's hut. Kettiajya and Yondalin kept them waiting as they enjoyed each other, both not believing how they felt. Eventually, they realised that the others were not going to go away until they had answers.

Yondalin rose and dressed as he watched Kettiajya's nervous anticipation of the reaction that the tribe would have upon seeing her with Yondalin. He reached for her clothing, knelt beside her, and assisted in dressing her. Not a word was necessary. They both knew that there was no turning back now.

"I will love you till I die," whispered Yondalin.

Kettiajya put her hand over his mouth.

They smiled at each other and embraced before Yondalin reached for the door hatch and stepped outside with Kettiajya's hand in his.

The response was joyous. Everyone approved and rushed forward to embrace and kiss them both. Many wanted answers as to when and what happened to bring them together, but no explanations were given.

Only Icemon showed no surprise. She had been out of bed for hours as she was every morning doing whatever it was that she did and was just returning to camp.

She stopped and gazed down to the campsite, watching the jubilant reaction to the news. She smiled for a second or two, and then it was replaced with a sad expression of acceptance.

As Icemon approached the campsite, Kettiajya stared at her, willing her to make eye contact.

She didn't.

Kettiajya found Yondalin's hand and held it tight. *She's wrong,* she thought to herself as she tried to put Icemon's prophecy out of her mind. She turned to see Tsulib watching them; tears were filling his eyes as he saw the change in Yondalin, knowing that this was going to change everyone's lives, especially his son's life.

133

As the days grew into weeks, restlessness overcame the tribe as they realized that they could not keep on running from the shorthairs to avoid conflict.

Extended discussions were carried out, lasting days and nights with only sleeping breaks. They all agreed that if a confrontation was inevitable, they needed to dictate where and when.

They had to be the aggressors and make the first strike, so teams were sent out every day to study the daily habits and movements of the opposing force—the shorthairs. Knowing the shorthairs' weaknesses was a must if a successful strike was to happen.

Sorrow enveloped everyone as they knew that many lives would be lost and it would be the young and fit who would die. Anyone who did not want to be involved in the conflict would have a role to play at the campsite by organizing an exodus if the worst scenario eventuated.

The daily workouts now included training with weapons in the form of poles and slingshots. Their main aim was for accuracy and surprise.

They learnt from their enemy also. The wrist wraps with stones entwined in them, common among the tribespeople, were adopted, and training was carried out to utilize them for reinforcing a fatal blow.

They trained at night time to get their eyes accustomed to night-time vision as they decided that an appropriate time for attack would be at between midnight and few hours before dawn; that would be a time when the enemy would be at its weakest and possibly under the influence of their beverages.

Since the incident with Taisha and the boys, the training master had been educating them all in the anatomy, showing them where to focus blows to ensure a sudden and definite fatal blow first time.

The scouts arrived early and appeared to be anxious.

"They're moving," he said. "They have packed their camps and have started traveling this way. I reckon about two weeks and they will be upon us."

134

Tsulib remained silent and walked towards the central hut; everyone followed.

"What do we do?" he asked. "We can move on and always be a week or two in front of them. They can easily follow our tracks so we may never be rid of them. Or we can bring forward our plans to attack them."

"The team is ready to fight," answered the trainer.

"Constant moving is extremely stressful and the threat of being found...We really don't have time to organize a move," said Taisha.

"There are only two weeks until a full moon that will make us vulnerable. We won't have the veil of darkness to assist us!" exclaimed Yondalin.

"And we won't know where they will be, doesn't leave us time to plan around their environment," Carlos added.

After a moment of silence, Tsulib called for everyone who had wanted to be heard to take their turn and be heard.

"I don't want to send my children to fight and risk them being killed!" stated a nervous mother.

"I have to agree," said another, "we are not prepared for this way of losing our families, some of us will die."

"I agree with you," Tsulib said. "However, we will be constantly on the run and hiding, waiting for the inevitable time when they find us. If that happens, we will not have an advantage. We need to be the ones who choose the time and place. We are outnumbered three to one. If we wait and let them surprise us, we may all die. Every one of us."

War

Tsulib built a map of the terrain on the ground, indicating the mountains and valleys in the vicinity of the proposed zone for attacking the shorthairs.

"We'll divide into four groups. Hector and Luis will go ahead with your groups and wait on the slopes of the mountains on either side of the camp. You won't begin closing down on the camp until we make contact. Yondalin's group will approach from the valley and head directly into the camp at the same level. The remaining group will wait behind the third group. That will be your group, Kettiajya. After we make the first hit, we'll retreat and you will all go forward.

"You message boys will need to resist joining the fight. We must be able to rely on you to relay messages between each group and also to keep the home camp informed of what is happening. You will be running your hearts out, so keep your food sacks topped up and make sure you remember to eat and drink regularly.

"We have three nights before full moon to complete this."

As the dawn approached, Yondalin signaled his group to begin moving toward the shorthair camp. As they became closer and entered the camp, Yondalin felt uneasy and signaled to stop. He stood listening and looked for the shorthairs who were normally sleeping at the fireside.

There were none.

He also saw no tools or weapons scattered as they usually were.

No captive animals were there either. The camp appeared to be too tidy and the feeling was tense.

Yondalin decided to signal his group to retreat; he raised his arm to signal.

Suddenly, the hut flaps flew open and shorthairs burst into the camp area.

Yondalin didn't have time to direct his group as they found themselves in a position of fight or be overcome.

Many of Yondalin's group found it very difficult to be the aggressor; they reverted back to protection moves and found themselves being pushed back and knocked to the ground by the brute force of these big shorthairs. Yondalin called upon all his strength to make the first fatal blow but didn't have time to consider what he had done as another two shorthairs lunged toward him. His survival instincts took over and smoothly ran through the moves that he had been taught and dealt with them in seconds.

Yondalin then ran back to the few who were having difficulty putting the learnt actions into practice, and his heart ached when he saw two of his group slain before him. He moved in front of the others and stood between the aggressors and his friends, then proceeded to swing himself into action, willing the others to follow suit.

He was disappointed to see that only a few followed his example; others were still only defending themselves.

The shorthairs' numbers were growing very fast and Yondalin feared for the other groups that were now spilling down the slopes. He turned quickly to signal a retreat to them and was pleased to see Hector and Luis's groups make contact with the shorthairs without hesitation and with great offensive skills.

Kettiajya and her group were waiting for the signal from Yondalin to join them but it never came. She sent one of her people, a young woman named Molly, up to a high point to overlook the fighting and bring back news of the progress.

When she reached the top of the ridge and looked down upon the surrounding terrain, she saw that the three groups were holding their ground and may have made some progress despite the surprise of the shorthairs' apparent knowledge of their approach. As she sat and watched the fighting, her attention was distracted by a herd of woolly creatures running very fast up the mountainside, disturbing flocks of birds from the grasses. Knowing that it was unusual for these creatures to run directly up a steep slope for a large distance, Molly stood up and walked closer to the edge of the ridge.

She was shocked when she saw a large group of more shorthairs on the other side of the river. As she watched, half of them crossed the river and began working their way up the mountain towards them. The remaining shorthairs stayed on the opposite side of the river out of sight.

Molly immediately ran down to Kettiajya and her group and described what she saw.

Kettiajya knew straight away that a preplanned ambush by the shorthairs was about to take place. She sent a runner to Yondalin to warn him and instinctively withdrew her group further back to ensure they did not get trapped inside a ring of shorthairs.

Yondalin was very concerned to hear of the impending ambush and saw that his group could not retreat and leave Hector and Luis's groups. Instead he directed his group to try to join the other two groups down near the river, hoping that the combination of all three groups would be large enough to make a formidable force. A few more souls lost their lives before reaching the river and joining the other groups, who had secured a high spot overlooking the river. The shorthairs had not followed them, which concerned Yondalin. They soon realized that the

139

other groups of shorthairs had reached the site and had closed all escape routes.

Shorthairs were on the opposite side of the river and also at each end of the valley.

"We have underestimated these people," exclaimed Yondalin. "Fighting may be their way of life; they have skills that we never expected." He stood, silently looking at his tribe. Many had received wounds, some appeared to be quite serious, and the general attitude was that of a defeated tribe.

Two days and one night passed with an occasional test from both camps, but it appeared that the shorthairs were more than willing to wait and appeared to revel in prolonging the obvious outcome.

Kettiajya looked down with a heavy heart upon Yondalin and his group and the shorthairs who had all escape routes blocked.

Hepsibarb had joined her and Paterson, but upon sighting Yondalin in the valley, Hepsibarb's anxiety overcame her and became very restless, snorting and striking the ground with her hooves. Kettiajya tried to calm her, but Hepsibarb sensed that Yondalin was in desperate trouble.

Without warning, Hepsibarb threw herself over the ridge and began making her way down towards Yondalin. Kettiajya held her breath as she watched the magnificent mare pick her way over the rocky outcrops gaining speed as she continued her run towards Yondalin.

Kettiajya whistled to draw Yondalin's attention to Hepsibarb. He responded and ran to the perimeter of the group to see Hepsibarb surging down the mountainside towards them. He called, "No, Hepsibarb, no!"

She didn't miss a step as she continued lunging down the steep slope.

Everyone from the top of the mountain, looking down to the groups in the valley who were looking up, stood in awe of this beautiful mare following her instincts to care for her companion in need.

140

As Hepsibarb approached the cloud forest above Yondalin's group, Kettiajya drew a deep breath as she saw many shorthairs running towards her in an attempt to intercept her before she could access Yondalin and the others.

Hepsibarb, however, brought her front legs straight and firm, bringing her to a sudden stop before the cloud forest.

Her ears pricked and turned to every direction as she scanned the forest. Within seconds she leapt forward once more and galloped around the edge of the cloud forest before lunging into the clouds and disappeared.

Kettiajya and Yondalin's groups fell silent as they waited hopefully for her to emerge safely somewhere.

Yondalin stood as close as he could without drawing attention to himself and willed her to survive.

Noises of thrashing undergrowth and shouting voices seemed to go on forever before movement was seen. Yondalin's heart missed a beat as he saw Hepsibarb emerge from the forest followed by many shorthairs, who were loading their slingshots as they came into open ground. They stopped and began swinging and taking aim at Hepsibarb. Yondalin yelled at his group to distract them by feigning an attack down the hillside toward the shorthairs. Unfortunately, the shorthairs had time to deliver a barrage of shots towards Hepsibarb, many making contact with her rear legs and thighs. She stumbled for a moment but found the strength and courage to continue up to Yondalin, where she pushed and nuzzled against him.

Yondalin wrapped his arms around her neck and patted her bulging stomach.

"Heps, you scared me big time," he said. "What..." He stopped.

He knew she was strong-willed and nothing would have stopped her coming to him. He talked quietly to her as he stroked her, looking for injuries. She winced as he ran his hand over a large wound on her left hind quarter.

Yondalin took nettles from his bag and chewed them before placing them on the wound, and stood holding them against the wound until all the moisture had dried. He placed his hands and ear against her stomach and smiled when he felt movement.

The following morning found Hepsibarb with a very sore rump that caused her to limp on her left leg.

Kettiajya continued observing the situation from high above, where they had a good view of the whole area. She could not see a way to prevent all the young men and women in the groups trapped below to be freed from their virtual prison.

The concern about their lack of knowledge about warfare had now become a matter of survival.

Two days and two nights had passed with no sign of action from the shorthairs, who would know that food and water would soon be having an impact on their prey.

Yondalin was becoming anxious and others were looking to him for guidance and leadership. He had run through every possibility to get his group out of this predicament.

Their hilltop was surrounded by cloud forest around the base and shorthairs were on two sides. He had considered the river which was on one side at the base of the hill that they were trapped on. The river was wide and flowing fast over large outcrops of rock—and freezing as it came directly off the snow-capped mountains. They could only use the river as a last resort for escape, but it would almost certainly cause many lives to be lost or carried downstream if they tried to cross it.

The only other way out was straight up the mountainside towards Kettiajya, but it would take a very strong group to get up there while fighting off the shorthairs from two sides.

The shorthairs appeared to enjoy the waiting and watching prolonging the inevitable as they continued with festivities.

As the day passed by, one brave person in Yondalin's group decided to test the shorthairs by making a run straight up the mountainside. He soon became exhausted before he was half-

142

way to the top, and as he sat down to rest, a single stone from a slingshot struck him in the head.

His body tumbled back down the slope into the cloud forest.

Kettiajya instructed her group to gather all the stones and rocks in the area and bring them to the ridge overlooking the fighting zone below. It was an attempt to occupy them and could be used to trigger a slide of stones if they needed to.

The shorthairs had begun to light a fire and Kettiajya watched in horror as they brought a large woolly animal to the fire and killed it. They then tied it over the flames of the fire and large gourds of drink were brought in from the outer areas.

Over the following hours, the shorthairs rotated their men and allowed them to take turns ripping flesh off the cooking animal and drinking with others who were on guard at the perimeters.

When a messenger arrived back at the camp with the news, Tsulib instructed those left at camp to begin packing up personal belongings in preparation for moving on before he set out to the site of the conflict. He did not arrive until one day later and was very agitated while traveling as he anticipated the worst scenario. However, when he saw Kettiajya and her group camped on the top of a ridge, his feelings were torn between hope when he saw Yondalin and most of the three groups safe on a small rise near the river and that of desperation when he saw that their avenues for retreat were nonexistent and the numbers of shorthairs was growing with a continual flow of men arriving to join them.

Tsulib now accepted that their way of life over the past two generations was idealistic but not realistic. He had rejected thoughts from others about educating the tribe about violent and deceptive natures of the human being, believing that all humans would choose peace and friendship over the negatives if they had a choice.

He had passed off the Taisha incident as a remote incident and was not in favor of this fight, but he now realized that these

143

shorthairs were an organized fighting tribe who obviously reveled in and celebrated the stimulation of war.

Considering the shorthairs' lifestyle of over-indulgence and personal neglect, Tsulib had to admire their tactical abilities and saw that his own tribe was at their mercy because they did not have the skills to counter the shorthairs.

As the third day approached, desperation was settling into the minds of both Yondalin and Kettiajya and those up on the mountaintop looking down on the impossible situation controlled totally by the shorthairs.

Kettiajya found a place away from the group where she could release her emotions freely without causing concern to her group.

She found that it was very hard being a member of a community where everyone relied on each other for morale support and always focused on a few to lead.

She shed a few tears as she looked down upon Yondalin. She wondered how she came to be in this situation whereby her whole being was caught up in another person's life.

She was startled by Paterson approaching her. He stood quietly next to her.

"You too, huh?" she said. "Things have changed haven't they? We need to find a way to help them, Paterson, but…how?"

She sat for many hours observing the surroundings and then lay on her back looking at the sky. She watched the clouds passing overhead going in different directions as they became caught in different altitudes. She noticed a large bird cruising the thermals.

She sat up suddenly and looked at Paterson. "Full moon tonight, Paterson," she said excitedly. "Can you please get me to the Misha before sunset?"

Paterson responded immediately by pushing himself to his limit. With Kettiajya on his back, he galloped down the mountainside to the river and followed it until it reached a point where it divided and continued in two new paths. He took the path to

144

the left and followed it many hours before Kettiajya forced him to stop at the base of another large mountain.

"Time for a rest, Paterson, then we'll tackle that," she said as she pointed up the mountainside. She took a cloth from her bag and began rubbing Paterson down as he drank from the river.

"OK, baby?" she asked. "We've got to try this, Paterson; it might be the only chance they have."

Paterson drew on every last bit of energy and strength to get himself and Kettiajya up to the mountaintop and continued across the top of the ridges to take them to the domain of the Misha.

As they approached the sun was beginning to set, making the sweat and froth on Paterson's chest and shoulders look like molten gold. He slowed down to a prancing trot, holding his head high, pleased with himself for getting to the Misha in record time.

Kettiajya slipped off his back. "You're the best," she said as she kissed his forehead. "Now you rest here, I have work to do."

As Kettiajya approached the grid blocking her entrance, a neophyte Misha appeared. Kettiajya slapped her thigh, formed a fist, and opened her palm facing down and then placed her open hand on her solar plexus. Recognizing the gesture, the neophyte released the grid and allowed Kettiajya to pass but not without pulling her hair as she walked by.

Kettiajya smiled.

Kettiajya was happy to hear that noise and excited chatter was higher-pitched and faster than usual as she approached the main compound of the Misha camp, where a violet hue had penetrated the hovering mist.

"Ah, Kettiajya," called leader Misha. "Come join us for our Luna festivities."

"Thank you, it's been a while hasn't it?" said Kettiajya, feeling a little guilty, knowing that she was only there to take advantage of the Misha moon-induced carelessness.

As the moon rose higher in the sky, the Misha exhilaration increased to a frenzy of singing and animated dancing. The

145

younger Misha began pushing and shoving each other. They soon tired of each other and began to surround Kettiajya, pulling her hair and squeezing her uncovered arms while screaming.

Leader Misha called everyone to the large bonfire in the centre of the compound and started a chant that initiated synchronized dancing and the tossing of dried plants onto the fire. Some of these plants caused a flash of flames and strong aromatic ash to drift into the air, to settle back down onto everyone. After many hours, everyone was covered in a film of violet-coloured ash, giving them a coating that glistened in the moonlight. Kettiajya continued to participate in the festivities, waiting for the leader Misha to reach her peak of stimulation, which was when the moon was directly overhead.

Kettiajya slowly moved herself around to get next to leader Misha, who offered her a herbal brew.

"Here, Kettiajya," she said in a state of excitement.

Kettiajya took the drink and put it to her lips pretending to drink it but not daring to, knowing that she had to stay alert. She would only get one chance to trick leader Misha.

She discretely poured the drink onto the ground and asked for a refill. "Come on, let's have some fun," she challenged leader Misha. "Tell me something I don't know about Misha."

"There is much you do not know about us, what do you want to know?"

"Tell me about the grids," said Kettiajya as she pretended to be consumed by the moon. "I was told that you can move the grids, is that true?"

"I can move energy, yes!"

"And the grids?"

"Of course I can if I want to ,but there's no point in moving the grids," said leader Misha. "I only do it to surround our compound, you know that."

"Can you teach me?"

"No!"

"Why not? Can I have another drink; it's a nice brew isn't it?"

146

Leader Misha called to her neophytes, "Bring another here for Ketty."

Kettiajya smiled when she heard her name shortened. *It's now or never*, she thought.

"I don't believe you can really move the grids," laughed Kettiajya as she playfully pushed leader Misha, making her fall backwards onto her back.

"Oh you don't think I can, do you?"

"No!" Kettiajya said as she put the cup to her lips and gazed into the bonfire.

"Well now, come with me, dear girl."

Kettiajya climbed to her feet and followed leader Misha on a path to the top of the ridge overlooking the compound. She chatted and laughed as she followed and deliberately stumbled a few times, causing leader Misha to laugh.

"OK, now what? Move the grids for me, big leader Misha," said Kettiajya. "Amaze me with your power!"

"Firstly, walk that way," said leader Misha, pointing to her left.

Kettiajya began walking and was knocked to the ground as she ran into a grid.

She giggled and turned to see leader Misha making a movement similar to reaching from the ground and dragging something over her head and throwing it towards the grid.

"Now try to pass and then tell me that you were wrong and I was right."

Kettiajya stood up and began walking toward the grid again and found that it had gone.

"All right then, what did you do with it? Is it destroyed?"

"No, you know energy can't be destroyed, I just moved it."

"So what happens to it now?" asked Kettiajya. "Does it stay there?"

"No, it will only stay there for three cycles of the sun then it moves back to where it is supposed to be."

Kettiajya stood silent for a while thinking of the possibilities.

"Impressed?" asked Leader Misha.

"No, it's no big deal moving a straight line of energy."

Leader Misha became agitated. "Come on, Ketty, what do I have to do to impress you?" she said as she turned and began walking back to the compound. "Why am I trying to impress you anyway? Come on, that's enough of this nonsense."

Kettiajya panicked, "No, no let's try something. Come on, Leader, entertain me!"

Leader Misha stopped but didn't look back to Kettiajya.

Kettiajya looked up at the moon. *Nearly out of time*, she thought.

"Just one more," she said. "Please?"

"OK, what will do it?"

"Can you make a grid of energy follow a river?" she asked.

"Too easy!" answered leader Misha. "I've had enough, this isn't fun anymore." As she proceeded to follow the track back down to the festivities.

"You can't do it! Leader Misha can't do it!" chanted Kettiajya.

Suddenly, an angry leader Misha was standing next to her.

"Tell me now, tell me precisely what I need to do to prove to you and then leave my compound," she shouted.

"Don't be angry, I thought we were having fun?"

"Tell me!" she demanded.

"Move a grid to follow the whole length of the major river from here to a length that I can travel on for three days."

"Easy, anything else?"

"Following the river exactly would be too easy, so make it run on the sunrise side of the river about one sector of the sun's movement away from the river."

"About one sector? About? Be precise or don't waste my time."

"One sector!"

"Is that all?"

"No, have the grid move towards the rising sun at sunrise on the second day and keep moving it until it runs out of energy and returns to its true place on the third sunrise."

148

"That's not a challenge, Kettiajya!" shouted leader Misha as she threw her arms into the air and disappeared.

Kettiajya was left standing alone in the moonlight. *Have I pushed her too far?*

She hurried back to Paterson, who was tired but happy to see her.

"I think I'm going to pay for that, Paterson," she whispered. "Must get back."

At first light, Kettiajya and Paterson were once more crossing the high ridges on their way back to the conflict with the shorthairs.

Upon their arrival, Tsulib informed her that there was no change but he was worried that there was no food or water for Yondalin, Luis, and Hector's groups and still no ideas on how to help them.

Kettiajya sat and observed the scenario and noticed that the shorthairs had become more vocal and dust was rising above the trees indicating that they may be moving or regrouping.

She needed to test the grid's presence before she told Tsulib what she had planned. She asked Paterson to take her downstream to the conflict site and approached the river slowly from the direction of sunrise.

Paterson sensed the grid barrier before they hit it.

Exactly how I ordered it, thought Kettiajya, noting the distance from the river.

Tsulib watched as Kettiajya and Paterson found their way up the mountainside back to their group overlooking the conflict. He suspected that she was going to abandon them but trusted that the relationship with his son would keep her close and this was confirmed as she approached him.

"Tsulib, I have a plan," she said. "Please don't ask how or why, just trust me. Are you aware of energy grids in these mountains?"

"I've never encountered one, but yes, I have heard of them."

"OK, I have negotiated with the Misha to move one and have just checked to see if it was installed. It was!"

149

"How does that help them?" he asked pointing down into the valley.

"The grid is impassable! The shorthairs don't know yet, but they cannot touch our people, they can't get through the grid."

Tsulib was speechless.

"Our problem now is that Yondalin and the others don't know it's there either so they do not know they have protection for the moment."

"For the moment? It's not permanent?" asked Tsulib.

"No, two days and it'll go back to its designated course, but for now the whole grid is one sector this side of the river," explained Kettiajya. "At sunrise tomorrow, it will begin moving east."

"And...?"

"Well, anything that is not of the earth will be moved with it."

Tsulib thought for a moment then he smiled and lunged toward Kettiajya to hug her but Paterson moved between them and forced Tsulib to back away.

They laughed and Kettiajya moved around Paterson and grabbed Tsulib's hand.

"We need to find a way to let Yondalin know what's happening. Any ideas?" asked Tsulib.

"Someone has to get in to them but the grid will also work against us by not allowing anyone through," said Kettiajya. "Unfortunately, it is not selective."

Tsulib gathered the group on the ridge together to tell them about the plans. There appeared to be no confidence in the grid. Kettiajya tried to explain to them. "Remember when Taisha was very ill and the Misha came to take her away and then returned her transformed?"

"What does that have to do with the grids," they asked.

Kettiajya paused, "You didn't see them take her, did you?"

"No."

"OK," said Kettiajya. "I can't explain it then, I'm sorry."

She stopped. "Yes!" she exclaimed. "Taisha, where's Taisha?"

150

"She's a messenger at the first post that way," said Tsulib, indicating the direction towards home camp."

"How long will it take to get her here?" asked Kettiajya.

"It's quite a distance, maybe quarter of a day's walk and another quarter to get back."

Kettiajya looked at Paterson. She took him aside. "Paterson, my darling, I know you're tired but we need you to bring Taisha here." Tears came to her eyes, knowing that he had been a champion to get her to the Misha and back and now she was asking for more.

She took him to the top of the ridge where he could see Hepsibarb.

"Paterson, we all need you to do this...Hepsibarb and her precious cargo too."

Paterson became agitated and pulled at Kettiajya's arm.

"Thanks, baby, I'll take you to Taisha then you bring her here."

They set off once more but maintained a steady pace to preserve Paterson's energy as he would need to make an immediate return. He appeared to be content to keep up a slow canter, holding his head high as Kettiajya talked to him continuously.

They reached the first messenger post in good time and Taisha and two others welcomed them and anxiously asked about the conflict. They were very unhappy to learn of the three groups' demise.

Kettiajya told them about the grids but only Taisha understood and assured the others that it was a viable plan except for the grid not allowing anyone through to advise Yondalin's group that they were safe for a while.

"That's why we need you, Taisha," said Kettiajya. "The Misha gave you a medallion, do you have it?"

"Yes, here," she answered as she clasped it. "No matter how careless I am with it, can't seem to lose it."

"Good, I believe that it is a key to pass through the grids."

"Believe?"

151

"Mm, we're counting on it."

After Paterson had rested and eaten, Kettiajya assisted Taisha to get onto the back of Paterson and indicated them to leave.

"I'll follow on foot, won't take long, but you, Taisha, have to figure out how to pass through the grid and let Yondalin know that they are safe for a while. Tell him that the grid will move east, pushing anyone east of it over the mountain at sunrise tomorrow morning. They'll have some time to leave their position."

"And then?"

Kettiajya hesitated before shrugging her shoulders and saying, "I don't know, Taisha. I hope Yondalin will think of a way to utilize it."

Tsulib heard the sounds of a distressed Paterson as he galloped up the mountain towards him with Taisha on his back. He had white froth on his chest and was snorting with every exhale but was not slowing down. When he reached Tsulib, Taisha dismounted and Paterson turned without hesitation and began retracing his steps back down the steep slopes.

"Paterson!" called Taisha.

"Let him go," said Tsulib. "You won't stop him from going back to Kettiajya even if it kills him."

They both watched helplessly as he disappeared down the mountain.

Taisha told Tsulib what Kettiajya had told her to do and asked for directions to a remote part of the grid where she could try to make a crossing.

As Tsulib was giving her directions, Taisha then realized that the shorthairs were on the eastern side of the grid as they were. As she gazed over the terrain from the mountaintop, she planned to go back down the eastern slope and travel in a southern direction to approach the grid from a considerable distance downstream, hoping that she would put a good distance between her and the shorthair encampment. Once through the grid, she would then travel north alongside the river until she reached Yondalin. Tsulib agreed that it would be the best plan.

152

"We will begin to travel south now," said Tsulib. "We need to be well past the grid before it moves or we'll be dragged east with the shorthairs." He held her close. "Good luck, Taisha, I'm sorry we have laden you with this."

Taisha smiled and touched his cheek with her hand before she headed off in a southerly direction.

She thought she had put a considerable distance between her and the shorthairs before turning and headed west towards the river, hoping that she would encounter the grid.

Two shorthairs scouting the area saw her as she entered the cloud forest and immediately began running in an effort to trap her at the river, which was impassable. Their demeanor was excitement as they grew closer to Taisha and realized that she was a woman and their pace increased to a sprint.

As Taisha emerged from the cloud forest and saw the river a short distance away. She smiled and wondered how far away the grid would be. She was startled to hear footsteps and excited chatter close by and turned to see two shorthairs running towards her. Fear struck her heart as she tried to run, but her legs would not cooperate as she froze, staring at the two men who had slowed down as they approached her. They stood looking at her. It was when they began walking slowly toward her that Taisha snapped herself out of the moment and grabbed her robes above her feet and began running for her life towards the river. She suddenly found herself knocked to the ground. As she tried to pick herself up, she looked up to see the men were standing over her. She slowly lifted herself to her knees and felt a blow to her back, forcing her down again. She immediately tried to crawl towards the river but she saw one pair of feet was next to her, teasing her by letting her crawl before pushing her over with a kick to her side. As she rolled from the force of the kick she panicked as she was forced against what she thought was a tree stump but was surprised when she tried to use it as a lever to stand.

There was nothing there but she could feel something stopping her.

153

She pushed herself against the barrier as she rose to her feet.

Realizing that she had reached the grid, Taisha turned to look at her tormentors but only one of the shorthairs was close to her. The second man, who was standing about twenty steps away, stared at her. The shorthair close to her began removing his weapons and dropping them on the ground as he loosened his waist ties as the second shorthair suddenly began sprinting toward them with his club swinging above his head. Taisha watched him and opened her mouth to scream as she realized her desperate situation.

Suddenly, the shorthair wielding the club struck his companion across the base of his head as he lunged forward while trying to push Taisha clear. She found herself pinned between the grid and the second shorthair.

The other shorthair was struggling to get to his feet, blood gushing from his head. He reached out and gripped the leg of the shorthair who had struck him; his face was distorted with aggression. He forced him to the ground where a vicious struggle took place.

"Go, girl," yelled the second shorthair. "Go!"

Taisha instinctively reached for the Misha medallion around her neck with one hand and leaned against the grid as she slapped her thigh, formed a fist, and opened her palm facing down and then placed her open hand on her solar plexus with the other hand.

She felt herself falling as the grid pushed her through and beyond it.

When she stopped rolling, she looked back to see where the shorthairs were.

She was not surprised to see one very angry man trying to pass through an invisible barrier. The other was standing a distance away just staring at her.

She stood up and brushed herself clean and lightly touched the medallion.

"Thank you," she said.

154

She began running north alongside the river but stopped to look back to the shorthairs when she felt confident that she was safe.

She was surprised to see only one man, the less aggressive man, still watching her. There was something familiar about him but she didn't know what, so she turned to continue her course to Yondalin.

She had only taken a few steps when she remembered. It was the shorthair who helped her escape from their camp many moons ago.

Taisha turned once more to find her helper once more but he was gone. She felt cheated of the chance to thank him for saving her life.

The shorthair named Tarian was surprised when he recognized the girl whom he had helped leave their camp. He had left his companion bleeding on the ground close to where the girl had passed through the grid.

He stood in the cover of the cloud forest watching her as she ran alongside the river toward her trapped fellow tribespeople.

His fellow tribesmen had suspected that he was the one who had made a hole in the hut for her to escape, but Tarian had denied it. He now knew that he had exposed the truth to his companion, but was sure he had killed him.

Tarian didn't hear a sound or feel the sickening blow that killed him instantly.

Yondalin ran towards Taisha when he was told that she was approaching them from the south.

"What are you doing?" he yelled. "How did you get past the shorthairs?"

"There's a power grid in place, I'll explain later," answered Taisha. "You only have till first light tomorrow until the grid will

155

begin moving east for one day and will move any living animals including humans back up and over the mountain and beyond until it loses its power and goes back to its correct position."

"Misha?"

"Mm, Kettiajya tricked leader Misha on the full moon."

"Kettiajya," Yondalin said softly as he smiled.

Taisha slapped his arm. "Come on, Tsulib suggested resting now that the threat of an assault has gone, we'll all have to make a run for it as soon as the grid starts moving. Tsulib has already begun their trek south to get out of the way of the grid when it begins to move."

"Why not now, they can't follow us as long as we are this side of the grid?" asked Will.

"It would be better if they don't see what direction we head, we'll wait till the grid starts moving. The shorthairs will be too busy staying alive to watch us," answered Yondalin. "Are you OK? You're bruised," he asked Taisha.

"Shorthairs," she said. "That's another story."

The shorthair tribe became extremely agitated when the surviving shorthair struggled back to camp with the news of Tarian's betrayal and the existence of a power grid.

"Can't be, we crossed there just a few days ago."

"It's there now, I couldn't cross it," said the injured man. "The girl passed through somehow and I couldn't follow after I dealt with Tarian."

Their leader began pacing as he consumed liquid from the gourds.

"We'll make a line along the grid. Show everyone where the grid is and move along it north and south, there has to be a gateway somewhere. Start where you saw the girl go through, it must be there somewhere."

During the night as Yondalin and his group tried to rest, a feeling of uneasiness prevented him from sleeping. He stood up and paced many times in the darkness and couldn't understand

156

why he was very anxious. The night was very dark as the moon and stars were shielded by heavy cloud, and the dampness in the air exaggerated the coldness. He finally grabbed a few hours of rest before the first light highlighted the outlines of the surrounding mountains.

He began waking everyone to prepare for their flight to freedom when the morning light would hit the grid line and trigger its movement.

As everyone rose to their feet, a heavy silence overcame them as they looked east towards the position of the shorthairs. There, only fifty paces away from them was a thick line of shorthairs. The line extended as far as they could see both downstream and upstream of the river. They were still and silent, which unsettled the Tsulib tribe, greatly turning the confidence into fear and trepidation.

"Don't fear them," said Yondalin. "They are on the other side of the grid."

Yondalin loaded his slingshot and threw a stone toward the shorthairs. The stone flew through the air and came to a sudden halt directly in front of the line of shorthairs and fell to the ground.

A few courageous men slowly walked towards the grid and stood face to face only one step away from the shorthairs as the sun's rays slowly slipped down the mountainside towards them. Only the energy of the grid separated them from each other.

The shorthairs began chanting and beating their weapons, creating a terrifying rhythmic sound just as the grid was stuck with sunlight.

All Tsulib's tribe could do was watch as the shorthairs were pushed by an invisible force, slowly at first but quickened as it gained momentum. Those shorthairs who were fit and strong enough tried to outrun the moving force as it took all living creatures with it up the mountainside. Those who could not keep up the pace to stay in front of it were dragged until their hearts stopped beating and were left behind.

157

Yondalin instructed his people to head south alongside the river and only stop for short resting periods.

"We need to put as much space between us and them while the grid is still active."

Hepsibarb stayed close to Yondalin as he watched over the tribe and assisted the wounded and stragglers. They pushed themselves until the sun was overhead and Yondalin was happy with the progress that they had made; he called for a rest, which was welcomed by everyone.

Kettiajya was very restless as Tsulib's group had followed the grid southwards and put a good distance between them and the shorthairs, realizing that they had traveled far enough to clear the grid. As the group settled in for their second night, Kettiajya decided to head north again, hoping to intercept Yondalin and the others on their way south.

Paterson joined her as she began running, following the river north.

The darkness forced them to stop as the clouds settled low in the valley, but sleeping was difficult with no news of the fighting groups. She had anticipated meeting with them at this stage as they were all traveling the same distance, with Tsulib's group only half of one day ahead.

The following morning was welcomed with much enthusiasm by Kettiajya. "They must be very close," she said to Paterson. "Can't be far now."

Paterson urged Kettiajya to climb onto his back and he headed off into a steady canter along the worn track beside the river.

Large, rocky outcrops intruding into the river forced them to take detours up the hillsides.

Kettiajya became anxious as each corner and rise failed to reveal the fighters. Paterson sensed the mood and increased the pace, slowing only at Kettiajya's request as they approached rises

158

in the terrain. As they reached the top of a large rise, Kettiajya dismounted and stood silently. She stood with her arm under Paterson's neck, stroking his face as she scanned the valley below for any movement or sound.

Suddenly, Paterson's ears pricked up and he began to whinny moments before Kettiajya saw people coming through the thick growth down in the valley near the river. She reached into her kutcha bag for her bamboo whistle and blew her signature whistle. The people in the valley stopped and looked up towards Kettiajya and Paterson, waving their arms.

"Yes, come on, boy," she said. "They're OK."

Down in the valley, the word was passed down the lines to Yondalin, notifying him that Kettiajya was here.

He immediately began sprinting past everyone towards Kettiajya, who was half-running and half-sliding down the steep hillside towards him. He stopped and stood watching Kettiajya as she disappeared behind large outcrops of stone to emerge again much closer. She was laughing and calling his name, followed closely by Paterson. When she finally reached Yondalin, tears of relief began flowing from her eyes.

No words were spoken as they held each other tightly before joining the tribe and unloading the bags of food from Paterson's back. Everyone laughed as they feasted on the very welcomed food. Kettiajya and Yondalin wandered away from the group and found a secluded space and settled in for the night.

The following morning as they prepared to move, feeling refreshed and happy after their rest, Hepsibarb and Paterson became agitated. Yondalin was worried about the injuries Hepsibarb had acquired and approached her, hoping that her foal had not made the decision to arrive at this time. He rubbed his hands over her stomach and was confident that she was not in labor.

"Just hang in there, Heps, we'll soon be out of here," he said. "We're out of danger now."

159

Suddenly, the sound of crashing footsteps and fierce yelling broke the peaceful moment as a group of thirty or more shorthairs came rushing towards them with weapons raised. They came from the north, indicating that they must have been west of the grid line before activation and had followed them.

Yondalin pushed Hepsibarb away from him. "Go, Heps go," he yelled as he drew his club and ran towards the oncoming shorthairs.

He was joined by Kettiajya and the others of his tribe and formed a barrier between the wounded and the approaching shorthairs.

The two opposing groups met with the sickening sounds of wood and stone striking flesh.

The Tsulib fighters attacked with more precision this time, as the promise of escape and survival had lifted their spirits and given them courage. They fought with confidence and instinctively followed the movements they had been taught, inflicting fatal blows quickly and efficiently. As the shorthair numbers dwindled, it became apparent that they were going to fight until death.

After losing fifteen of the Tsulib tribe, Yondalin brought down the last of the shorthairs. The surviving fighters then walked silently amongst the slain, assisting the wounded and gathering the dead of the Tsulib tribe. The dead shorthairs were stacked a short distance away and those still living were given a final blow to the head.

The fight had taken its toll both in lives and injuries, so they decided to stay another night where they were and tend to the injured and construct frames to carry the incapacitated.

A long and uncomfortable night ahead was anticipated. The comfort of a fire was out of the question as they had to consider that there might be more shorthairs in the area.

After placing their dead amongst the rocks a short distance up the mountainside and removing their kutcha bags to be taken back to their families, Yondalin and Kettiajya decided to stay at

160

the rear of the moving tribe keeping a constant look out for more shorthairs who might approach from the north. If trouble was imminent, Yondalin would blow his signature whistle to alert the tribe to the danger.

Yondalin and Kettiajya told the surviving tribe to begin moving at first light; he and Kettiajya would follow but keep a distance behind them. They traveled a short distance back north in the direction from where they had come and found a high position with views both upstream and downstream. Hepsibarb and Paterson did not follow their instructions to stay with the tribe and chose to follow their companions to their lookout but remained at the lower level near the river.

The shorthair had watched the tribe overnight knowing that he was only one against many and was pleased to see the tribe move on, leaving only a man, a woman, and two horses to follow behind the tribe. He smiled at his good fortune in being presented with the opportunity to take a horse to carry him away from the place where all of his companions were killed. He could see no purpose in trying to take revenge by confronting the people and possibly losing his own life.

He watched as the two people began to climb up to the ridge overlooking the river and took advantage of their obvious preoccupation with each other to move closer to the horses.

He liked the look of the black stallion but doubted his abilities to capture and then to control him. The mare looked much more passive, and he slowly worked his way toward her while watching the man and woman climbing the hill. Paterson, however, was aware of the shorthair's presence and became increasingly restless as he drew closer.

Kettiajya sensed his restlessness and stopped to look down toward him and Hepsibarb in time to see the shorthair running along the river's edge toward Hepsibarb.

She cried out for Paterson at the same time as Yondalin threw himself down the hill, sliding and leaping as he kept his eyes on Hepsibarb, whose reflexes were much slower with the pregnancy and weary after the days of fighting.

She was confused and fearful by all the action and began running toward the river not knowing that she was going toward the shorthair, who was crouching in the shrubs waiting for the opportunity to leap onto her back and escape from the area. Paterson was caught between his devotion to Kettiajya and love for Hepsibarb, but after seeing Kettiajya safe up on the hill, he rushed to Hepsibarb.

The shorthair panicked when he saw the stallion running toward him, and the man was heading for the mare. His only chance was to take his chances with the stallion and make a run and try to get the mare before the man. As he ran, he unwound the rope that was wrapped around his waist, hoping he would get the chance to throw it around the mare's neck and drag himself onto her back.

Yondalin was bruised and exhausted by his flight to Hepsibarb but still found the strength to pull his club from his waist wrap as he called to Hepsibarb to go quickly.

The shorthair felt that his chances were not very good as he saw the man and the stallion focus on him. He stopped and drew his sling from his bag and picked up a large stone from the ground as Paterson was just a few strides away from him. He took deliberate aim and fired the sling toward Yondalin and the mare.

Yondalin anticipated the stone which was going to hit Hepsibarb and lunged forward, putting himself between the stone and Hepsibarb.

The shorthair did not see the stone reach its destination before Paterson pounded him with his hooves again and again until he was battered and lifeless.

Kettiajya felt helpless as she watched the events unfold in front of her. She screamed Yondalin's name as he took the stone at close range into his abdomen leaving a bleeding wound under

162

the left rib cage. He picked himself up off the ground and fell towards Hepsibarb. He threw his arms around her neck to steady himself but she was too exhausted to stand firm and fell toward the river's edge, slipping into the water with Yondalin's arms gripped tightly around her neck.

"Paterson," she cried. "Quickly, boy!"

The waters carried Yondalin and Hepsibarb downstream very quickly. Kettiajya jumped onto Paterson's back and they galloped downstream, trying to get ahead of them and looking for a narrow part of the river where Yondalin and Hepsibarb might get trapped long enough for Paterson and Kettiajya to help them.

They had a natural affinity with the river and didn't doubt for a moment that they would be able to help them.

The riverbanks were very rough and forced Kettiajya and Paterson to leave the riverbanks and travel around obstacles and impassable rises.

As they reconnected with the river and continued the sprint downstream, she saw an area where the swollen banks had eroded into a steep rise and had destabilized a large tree by exposing its roots and causing it to fall into the river.

She was shocked when she recognized the golden form of Hepsibarb caught in the fallen tree.

Paterson did not need any encouragement to find the quickest route to the banks of the river closest to her. He immediately entered the water with Kettiajya still mounted and forced his way against the tree trunk near Hepsibarb.

Kettiajya climbed onto the fallen tree and clawed her way towards Hepsibarb, who appeared to be still alive but was struggling to keep her head above the strong force of the waters. As she reached Hepsibarb, Kettiajya saw Yondalin still clinging to Hepsibarb under her neck, jammed between her body and the fallen tree. A stream of blood was coloring the waters as it flowed from Yondalin's wound. Kettiajya did not hesitate to enter the water and struggled to pull Yondalin under Hepsibarb's neck to

163

get him on the upstream side of her where she attempted to lift him onto her back.

Paterson had found the bottom of the river with his feet and stood firmly behind Hepsibarb, offering his body as leverage for Kettiajya to pull Yondalin under Hepsibarb neck to the upstream side of her. She tried to drag him along Hepsibarb's body towards the shore. The current of the river was far too strong and fought to keep him within its clutches. Kettiajya had no choice but to get under the water and try to lift Yondalin onto Hepsibarb's back, which she did after many tries. She pushed him onto Hepsibarb and took his hands and yelled, "Hold on, Yondalin, please hold on!"

Yondalin used the last of his strength to tighten his grip on Hepsibarb's mane.

Kettiajya then called Paterson to the shore, tied a length of rope around his neck, and plunged herself back into the river, taking the other end of the rope. She fought the river to wrap the rope around the flanks of Hepsibarb.

She then cried out to Paterson, "Pull, Paterson, pull," as she clung to the fallen tree and tried to reassure Hepsibarb and Yondalin that it would all be OK.

Paterson dug his hooves into the muddy banks and slowly began to gain momentum as Hepsibarb's head became more exposed as she was dragged closer to the shore.

As they drew closer to the shore, Kettiajya found the riverbed with her feet and leaned against Hepsibarb's flanks and pushed.

Hepsibarb slowly reached the bank of the river but it became increasingly harder for her to lift herself and Yondalin out of the water, which had given her buoyancy.

Kettiajya soon realized that Hepsibarb was far too weak to raise herself and Yondalin out of the river. She untied the rope from Paterson's neck and called him to the deep side of Hepsibarb, where he stood higher than Hepsibarb. Kettiajya then called, "Yondalin, we need to get you onto Paterson's back, I'm sorry. Please stay with us, please!"

164

Kettiajya then climbed onto Paterson's back and called upon all her reserves to drag Yondalin up onto Paterson's back. She took his hands and pulled him as she slid over the opposite side of Paterson, draping Yondalin over with the top half of his body over one side and the bottom half hanging to the other.

Yondalin cried out in pain.

"I'm sorry, my dear, but I can't think of another way to do this," cried Kettiajya. "Please hold on, we'll get you out now!"

Paterson then forced himself with Yondalin on his back up the banks of the river, where Kettiajya dragged him off Paterson's back and laid him on the ground.

She looked up to see Hepsibarb, now free of her burden; the mare had become lighter and had dislodged from the tree and was being dragged downstream again.

As she jumped to her feet, Paterson immediately lunged into the river and began swimming frantically towards Hepsibarb. As he drew alongside her, he forced himself against her as he pushed and swam towards the shore. Finally, he had her in shallow water, where they stood still for a moment as Paterson nudged and nipped her neck, keeping her alert.

After standing in the shallow water for some time, Paterson nudged and encouraged Hepsibarb to begin climbing out of the river. She did so but very slowly, one step at a time, until finally they were on the banks of the river.

Kettiajya had run downstream and met them both. She was shocked when she saw Hepsibarb standing still with her head hanging very low and covered in blood which appeared to be coming from the top of her neck and back and had run all the way over her belly. Then she realized that it was not Hepsibarb's blood, it was Yondalin's.

"Oh, thank goodness you are both OK," she said as she walked around each of them hugging and kissing their necks. She ran her hands over Hepsibarb's belly and cried when she felt movement. "Your baby is OK, Heps, it's OK."

165

She ran back to Yondalin and found that he had regained consciousness but was still lying on his back.

He smiled when he saw her approaching.

Kettiajya reassured him that Hepsibarb was OK but very weak.

She tore strips of cloth from her clothing and began to pack his wound and sat with his head on her lap as she pondered their situation.

She knew that both Yondalin and Hepsibarb were in a bad way but also knew that they would need to let them rest for a while before trying to get them back to the tribe, which would be at least one day from them.

She whistled for Paterson to join them but he did not. She knew that Hepsibarb was his first priority and it worried her that he did not respond.

She lay close to Yondalin to keep him warm as he drifted in and out of consciousness. Her body shook and her tears dripped onto Yondalin's face as she cried in desperation.

She then stood up and wandered around, keeping him in sight as she searched for the grey ghost plant. She lit a small fire and tossed the plant onto it and sat down with Yondalin again and waited.

Within moments she heard the sound of winds swirling around and getting closer until she was surrounded by leaves and dust swirling around her getting faster and faster.

"Misha!" she cried, "Misha, please help us!" She stood up and began running around amongst the swirling leaves and dust looking for Misha.

The movement finished suddenly and Kettiajya stood still, waiting for Misha to appear.

They didn't.

All she heard was a haunting, whispering laugh getting further away from her until it was silent.

Kettiajya stared into the darkness, not believing a Misha would deny assistance. She turned to walk back to Yondalin when she saw leader Misha fading away into the scrub. She was smiling.

166

Kettiajya fell to her knees and sobbed.

She settled into the night with Yondalin in her arms and sang songs to him as she tidied his hair. She was delighted to hear his song once more. She had only heard it twice before. The first time was when she turned him away and the second was when she returned to him. He responded occasionally by smiling and lifting her hand to his face before drifting into sleep again.

As the sun began to creep down the mountainside, she raised herself to her elbow and watched and stroked Yondalin's face as he slept, hoping that he was only sleeping. She stood up and ran downstream to find Paterson and Hepsibarb standing still and silent.

"Paterson, I need you to carry Yondalin," she pleaded. "Do you feel up to it?"

She checked Hepsibarb's belly once more and once again felt movement.

She looked a mess covered in Yondalin's dried blood, but otherwise she appeared to be fine considering what she had been through.

The horses followed Kettiajya back to Yondalin and were very surprised to see him sitting up. He was very weak but sitting up, which gave Kettiajya hope and joy.

She asked Paterson to lie down next to Yondalin, then helped him onto the horse's back. Paterson then raised himself to his feet and Kettiajya laughed and clapped when she saw Yondalin sitting upright on his back.

"We're going to make it!" she cried.

Yondalin responded with a smile.

Tsulib's tribe had reunited with the fighting team, who told him that Yondalin and Kettiajya had volunteered to be the rear guard and were following. They joked about them using it as an excuse to have private time together.

Tsulib was worried when he did not see Yondalin with the rest of the tribe but relaxed when he was told that Kettiajya was him.

167

Icemon, however, was very concerned and asked Tsulib if she could take a few companions back to meet them.

"Yes, good idea," he answered. "Take food as well, can't live on love alone," he said, smiling.

A girl named Georgia, who was a great, great granddaughter of Aida, volunteered with Yondalin's mate Carlo to go with Icemon.

They pushed themselves to increase their pace as she became increasingly anxious.

As the sun was completing its morning session and settling overhead, Icemon raised her hand and called, "Shush everyone!"

They stopped and listened.

Icemon was right; she heard a horse galloping through the cloud forest.

"Out of the way," she commanded as she swept her hand indicating to clear the track.

"It's Paterson!" called Georgia.

Icemon hurried forward and raised her hand to Paterson as he approached.

He ran toward her with his head held high and maneuvered his flanks toward her. She then saw fresh blood on his back and feared for him. He knocked her over as he nudged her with his flanks.

She stood up muttering to herself.

Paterson again knocked her over by pushing against her.

She lay on the ground looking up at him. He was extremely agitated.

"Where's Kettiajya," she called.

Paterson then lowered his front legs to the ground.

"Oh dear, you're going to take me to her, aren't you?"

Georgia ran forward and helped Icemon onto Paterson's back, and Paterson whisked her away. The others followed quickly.

Paterson took Icemon on a fast, rough ride but she sensed that he was on a mission knowing Kettiajya was in trouble.

168

She wasn't prepared for the sight that awaited her.

Paterson unceremoniously dropped her at Kettiajya's side.

Kettiajya was sitting on the ground with Yondalin in her arms. Her face was red and wet from tears. Hepsibarb was lying on the ground next to them.

"He's not going to make it, Icemon, please do something, she begged. "He's bleeding again, it won't stop!"

Icemon knelt down and touched Yondalin. She took a handful of simarouba bark from her kutcha bag and pressed it against his wound.

She ran her hands over him without touching him. She looked back at Kettiajya. "Stay with him, Kettiajya, help him go," she said quietly.

Kettiajya stared at Icemon.

"Leader Misha denied him, Icemon," she cried. "She denied us both!" she screamed as she squeezed Yondalin close to her breast and rocked him.

Icemon stood up and looked towards Hepsibarb.

She hurried to her side and looked up at Paterson, who was standing over her.

"What happened, Paterson, we have Yondalin leaving us and your baby arriving at the same time," she asked. "What happened?"

Finally Georgia and Carlo came running to join them. Icemon instructed them to leave Kettiajya and Yondalin alone. "You can stand by to help Hepsibarb, looks like she's in trouble too."

They were suddenly drawn to Kettiajya as she screamed, "Yondalin, please don't leave me, please don't..."

They turned to see Kettiajya stroking and kissing Yondalin's face and crying and sobbing inconsolably.

"He's gone," said Icemon. "Carlo, go and bring Tsulib and others to help."

Icemon then knelt down to Hepsibarb and noticed that she had run out of strength to give birth and the foal was frantically moving inside her belly.

169

"What can we do, she needs help," said Georgia.

Icemon didn't answer.

"Icemon…?"

Icemon sighed and then said, "We'll have to help the little one."

She then took a length of cloth from her kutcha, tore it into a long strip and crawled down to Hepsibarb's flanks. She made a loop of the cloth strip, made a loose noose in the middle section, and gripped it in her hand. She then pushed her fist into Hepsibarb's uterus. She felt around inside her, located two small feet, slipped the noose over them, and withdrew her hand while pulling on the noose. She then gently but firmly began to pull on the cloth strips.

Hepsibarb was too tired to offer any resistance or assistance.

The foal slowly began to appear and as Icemon leant back strongly on the noose, she fell backwards when the foal suddenly fully emerged. Icemon quickly crawled back to the foal and began massaging it as she cleaned the membranous tissue off it. The little creature began its struggle to live.

"Well, Hepsibarb, you've got a son. A beautiful son and he's just like you," she said as she carried him towards Hepsibarb's face, where the mare began nuzzling him. "Oh, he has a black mane and tail!"

Icemon walked over to Kettiajya, who was lying next to Yondalin, embracing him. She was silent. "Hepsibarb has a son, Kettiajya," she said. She waited for a response but did not receive one. She went back to Hepsibarb, who appeared to be showing some improvement and had raised herself to her feet as the foal had found his feet and her nipples. He was pushing and nudging Hepsibarb's belly as he tried to stimulate the milk flow. Paterson did not show much interest in the foal but continuously nudged Hepsibarb's neck.

A fire was lit as they settled in for the night to await Tsulib's arrival. They decided to sit beside Kettiajya and Yondalin for the night.

170

As dawn approached, Tsulib and many others arrived. Tsulib stood in disbelief as he saw his son Yondalin still on the ground in Kettiajya's arms. He approached and wept as he saw the blood on his body and the color gone from his face. He knelt down and touched his hair.

He stood and walked towards a group surrounding Hepsibarb, who was once more lying on the ground.

Icemon saw him approaching. "She died last night, Tsulib, this is her foal," she said, uncovering her robe to reveal the colt.

"She wouldn't have survived without Yondalin anyway," said Tsulib.

They looked up to see Kettiajya walking toward Hepsibarb with Yondalin in her arms.

They moved aside to allow her free access as she slowly laid Yondalin down with Hepsibarb.

"We need to bury them together," she said. "Right here where they chose."

It took all the rest of the day to dig a huge grave next to Hepsibarb and roll her into it. Kettiajya then lifted Yondalin and climbed into the grave to place him next to Hepsibarb. She cut a piece of his hair and a piece of hair from Hepsibarb's mane and placed it into Yondalin's kutcha bag and tied it to her waist. She cut a length of her own hair and placed it in Yondalin's hand.

She looked for Paterson but he was nowhere in the vicinity.

The evening was taken by talking about Yondalin and Hepsibarb and singing his favorite songs.

They would not sleep this night.

As the night grew longer, Paterson was seen entering the campsite, and following him was a mare with a foal of her own. Paterson walked directly to Icemon and nudged the foal under her robes. The foal reluctantly shuffled to his feet and objected when Paterson pushed him towards the mare. Everyone watched in silence as the mare sniffed the new baby and nudged him toward her nipples where her foal was feeding.

Hepsibarb's baby instantly copied the actions and began feeding greedily.

The following morning found Kettiajya lying on her stomach with arms stretched wide on the grave. She refused food and water and company.

"Leave her be," said Icemon.

"I need to know what happened to Yondalin," interrupted Tsulib.

"You'll have to wait till she tells us, Tsulib."

Kettiajya didn't move all that day and it was decided that they needed to leave the campsite early the following day with or without her.

Upon rising the following morning, Kettiajya was gone.

So too was Paterson.

The mare and the two foals were content to stay where they were, so Tsulib and his tribe quietly disappeared into the forest.

They followed the river along its course through many valleys, cutting its path into the mountainsides and falling down a multitude of ravines and gullies. They only stopped to rest as darkness descended upon them and they undertook the daily rituals of cooking and bathing and caring for the weak and wounded.

It was a silent journey as no one could get their minds around what had happened and how much their lives had changed in so little time. Tsulib followed the tribe, keeping his distance, nursing his grief in losing his only son. He did not speak to Icemon as he somehow blamed her for the prophecy that took Yondalin away from him.

The tribe heard him on many occasions half-crying, half-shouting, as he struggled to accept his loss.

After ten days of traveling, Tsulib had slowly worked his way to the front of the travelers and suggested looking for a suitable place to call home for a while.

172

Icemon had decided to stay with the tribe after the death of Yondalin to offer advice on choosing a home based on her knowledge accumulated while roaming the mountains.

She had suggested that they find their way east over two mountains to reach a river that she knew would lead them to the place where the river would fall into the low forests below the clouds. Icemon knew it would take three or four weeks of walking over extremely difficult terrain to reach their destination. The mountains that they had to cross were very steep and nearly impassable, covered in dense forest. She did not tell them of the task ahead of them and no one asked.

They were more than willing to let someone else make the decisions and were very happy that it was Icemon, who had a mysterious connection with the earth.

"A change of environment will do you all good," she whispered as they started their journey.

The walking was good for the tribe. It gave them all time to be alone with their grief and thoughts, and the physical exhaustion made them all sleep well at the end of the day.

Icemon encouraged them to find strength and push themselves each day, promising them a beautiful place to rest in many weeks. A place to call home for long enough to replenish food, rest, and talk about the things that had changed everyone's lives forever before asking them to pack up once more to continue their journey over the last mountain.

She gave them something else to think about as she deliberately took them on a very difficult trek and followed a stone path which was obviously manmade.

The path led them to the top of a very large mountain with deliberately placed stones forming a gateway that announced the view below them. It was a smaller mountain, which appeared to be nestled in the arms of a ring of large, sharply peaked mountains and wrapped in a ribbon of water at the base.

As they found their way through the overgrown vines and trees, they noticed remains of previous inhabitants' dwellings

173

and even suggested an overnight's stay at one place high on the mountain with views down the valleys every way but one: the path back onto the top of this place. There was a smaller mountain on the edge of this mountain standing like a vigilante guard watching over the remains of this place of many dwellings. The stones were still sitting strong in their original places, meticulously laid on top of each other, forming walls and windows with no mortar, which was not necessary as the joins of the stones were perfectly matched with no space even for a blade of grass.

Conversations were promoted by questions about how the stones were carried to this almost inaccessible place and why they chose such a place to build a settlement.

Clear freshwater still ran through the stone ducts, falling into baths which cascaded down the mountain. The question was, they were on top of the mountain, so where was the water coming from?

A few energetic boys decided to follow a track which led to the top of the small mountain overlooking them. The climb was hard and treacherous but was rewarded at the top with a view like no other.

The ruins below were indeed draped over a peak with one access point. The surrounding mountains stood sentinel. One of these stood alone and appeared to be not peaked but rounded at the top. It had a dark, foreboding, very masculine energy but was also very beautiful in its own way. Surrounded in cloud at its base and a veil of mist over the peak, it was offering an unquestionable protective energy to the central peak.

Icemon was happy to see the people's minds distracted for a while, and seeing the remnants of another race made it easier to accept that nothing stays the same forever...nothing.

The tribe had a chance to grieve for their lost friends and companions. Taisha had put her trauma behind her and others stopped talking about her experience with the shorthairs now that they all had lived through loss and pain.

174

She formed a much-needed friendship with a woman called Brodie, who had lost two brothers in the war and was left with no family. They were both happy to find a kindred soul to laugh with after so much unhappiness.

After five days rest and much exploring, the tribe reluctantly decided to continue their quest to find the lowlands that Icemon and Kettiajya spoke about.

Many felt sad to leave such a magical place as Icemon guided them off the mountain, continuing to show them the way heading south on a stone track which wrapped around the sharp peaks and fell into valleys. Animals used these paths, but the stones were placed too precisely and deliberately to be natural formations. The tribe became excited and chatted amongst themselves as they approached every mountaintop or dense growth in a valley. They had guessing competitions with each other on the chances of the engineered paths continuing. Cheers of amazement were sent into the air as the first person to see the continuing path screamed, "Yes!"

Even Tsulib appeared to cheer up a little to see his people delighted with such a simple distraction as a path.

After three days since leaving the ruins on the mountaintop, they finally reached a point where they looked down upon a large valley with a river flowing through.

They were silent as they looked over the valley in its splendor with the large, woolly animals walking along the narrow paths created by years of use.

"The animals have made this easy for us, we'll use their tracks," Icemon said. "This will lead us to a place where the valley stretches wider and two rivers run into one and abundant food grows. We can stay for as long it takes to rest and tend to our wounded and gather and prepare more food to continue."

"What about the shorthairs? What if they are following?" Brodie asked.

"We need a few volunteers to stay behind on the mountaintops and ridges to watch for that. That will be a part of our life

175

now; we need to be alert all the time. Come on now," she said. "We'll be there by sunset then we can talk."

Icemon smiled in anticipation of the tribe's reaction when they saw this place she had spoken of. There they would find many foods growing wild amongst the forest in the valley; remnants of gardens planted by past tribes had been revitalized by the annual flooding and protection of the forest growth.

She was not disappointed. As the tribe made their way down into the valley and the sun was slowly shielded by the mountains, excited chatter changed to uncontrolled laughter as their pace grew faster. Finally the valley floor exposed the remains of large retaining walls stretching down to the river.

The walls appeared to wrap around the mountain base where the two rivers merged to become one.

They found large plants of corn, potato, and yam plants, which promised large tubers below the ground. Large, colourful fruits hung like teardrops from trees.

The men carrying heavy poles with sick tribe members carefully stepped through the forest and found the remains of a dwelling with three walls intact, offering protection from the cold for the sick and injured. After large baskets of food were picked off the trees and vines and dug from the earth, large gourds of food were prepared and fires were lit to heat the stones for cooking.

Georgia was busy crushing, smelling, and tasting the small plants in the undergrowth, excited by the possibility of new herbs for food and medicine. The knowledge of identifying plants was handed down from mother to daughter since the cave dwelling days. Georgia loved to hear the stories about her ancestor Aida. *I wish she was here to see this*, she thought.

Tsulib found himself distracted from his grieving by the excitement and approached Icemon. He smiled at her and nodded his head, realizing that this was not a coincidence. She knew that this and the ruins that he suspected were far off the original course set by her, but was exactly what the tribe needed at this point in time.

176

She was offering a promise of better times ahead.

It was after the feast of known and new flavors that everyone grouped with the sick and injured and contemplated their good fortune to survive and reach new lands.

"Icemon, we need you to know how grateful we are for getting us here," said Carlos. "You are a bad-tempered old bag most times but…Well, thanks."

Laughter and rattling kutcha bags followed.

"Hmm," sounded Icemon. "Well, now you miserable lot need to talk about what you're thinking, get it off your scrawny chests." Having said that, she disappeared into the darkness leaving everyone with only the sounds of her signature hop-drag.

Taisha began the discussions. "I never thought we could get past the first shorthair incident with me and the boys, but here we are. We have survived more loss and unbelievable grief."

"We've never known such sorrow," whispered Tsulib.

"Do you think we'll ever get over this?" asked Georgia.

"Yes. With time, only time," said Rosa, the mother of Taisha.

"We'll need to be prepared for future altercations; there will be more sooner or later. Tsulib added. "We will need to develop warriors, specialists in different skills."

"What are you saying, Tsulib?" Carlos asked.

"Some of us do not like the fighting, these people will need to develop signals and stand guard at outposts surrounding our camps. They will need to invent ways to communicate from distances," he said. "We all need to think about what skills we have and how to develop them to benefit us all. Our priority at this time is protecting ourselves as we travel; think what you like to do and how you can use it."

"We could use these old places for lookout posts," Carlos suggested.

"For now, yes, but we will be a long way from here," Tsulib said.

"I think we will need to have constant travelers coming back this way to bring news of any changes," Taisha offered.

177

"That sounds logical, give us many weeks to anticipate visitors, friendly or not," Carlos agreed.

"I wonder where Kettiajya is," Georgia mused.

"Everything changed after she came to our camp, she destroyed us. Best she stays away," said Sinai.

"Contact with us also changed her life and gave her equal grief," Taisha pointed out.

"Maybe more, "Georgia said.

"Mm…everything changed after she arrived," Sinai said.

A long uncomfortable silence followed as most had not considered Kettiajya or where she was.

"No, it began with Taisha and the boys," Rosa said.

"It began with our neglect, not telling the truth about human nature," one of the elders said.

"Well, we didn't lie. We just didn't tell," another elder added.

Silence again consumed them.

"Can we stay here for a while? Maybe one or two moons before we move on? We all need the rest and our sick need to get well again," Georgia said.

"We need a bit of time to dry some of the fresh food here too," said Rosa...

"Why can't we stay here forever?" someone asked.

No one answered. No one was ready to think about a permanent home at this time. No one felt safe anywhere after their fight with the shorthairs.

178

Kettiajya Leaves Yondalin

After leaving Yondalin and Hepsibarb's grave, Kettiajya and Paterson headed back east to the comfort of their cavern. The walk back was long and slow and silent. Kettiajya walked with Paterson following, as they crossed mountain peaks but avoided deep river crossings where her bloodied clothes and hair would be washed. She found some comfort in carrying the blood of Yondalin with her.

For many days she cried and screamed at the mountain peaks; nights were spent sobbing with unbelievable grief as she longed for the warmth of Yondalin's embrace, knowing she would never feel it again. After three days she fell silent. No crying or sobbing.

Just silence.

When they finally reached the cavern, Kettiajya entered and lay down on her familiar resting place. She ran her hands over the covers and cried, "You never knew my special place."

She turned to face Paterson, but he had not followed her into the cavern. She returned outside and looked towards Veronica as tears flowed down her face. She turned back to her bed and lay down finally closing her eyes, exhausted.

Many days later, Paterson returned, entered the cavern, and nudged Kettiajya, encouraging her to rise. She reached out for his nose and struggled to sit up to stroke him.

She rose and walked to the cavern entrance, removed her bloodied and soiled clothing and lowered herself into the river. She sat gazing up at Veronica; a hint of a smile crossed her face as she ran her hands over her stomach.

"We are three now, Paterson," she called to Paterson. "What are we to do, Paterson? How am I going to do this alone? Nothing can ever be the same anymore."

Paterson stood silent, watching Kettiajya.

She reached out and wrapped her arms around his neck. "We still have each other."

They stood watching the sun setting over Veronica. *Nothing is permanent, no plant and no river. Nothing stands still,* she thought as the last ray of sun disappeared.

She gathered her clothes which were red with the blood of Yondalin and carefully packed them into a basket. She placed the basket in a place close to her sleeping place.

Kettiajya felt an obligation to inform Tsulib about the pending arrival of the child of Yondalin. *Not right now, some time later,* she thought.

It was four months before Kettiajya felt revived enough and ready to confront the tribe, although at this time she felt that she could live forever with no other contact but Paterson. She felt like she had lost half of her soul, the only man she had ever known and loved, but Tsulib had lost his only son. She knew that he deserved to know that Yondalin lived on in her baby.

She anticipated that Icemon would lead them southeast toward the cloudy lowlands that they had both seen but never visited. She came to the conclusion that there was no other place that would offer the tribe a new beginning.

During the week before they left the cavern to find the tribe, Kettiajya took time to visit Veronica and her favorite places and to collect plants of jurubeba, chuchuhuasi, and atuaba to assist her with her pregnancy and the long trip ahead.

Paterson became restless in anticipation of the journey ahead and the responsibility of Kettiajya and her precious cargo.

180

They both felt relief and gratefulness for having made the decision to take another step forward, to leave the grieving behind but never the memories.

The memories would feed and keep her for the rest of her years.

Kettiajya set no measurement of time or seasons to find the tribe; she wanted to travel with Paterson as they did in the days before Yondalin. No plan, just go in the general direction which was east-by-southeast. Only now, there was an extra consideration: Yondalin's baby.

It was seven very relaxing and enjoyable weeks after leaving the cavern that Kettiajya and Paterson knew they were only a day or two from catching up with the moving tribe of Tsulib. They had found their tracks four weeks before but had deliberately slowed down their pace when she noticed that the tribe had left a very obvious trail to follow. She was concerned and wondered if the tribe had not learnt anything from the fighting with the shorthairs.

As they drew closer to the tribe, she made excursions in the dark of each night to get closer to the tribe and observe their behavior as she and Paterson did years ago.

She was pleased to see that they had posted watch people who traveled one day behind the main tribe, but was also unhappy to be able to get so close to these watch people without them seeing her or Paterson.

Kettiajya decided that the best way to show Tsulib the weakness in the watch people was to enter the camp unannounced.

The campsite had settled in for the night after eating and signals were exchanged between the watch people, indicating that all was well. Tsulib left the main group and walked towards his bedding, which was a small distance away from others.

As he walked away he turned to bid his companions a good night, he was shocked when he turned back and saw Paterson and Kettiajya standing only meters from him.

181

She was smiling and Tsulib felt a peacefulness generating from her. He now appreciated what his son had seen in her.

"Hello, Tsulib," she said softly as she walked towards him, offering him her arms. He said nothing as he held her tight, and they both cried, knowing that they both had lost the one person whom they would have willingly died for.

They then stood apart, holding hands, and looked at each other without speaking a word.

Kettiajya broke the silence. "I have news for you, Tsulib," she said.

"You are carrying Yondalin's child."

"How did you know," said Kettiajya. "Is it that noticeable?"

"I can't think of any other reason why you would want to visit us again." Tsulib paused. "We caused you so much pain, and you look beautiful."

"But it was worth all this pain just to have known Yondalin."

"Was it really worth it, Kettiajya? Now you will have a baby with no father."

"The baby has a father, Tsulib," Kettiajya said realizing that this was the first time Tsulib had called her by name. "Yondalin," she said firmly.

Tsulib looked at Kettiajya and dismissed any doubts that he may have had regarding the welfare of his grandchild. The child's mother would be a force to be reckoned with should any threat confront them.

It was then that he realized she had arrived at the camp site with no announcement by the watch people.

"How did the watch people greet you, Kettiajya?" he asked.

"I was not approached by anyone," she said.

"Did you see the watch people?"

"Yes, Tsulib, I saw many people on my ride into here with Paterson. Maybe they recognized me as a friend."

Tsulib did not comment as he knew that the tribe should have been advised on the arrival of anyone in the vicinity at least one day in advance.

182

Kettiajya realized that she was correct in guessing that the watchers had not seen her. It was fortunate that it was Kettiajya and not a stranger who had alerted Tsulib to a weakness in their primary defenses.

"I think we will keep your arrival to ourselves until tomorrow," said Tsulib. "Settle yourself in and have a good rest tonight, I am sure your presence and the news you bring will be received with delight."

Kettiajya offered Tsulib another embrace and quietly moved away into the darkness with Paterson.

Before dawn, Tsulib approached the watchers group and advised them of Kettiajya's arrival and let them discuss the possible consequences of someone entering the camp undetected.

He did not need to unsettle the tribe now that they had found a bit of contentment with the traveling and new experiences that Icemon had led them to.

Taking Tsulib's advice, Kettiajya kept her distance from the tribe until everyone had woken from their sleep and were busy doing their tasks to prepare food. She then quietly followed Tsulib into the main area, greeting those who saw her. The general reaction was excitement but the sight of her brought back many bad emotions for others, especially those who believed that she had been the beginning of bad things.

As everyone gathered to see what the excitement was about, Tsulib said, "We have wonderful news: Kettiajya is carrying Yondalin's baby."

Quietness descended upon them.

Taisha was the first to come to Kettiajya with tears and open arms.

"I am so happy," she said. "For you, for Tsulib. For all of us."

Others slowly approached Kettiajya. The whisperings became excited chatter and then cheers as their sadness for the death of Yondalin was overcome by the news of his child.

"Where have you been for five months, Kettiajya?" asked Taisha. "We have been worried about you."

183

"I needed time."

"You've been alone?"

"No, I had Paterson. He's all I needed."

Taisha began to weep. "Kettiajya, I wish I could've been there to hold you. I am so sorry that you had to do all that alone."

"Please don't be sorry," Kettiajya pleaded. "Yondalin left me with a beautiful gift," she said, stroking her stomach.

"How long will it be?"

"One moon, maybe more."

Kettiajya had noticed Icemon's absence and now felt excitement at the prospect of seeing her again. She looked around the site for a peak which offered views of the rising sun knowing that Icemon would be there.

Icemon was walking down the rocky path to the campsite when she saw Kettiajya sitting on the edge of the path, overlooking the valley and the settlement below.

"You could never sneak up on me, Icemon," laughed Kettiajya as she jumped up and ran towards Icemon and threw her arms around her.

They stood embracing each other in silence before Icemon held Kettiajya at arm's length and said, "How are you, my dear?" Her eyes dropped to Kettiajya's belly and then back to her face.

"Mm," said Kettiajya, nodding her head.

Tears welled in Icemon's eyes and she pressed her lips together in an effort to hold back her emotions.

"Icemon, are you OK?" asked Kettiajya.

"Yes, I am happy that Yondalin will live on. He was a lovely man."

They embraced once more, walked to the edge of the path, and sat looking down into the valley, talking for many hours. They discussed the days before Yondalin and the freedom of leading nomadic lives. They discussed their journeys and the plant medicine they had collected from all over the valleys and mountains. They exchanged plants from their kutcha bags and smelt, crushed, and tasted them to decipher their usefulness.

184

As the sun began to settle behind the mountain peaks, Kettiajya rose to her feet and helped Icemon move away from the edge of the cliff.

"It is so good to spend time with you again," Icemon said.

Kettiajya nodded her head and smiled as she leant over and kissed Icemon's cheek and said, "I wouldn't change anything, Icemon. It's been devastating, but," she paused. "I wouldn't change anything."

Kettiajya enjoyed the time in the camp. She enjoyed the pampering that the women insisted on bestowing upon her.

She was given many items for her baby, including clothing and a carry pouch, which she spent hours decorating with Yondalin's colors and family patterns.

Every day just a few hours before sunset, Kettiajya spent time with Icemon high up on the peak.

They were good days for all.

The Birth

The day of the birth of Kettiajya's baby was drawing closer and the women prepared a place for her to give birth. Kettiajya allowed them to make their plans for the birth, thinking it was good for everyone to be involved. However, one morning the women found Kettiajya's hut empty. They panicked and screamed that she was missing. Icemon asked them to be quiet as she knew that Kettiajya had gone to her special place knowing that the birth was imminent, and she wanted to do it in the comfort of her chosen place and time with only Paterson as a companion.

Paterson sensed long before Kettiajya that the baby was beginning to close down its reliance on her. Kettiajya was puzzled by Paterson's attentiveness since early that morning when he had pushed open the flap to her hut and stood in the doorway, watching her and snorting. It did not take too long before she realised what his attention was about as she felt a deep aching in her lower back and could not get comfortable. She quietly followed Paterson to the perimeter of the campsite, where he offered his back to her. He lowered himself to the ground for her to mount.

Paterson took his time carrying Kettiajya back to Veronica. It took him longer than usual as he chose every step carefully and took the easier tracks to protect Kettiajya from any unnecessary discomfort in this time when her body was preparing to present her baby. He sensed when she was having a contraction and stopped and waited until it had passed, then continued slowly as she tried to rest during contractions. As they approached the caves, Paterson chose the river access and slowly entered the water and swam across the rapids with Kettiajya clinging to his mane to stay mounted. He gently climbed up the steep slope leading to the entrance of her caves, where Kettiajya slipped off his back and proceeded to prepare for the birth.

She started a fire and filled a pot with water and added the leaves of emauba, vassourinha, and algodon to make a drink to give her body and the baby some assistance. She made herself a comfortable place close to a large stone for relaxing between contractions and for support during the birth.

As the day progressed, the discomfort felt by her was beginning to become more intense, and Paterson moved closer so that she could touch him for comfort if she needed to. Kettiajya was grateful to have him there, guiding her as she paced around the cavern.

As the sun was sinking over the mountains, the contractions grew closer and became constant, causing her to wince with every outgoing breath.

"Oh, Yondalin! I can't do this!" she screamed.

Her cries echoed across the valley into the night, causing the large woolly animals to stop and turn their ears to the wind to gauge the source of the cries.

Paterson also began to whinny in sympathy, causing Kettiajya to smile in her pain.

She suddenly had the urge to push and bear down. She reached out for Paterson and took a handful of his skin on his neck and gripped it as she lowered herself into a squatting position and leaned on the large stone as she cried, "Veronica! Help me!"

She leant on the stone with one hand, placed her other hand between her legs, and felt the head of her baby making its

188

first contact with the new environment. She continued pushing and threw her head back and groaned as the pain became overwhelming. As the baby's head slowly emerged, Kettiajya let go of the stone and squatted to enable her to support the baby with both hands as it completed its journey into the world.

She gathered the baby up and fell backwards on to the bedding with the baby held firmly in her hands.

She began massaging the tiny body and sighed when it began to cry.

Kettiajya then lifted the baby onto her stomach and rested for a short time before she ejected the placenta. She then took a smooth, round piece of wood and wound and knotted the umbilical cord between the baby and the placenta around it.

It was only then that she laid back and tears of relief flowed down her face as she put the baby to her breast.

She gazed at the little life and cried.

"Yondalin," she sobbed. "Yondalin, I need you!"

Paterson's first concern was for Kettiajya, and he snorted as he nudged her and she reassured him that she was fine. He then sniffed the baby before he hurried outside. Kettiajya heard him splash into the river and gallop away.

When he returned, Kettiajya had disconnected the cord and laid the placenta in a basket and covered it with dry leaves.

The baby was sleeping very contently.

"Well, Paterson," she said as she gave him a big embrace around his neck, "that was pretty bad wasn't it, but it's over now."

As she was embracing him, she felt a welt on his neck and apologised to him after realising that she had punctured his skin with her fingernails during the birth.

"I'm sorry," she said as she rubbed the wound and kissed his nose. "Thank you."

She slowly walked outside the cave, holding her still-enlarged stomach with her hands. She gently sat on the edge of the river with her legs in the cold water and plunged her naked body into the river. The water was soothing and made her feel revitalised.

189

As she climbed out of the river, she turned to face Veronica as she ran her hands over her still-bulging belly.

"So many changes," she thought as she turned and went back into her cave.

After rubbing herself down with a rough cloth and dressed herself in one layer of clothing, she gave her baby a soft kiss on the forehead and turned to pick up the placenta.

"Take care of the baby, Paterson," she said. "I'll be back very soon."

She held the placenta in front of her as she found her way step by step through the thick forest growth and emerged at the base of the waterfall.

She then placed the placenta into the folds of her robe and secured it with ties and began a slow, painful climb up the slope towards the waterfall summit.

Exhausted and tired, she pulled herself over the last ridge and sat on the edge of the waters.

Kettiajya then took a flat stone and began digging a hole into the banks of the river. She took the placenta and held it in her hands above her head for a few moments as she offered it to Veronica. She then buried it and placed many stones on top.

She turned and threw herself over the edge of the waterfall and fell with the waters to familiar territory at the base.

As she found her way back to the baby and Paterson, she thought about how her life had changed in the last twelve moons. Tears began to flow as she remembered Yondalin.

Her pace quickened as she heard her baby crying and the sound of Paterson trotting toward her.

"It's all right, Paterson, I'm coming," she said as he saw her and greeted her with an impatient nudge. "Feeding time again is it?"

The climb up the waterfall had been painful and hard on her body, but Kettiajya felt cleansed and revitalised after the physical strain had assisted to clear debris from her body. Now all she

190

wanted to do was to rest and focus on her baby. She sat gazing at her baby as she sipped a brew of scarlet bush and abuta.

It was after one full cycle of the moon that Kettiajya was sitting with Paterson high up in the valley overlooking her cavern, watching the full moon follow its course across the sky, that she decided that it was time to return to the site where Yondalin and Hepsibarb lay.

"Feel up to a visit, my dear?" she asked Paterson, knowing that he understood exactly what she meant. He did not react, not positively or negatively.

"Mm," muttered Kettiajya. "It will be tough for me too, but it's time we do it. Maybe we'll see your baby too?" she added.

Paterson snorted, shook his head, and scraped the ground with his foot.

"OK, I'll go alone," said Kettiajya.

They sat silently. The only sound was Paterson's tail flicking at a persistent insect intent on settling on his rump.

Kettiajya was thinking that it might be time to also introduce her baby to Tsulib. The tribe would be closer to her cavern than they had ever been now that they were heading south in search of a new environment which would offer them a fresh new future to look forward to.

"OK, Paterson, first sunlight tomorrow I'll be heading off west to spend a day or two at Yondalin and Hepsibarb's resting place, then south to find the tribe," she said. "Coming?"

She turned to face Paterson to see him staring at her with his head lowered. She stood with the baby in her arms and walked towards him.

He raised his head as she approached, allowing her to lean on his neck, and then pulled her and the baby closer to him by placing his head over her shoulder. Kettiajya held the baby with one arm and wrapped the other around Paterson's neck.

"We have to move on, Paterson," she said, "whether we like it or not, we've just got to do it."

191

Kettiajya was woken by Paterson the following morning as the sun began its passage over the mountain. He was eager to get this day done.

The forest had reclaimed the ground where Yondalin and Hepsibarb lay, but Kettiajya had no doubts about the place she had said goodbye.

She stood and cast her eyes over the ground as they approached the place that she would never forget.

All the memories of that last day ran through her head as she wiped her fallen tears from her baby's cheek. Paterson slowly nudged past her and walked directly to the grass-covered mound that held their most-loved companions.

Kettiajya joined him and sunk to her knees.

"Your son," she whispered as she laid the baby on the grassy mound.

She sobbed with her face in her hands. She took the tuft of hair that she'd taken from Yondalin out of her kutcha bag and held it to her breast before placing it in the baby's kutcha bag. It made her sad when she could not detect the smell of Yondalin in it anymore.

Kettiajya joined her sleeping baby on the ground, knowing that she was physically very close to Yondalin but separated by eternity.

She awoke to her baby's happy chatter. Paterson also appeared to be much more at ease and she was surprised that she too was feeling refreshed, like a burden had been lifted from her shoulders. She smiled and stroked the ground beneath her and began singing Yondalin's song to the baby, who responded joyfully.

Five weeks after Kettiajya's disappearance, Icemon kept constant vigil on the track leading to Kettiajya's retreat. *She should have returned by now,* she thought. She didn't sense any danger or trauma from Kettiajya, but she was beginning to worry as she knew Kettiajya would be aware of the anguish being experienced by the tribe in relation to her delay in presenting the baby to them.

Icemon decided to go to Kettiajya under the guise of offering her blessings to the baby.

She did not travel very far as she came upon Kettiajya astride Paterson, who was walking at a slow, steady pace, picking his way through the forest towards the village. Kettiajya had a bundle in her arms but she had a concerned look on her face.

Icemon smiled at Kettiajya, who smiled back to her. She slipped off the back of Paterson with the bundle in her arms, went to Icemon, and fell to her knees, crying with the bundle in her arms.

"Something is wrong, Icemon, my baby has something wrong!"

She unwrapped the little bundle for Icemon to see. The baby was very content and had its fingers in its mouth, indicating hunger.

Icemon had not spoken a word but gently completely exposed the baby.

Kettiajya cried and pointed to the genitalia. "See, Icemon, something is wrong here."

"No, everything is as it should be, dear Kettiajya," she said. "Your baby is both male and female, as it should be."

"Why? Why should it be like this?"

Icemon wrapped the baby up and offered it to Kettiajya to be fed.

"Your baby has a special role to play in its life, Kettiajya, that is why he—can we call your baby he at the moment?" Kettiajya nodded. "This baby is destined to be a leader and to bring peoples together, he will need both male and female qualities to do this." She paused before continuing. "This is why he is both male and female."

Kettiajya sat silently, feeding her infant.

"Do you love him less for being what he is?" said Icemon.

193

"No, of course not—he is very special like you say. But what do I tell others, how do I protect him from those who will say he is not normal?"

"Introduce him like any mother would—as yours and Yondalin's son, they will see that he has qualities unlike other people as he grows. He is complete as he is meant to be—like any other baby. They already have expectations of Yondalin's son. Come, Kettiajya, come and introduce your son."

Kettiajya smiled proudly and wrapped her baby up tightly and began to walk with Icemon.

As they approached the village, Paterson began to step in front of Kettiajya, preventing her from going any further.

"Paterson, what is the problem?" He snorted back at her, nuzzled the baby, flicked his head to his side, and nipped his own back with his teeth.

"That horse has a major problem, Kettiajya, he is one temperamental son of a bitch," said Icemon.

Kettiajya laughed.

"So what's going on?" asked Icemon.

"He wants to carry us into the village," Kettiajya said. "This is his moment too! OK, Paterson, here we go." Kettiajya laughed as she climbed onto Paterson's back. "Let's go."

Icemon was left standing behind as she shook her head and grumbled to herself.

Every step that Paterson took as he carried Kettiajya up to the top of the ridge overlooking the camp was proud, sure-footed, and calculated, knowing that he was bringing his precious load home. They were followed by Icemon, who was forced to stumble along behind them.

After Icemon's departure to join Kettiajya, the tribe had kept constant look out for the first signs of their return over the ridge. At last they saw Paterson's head and Kettiajya's shape on his back slowly rising over the top of the ridge. They saw the bobbing of Icemon's head as she followed close behind, working her way to the top. Her step-hop walk made her head bob into view and

194

then disappear until she reached a height where her whole body was visible, bouncing along behind Paterson.

The tribe members laughed and cried in happiness when they saw that Kettiajya had a bundle in her arms.

They rushed to welcome them but Paterson kept them at a distance by nudging them when they pushed to close. He walked in a proud, tall gait, lifting his front legs high with each step and holding his head tall as he delivered them to the entrance to Tsulib's hut where Kettiajya dropped to the ground. Paterson pushed his head to sniff the baby.

Kettiajya put one arm around his neck. "Thank you, Paterson; I could not have done this without you, none of it."

She held up her baby to the crowd.

"This is my son; the son of Yondalin. His name is Dilahn." Everyone cheered and some cried.

Suddenly, a gush of wind picked up the dust and swirled around Kettiajya.

Tsulib suddenly ran forward and stood in front of Kettiajya and screamed, "No!"

Kettiajya stood, staring at the Misha leader standing in front of her, and looked at Tsulib.

"What is troubling you Tsulib?" she asked. He did not answer; she looked back to the Misha.

"Misha leader! Why do you visit now? Have you heard already that I have a son? It is not like a Misha to respond to good news."

"Yes, I heard of the child's birth but I am not here to visit. I am here to claim payment for the assistance we have given this tribe over the years."

Kettiajya stared at the Misha leader. She looked down at her infant and then back at the Misha.

"No...No! You can't have Dilahn. He belongs to me!" she screamed as she stepped backwards.

Tsulib pushed forward to grab the baby but the Misha very calmly said, "Don't fight this! The infant is your payment. Why are you angry? We have assisted you many times voluntarily and

195

by trickery," she said as she looked Kettiajya in the eye. "Haven't we, Kettiajya, hmmm?"

The silence was numbing.

"You have always known that we would sometime ask for payment. That time is now and the place is here and the payment is the child."

"Yes, but please not this, please!"

Kettiajya was frozen in disbelief, tears filling her eyes as she shook her head in disbelief.

The Misha walked slowly toward Kettiajya and reached out her arms, taking the baby. Then she turned and walked toward the central area and disappeared as quickly as she arrived with a gush of wind as she mounted the grids.

Kettiajya stared at the space left by the Misha. She fell to the ground screaming and sobbing.

Icemon sat with her on the ground. Kettiajya looked at her, punched her, and said, "You knew this would happen didn't you? Didn't you, don't lie to me, Icemon?"

"I only knew that this child would be different and would require special training and taught to develop certain skills," she said. "I did not know it would be this way."

Icemon supported Kettiajya and guided her into her hut, understanding her sorrow but not knowing how to console her.

She reached into her pouch of herbs, took a handful of maracuja leaves, and dropped them into a gourd of hot water.

"Please, Kettiajya, sip this. I understand but I confess I don't know your sorrow at this time. Stay with me until you can better access the situation and we will talk about what to do."

Kettiajya stood up and amidst the tears and grief, she said, "No, Icemon! If what you say is true and this is all a part of my child's destiny, OK. However, if I cannot have Dilahn here, I will go to him. I know the Misha and their powers well. I cannot go against them but I can go with them until they allow my son to choose his own life. They will allow it, Icemon…someday they will allow it. I will wait with him."

196

"Won't you stay until your body has recovered from the birth?"

"My body is healed, Icemon. Veronica saw to that! I need my baby."

Icemon knew she could not stop Kettiajya. She had always been answerable to no one, but now she was bonded to another life, and nothing and no one could stop her now.

Kettiajya stood up and approached Icemon.

"Thank you, Icemon, I'm sorry to get angry with you. You of all people do not deserve it!"

"I understand. You are now a mother, forces greater than friendship will govern you."

Kettiajya went outside to an agitated Paterson, who was waiting, knowing the decision she would make; he was ready to carry her to the place of the Misha.

Without a word she ran towards Paterson and threw herself up onto his back. Together they swiftly disappeared into the forest, leaving Tsulib and everyone from the tribe devastated by the events that had gone from joy and celebration of the arrival of the baby and swiftly turned to shock and grief to having him taken from them.

Tsulib thought as he watched Kettiajya, in grief once more, *How much more pain does this girl have to bear?* He turned and walked away as Paterson took Kettiajya in pursuit of her baby, Yondalin's son.

"I told you didn't I, she's trouble. Every time she shows up we have nothing but more suffering," mumbled Sinai.

"Hey, did you stop to think of how she has suffered and still is?" shouted Taisha.

"Come on, don't get angry," said Georgia.

"No, someone needs to tell this woman a few truths," said Taisha. "Kettiajya was very happy with her life until she met us. She walked away from Yondalin the first time but came back to him. All she did was love him, everything that has happened since then has caused her more pain than you will ever comprehend,"

197

she yelled as she paced forward, causing Sinai to keep stepping backwards and fall when she stumbled into a hole.

Taisha continued as she stood over Sinai, "If you want to start blaming people, then blame your parents and mine and all the originals for making us believe other people were peaceful." Then she added, "Just knowing you should have given us an idea about that, shouldn't it?" She turned and strode off, leaving Sinai and others speechless.

No one interjected as they knew the words that Taisha spoke were true.

Paterson knew very well the way to the Misha as they had been there many times. Feeling her grief, he carried Kettiajya swiftly back along the ridge overlooking the tribal village and down to the river. Without missing a step, he continued to push himself along the steep and narrow pathways around the mountain ridges and along the river without slowing down. He wanted to join Kettiajya with her precious baby before sunset and knew he had to get to the Misha sentinel point before sunset to be allowed passage into their domain.

Exhausted and covered in sweat and froth, he finally arrived to the point where a strong magnetic wall prevented him going any further.

In a matter of seconds, a Misha manifested in front of them.

"We've been waiting, come this way," she said.

Kettiajya knew better than questioning the Misha and followed silently, exhausted both physically and emotionally, anticipating being reunited with her child.

As they approached the home of the Misha, Kettiajya heard the cries of her baby. She slid off Paterson and started running toward the sound, which led her to a hut.

With tears flowing down her cheeks, Kettiajya rushed into the hut saw the very irate baby Dilahn in a cradle, kicking and waving his legs about, sucking his fingers in hunger. She picked him up and offered her breast, which he welcomed with enthusiasm.

Leader Misha entered the room.

"We expected you sooner, Kettiajya; your baby has been hungry."

Kettiajya looked at her in disbelief. "Didn't you consider that he would need to be fed when you stole him?" she said in anger.

"Stole him? We have no need to steal. Just collecting our dues. Feeding the baby was never a problem, we knew you would come," she said calmly. "Motherhood is a strange condition for your species. Makes you very predictable and vulnerable. Very strange."

She turned and started to walk away, leaving Kettiajya very confused and tired but happy to be reunited with Dilahn. Leader Misha stopped and turned to Kettiajya, "A neophyte Misha will assist you, she didn't know what to do about all that mess your baby was making," she said. "You will explain that it's normal for humans, won't you?"

Leader Misha turned to walk away but paused and looked back to Kettiajya. "Oh, you should know that Yondalin was close to death when you called us, we couldn't have helped him."

Kettiajya didn't answer. She acknowledged everything that leader Misha said was true.

They all knew that Misha were going to claim payment one day and she did trick the Misha leader into moving the grids.

199

Moving On

Once more Icemon made the decision to move on. It had not been easy to raise discussions about leaving but they had stayed much too long at the joining of two rivers with terraced grounds. Suggestions to move on had been made many times but the majority of the tribe elected to stay at this place where two rivers merged. It supplied everything they needed: many fresh fruits and vegetables, water direct from the mountain snows, protection from the icy winds.

However, some complained about the short hours of daylight due to the height of the mountains blocking the early-morning and late-afternoon sun, and the days were getting colder.

The sick and injured had healed and two who had severe injuries and died were put to rest on a high terrace. Although some wounded in the fighting were left with permanent injuries, tools had been created to help them move around easily, but still they always found a reason to stay. The incident with the Misha taking baby Dilahn had reminded everyone how they came to be there and drew their thoughts back to their original plan to find the lowlands that Icemon spoke about.

Two of the watch people, Jose and Daniel who had travelled two days ahead with Icemon, returned to the main group after many days with news of a settlement of many people in the ruins of an old stone village in a large valley.

"There are many people living there," Jose said.

"Are they shorthairs?" Carlos asked.

"Didn't look like they were, there were women and children, answered Jose."They were living in old structures similar to the ones on top of that mountain we stayed at for a few days. I believe they are friendly, we were quite close and never saw any watch people," Jose added.

"They probably haven't met the shorthairs. Do you think we should contact them and warn them?" Carlos asked as he looked at Tsulib.

Tsulib thought for a moment and said, "No, we can't take the risk of letting others know where we are. I think we should let them be and carry on with our own journey."

"OK, but I would like to see the place. Can we go and look from the distance?" Daniel asked.

"Yes, we will stay here for two nights so any of you who are curious can go," Tsulib said. "Just make sure you're not seen, OK?"

The small group who decided to go to look at the village were speechless when they saw the ruins of a large city nestled in the valley squeezed between mountain peaks with a snow-capped mountain standing tall at the end.

The ruins were fallen and in disrepair except for the bases. These were still standing strong as solid large stones that had been carved to fit against another.

Two of the boys noticed an outcrop of these stones a short distance from where they were overlooking the city and slowly crept towards them. They were pleasantly surprised to see many rows and walls of very large stones, some three times their height, standing fitted and stacked perfectly. The view of the city from there was magnificent and lured them forward to the crest of the hill to appreciate the view.

Suddenly a large sound penetrated the air and all the occupants of the village began running; within a few moments, they had disappeared.

"Jose! We've been seen, come on quick. Back to the camp and warn the others."

Jose didn't move. He was mesmerised by the city and the activity.

"Jose. Come. Are you stupid or what?" said Daniel as he ran and grabbed Jose by the arm. "Tsulib's going to be real angry with us, come on hurry."

"OK, you go, I'll follow soon," said Jose.

As they entered the camp, yelling the situation, everyone began packing their possessions as the watchers nervously headed back in the direction of the village to assess what was happening. Meanwhile the tribe headed off to the west into very barren and exposed terrain with a large river to cross.

One day later, the watchers returned to the tribe and brought strange news.

"They haven't moved," they said. "We didn't see anyone all day, it was like they disappeared."

"I'd guess that they have been attacked before and went into a defensive plan," added Jose.

"I'd like to know what the plan is, not a soul was visible," said Daniel

"Go back and follow behind, their plan might be to follow us and choose a place to attack us," said Tsulib.

Many days passed and there were no indications from the watchers that the people from the valley village were going to cause concern, so the tribe concentrated on crossing a very high mountain range and many rivers. The environment was harsh with cold winds and little or no plants or trees to offer shelter. The mountain sides were very steep, and direct routes to the east were impossible. This extended their journey by many weeks as they sent forward scouts to seek easier tracks where the risk of falling down the sides into the ravines would be minimal.

After many weeks of hard walking and having to abandon many of their possessions to make the going easier, the terrain slowly changed, with each day offering more plants than the previous day. The mountains were now lower and covered in trees and shrubs, which were inhabited by a vast range of magnificent coloured birds. The spirit of the tribe was lifted tenfold, and rest periods were shorter each day as they anticipated many more surprises each day.

It was at midday on one of these days that Icemon led them to a high ridge that took them to a peak overlooking a large valley filled with cloud or mist.

It ran like a river through the valley, meandering through the valley and continued for as far as they could see.

"OK," said Icemon, "A bit further and just after dark we'll set up camp for a few days."

"After dark, Icemon?" asked Tsulib.

"Uh huh," she answered without stopping.

Tsulib did not question her further as he was aware that she had a plan and loved playing games.

Setting up camp in the dark was not a problem as there was indeed a large area with no obstacles. Once a fire was lit, it was a still night with clear skies. The night air became moist and cold as the clouds settled down into the valleys, leaving the evening sky clear and the stars exposed in all their glory.

The following morning found everyone awake early and busy with food preparations as the light of the sun began to shed a golden haze on the horizon. As the minutes slowly passed the golden hues changed to orange and red until the sky was totally illuminated. The mists and cloud below picked up the colours and stretched them back to the mountain ridge they were standing on.

One by one, tribe members were drawn to watch the spectacle from the edge of the ridge. The view was one that they had never before witnessed; there was nothing but cloud below them and sky above. The sun was slowly emerging above the low-lying

204

clouds, and a trick of nature gave an impression of two or three suns moving across the clouds.

If ever they thought the earth had an end then this was it.

The colours intensified as a golden crescent of the sun finally peered above the misty horizon and sent rays of gold stretching across the blanket of cloud to finally reflect upon the faces of the people standing on top of the ridge.

Gasps of awe were heard as the spectacle before them continued, changing with every moment.

As the sun continued its journey to rise above the horizon on its predestined path, the colours receded and the perfect orb of the sun broke free of the horizon. The warmth of the sun encouraged the mists and cloud to begin their part in this spectacle by commencing a slow rise, and the damp wave of mists enveloped the tribe once more, leaving minimal visibility around them.

Still no one moved or spoke in anticipation of more surprises as Mother Nature continued her visual opera. Eventually, the mists slowly dissipated and exposed the secret it was hiding beneath the blanket of clouds.

The view was one of lush green lowlands like none they had ever seen. The river in the valley below flowed down into a series of waterfalls and busy waters to disappear into a sea of trees, which stretched as far as the horizon with no interruption.

Icemon smiled as she sat back and watched as everyone reacted in their own way to the sight before them. Some were excited and some nervous about the unknown.

Tsulib approached Icemon, placing his hand on her shoulder. She put her hand on his and nodded her head.

"This is where I leave you, Tsulib," she said. "Take them down to the lowlands following the river and use all your skills to lean about the fruits and plants."

"Won't you come with us, Icemon; we will need your help to learn about new foods and dangers."

"No, now the tribe will need to use all its resources to build a new future. Of course you will make mistakes, but use them as lessons and start again. Watch the birds and animals, see what they eat. Remember that you cannot eat everything they eat so be diligent and figure out what creatures have similar digestions as you. You will encounter new challenges with the weather, and insects and animals that will push your patience to the edge, so do not take anything for granted. What awaits you down there in the jungle is new. It is nothing like the places you have lived in before. It can be dangerous and wonderful at the same time, and new leaders will step forward as existing leaders become challenged. Watch, Tsulib. Watch your people and be prepared to make hard decisions if you are forced to. Let each person decide their own fate. Remember the stories told by your ancestors, the stories of greed and ambition that brought billions of people to the brink of extinction." She reached out, took his hand, and looked him in the eye. Tsulib returned the eye contact and smiled into Icemon's eyes. The sun cast a golden light onto her face, accentuating the scarred and knotted tissue. He jumped to his feet to stop Icemon seeing the tears beginning to form in his eyes.

"Where will you go?" asked Tsulib. "We will miss you, you beautiful, crazy woman."

"Beautiful?" she laughed. She reached out to brush his face with her hand. "Never you mind about that, Tsulib. Please learn from the land and the creatures, Tsulib, they have all the information you need to survive."

Everyone was too busy looking at the new world in front of them to notice Icemon head back to the track leading west. She stopped and looked back at Tsulib and called, "I'll be back; you haven't got rid of me yet."

Tsulib smiled and raised his hand to wave but she had gone.

206

Educating Dilahn

After claiming the baby Dilahn, the Misha left Kettiajya and the baby to themselves for the passing of one moon. The only interaction was when food was taken to Kettiajya two times each day. Sometimes a neophyte Misha would deliver it, but every few days the leader Misha would take the food to Kettiajya and hold the baby while Kettiajya ate her meal. It was these times Kettiajya tried to convince the leader Misha that baby Dilahn needed to be with humans who were the same as he was.

"Kettiajya, we both know that he is not the same."

"He is a normal child; he needs to be with others."

"Everyone is normal, Kettiajya! Some have more potential than others."

Kettiajya sighed and thought, *I'm wasting my time trying to reason with this Misha.*

"So what's the deal, leader Misha? What do you plan to do with Dilahn?"

Leader Misha smiled at her and said, "Give him the knowledge he will need in his life. You should be happy about all of this, Kettiajya, he will learn many things. You will see."

"How long do you plan to keep him here?"

"That depends on how he develops, how much he understands," said leader Misha as she stood and started to walk towards the door. "We will begin with him after the next moon ceremony."

Kettiajya stared at the door as she pulled the baby close to her and kissed his cheek.

Kettiajya awoke early on the first day after the full moon. She expected leader Misha to be true to her word and come to visit Dilahn. She was not disappointed. Leader Misha appeared at the hut as soon as the sun had lifted the mists from the valley. She entered Kettiajya's hut and reached out her arms for the baby. Kettiajya hesitated but reluctantly stood with the baby in her arms and handed him over to leader Misha, who turned without speaking a word and walked outside. Kettiajya followed, but leader Misha turned and shook her head as she said, "No, this is only for me and Dilahn."

"How long will you be?"

"However long it takes."

"Please, leader Misha, please give me an idea when you will return him."

Leader Misha smiled and walked away with Dilahn in her arms. Kettiajya started to follow but stopped when she heard leader Misha talking to him in a soft, nurturing tone. She watched them until they were out of sight before she ran to meet with Paterson, who waited for her every morning outside the grid above the Misha settlement.

Paterson appeared to be anxious when he saw Kettiajya alone.

"It's all right, Paterson, he's with leader Misha," she said while reaching out to stroke his nose. "He will be fine with her, there is nothing I can do to stop it now, but..." she paused, "I must admit I feel all right about it."

She pulled herself up onto Paterson's back and he took her for a long-awaited run down into the valley, where they sat near the river before continuing up the other side of the mountain. Kettiajya sat watching and listening to birds cruising the thermals until she drifted into a sleep.

She awoke startled by Paterson nudging her and snorting.

208

"What's wrong, Paterson?" she asked as she jumped to her feet. "Oh," she continued as she clasped her breasts, "Dilahn will be hungry."

Paterson returned her to the grid entry quickly and ran to the hut to find leader Misha waiting for her with Dilahn.

She didn't speak a word but her attitude let Kettiajya know that her lateness was noted.

And so the training of Dilahn began at this very young age. As the years passed by, Dilahn did not seem to mind the time he spent with leader Misha, and Kettiajya grew to enjoy the time each day when she could go with Paterson.

Leader Misha allowed Dilahn to go with his mother every year for five days to coincide with his birthday. Kettiajya always took him to her cavern in the mountains and never ventured away. Dilahn enjoyed these times because his mother had many collections of stones, bones, feathers, plants, and many items of clothing which had patterns of colours and adornments on them. He loved foraging in the cavern discovering new things.

Every year Kettiajya made a new robe for him and as the years passed by, Dilahn was beginning to have favourite patterns and stones which became a part of every new robe.

On the year of his sixth birthday, Kettiajya took him to meet Veronica. As they climbed the steep cliff, Kettiajya explained to Dilahn how the energy of Veronica had supported and regenerated her all of her years.

When they reached the top of the waters, Kettiajya asked Dilahn, "Are you ready to come with me?" as she pointed to the waters below.

"In the water?"

"Uh huh."

Dilahn thought about it for a few seconds and replied, "Do you think I can do it?"

"Only you can answer that, my dear."

"You go, Mima, and I will think some more."

209

"No, I want a decision," she said. "If you decide to come with me then you need to hold my hand and we go together."

"OK," he said nervously. "Let's do it, but please, Mima, hold on to me very tight, won't you?"

Kettiajya took his hand and pulled him over the edge of the waterfall before he could change his mind.

Paterson looked up when he heard the screams of Dilahn and watched as Kettiajya fell into the waters with Dilahn. He entered the waters and offered Dilahn his back as he raised his head out of the waters screaming with delight.

"Oh, Mima! That was very scary but good," he called. "Can we do it again?"

"Not today, sweetheart," she answered. "It's not a game."

"After doing that I reckon I can do anything now!"

Kettiajya smiled and helped Dilahn onto Paterson's back. "I am very proud of you. You are very brave," she said.

It was during this annual visit that Kettiajya and Dilahn visited the gravesite of Yondalin and Hepsibarb. They made it a part of the journey back to the Misha at the end of their time together.

Dilahn was sad to be leaving their home once again but excited because he always saw the son of Hepsibarb and Paterson near the gravesite.

He ran ahead of Kettiajya as they drew closer to the site.

"Heps! Heps!" he called. "Here, Heps!"

"Who?" called Kettiajya.

"Heps. I call him Heps like his ma," answered Dilahn as he ran ahead.

Paterson also began to trot ahead, leaving Kettiajya to follow behind.

As she approached the gravesite she stopped and smiled to see Paterson and his son greeting each other and Dilahn walking slowly toward them.

Heps had grown into a beautiful stallion, short and stocky with golden colours of Hepsibarb, but he had a tail and mane of black ebony like his father.

210

"He's beautiful, don't you think?" asked Dilahn.

"He certainly is, Dilahn, he is magnificent."

Dilahn approached Heps and reached out to him. Heps did not mind at all and lowered his head to offer his nose to Dilahn.

Kettiajya felt sad as she thought how complete they would all be if Yondalin were alive and could see his small son reaching up to Heps.

"Mima, do you think Heps can come back to the Misha and wait for me like Paterson waits for you?"

"You will have to leave that up to him."

"Can't we just take him? I want to keep him for me."

"No," said Kettiajya. "Heps belongs to no one. He must decide if he wants to be with you. Do you understand?"

Dilahn was quiet as he thought about his mother's words.

"Mm..." he said. "Yes, I understand, but I love him, Mima. I want him to love me and be with me like Paterson is with you."

"Give him time to know you and trust you, Dilahn."

"OK. I will wait for him," said Dilahn as he ran towards the gravesite and lay down on the grass covered mound. Kettiajya joined him and answered all of his questions about his father until they dozed off.

Dilahn was woken by the hand of Kettiajya his hair.

"Come, sweetheart," she said. "We must go, time to return to the Misha."

Dilahn was sad, but he also accepted the regime and deep down enjoyed the learning with leader Misha.

They said their farewells to Yondalin and Hepsibarb, gathered their kutcha bags, and headed off in the direction of the Misha camp.

After many hours of walking, Dilahn began to scream in delight when he saw Heps following at a distance. Dilahn had noticed that every time he stopped walking, Heps would stop and look away. The horse had fun, making a game out of it.

By the time they had all reached the entrance to the Misha camp, Heps had joined the group, but Dilahn was asleep in the arms of Kettiajya on the back of Paterson. Dilahn awoke when the soothing motion of Paterson walking had stopped and Kettiajya lowered him to the ground. He squealed quietly when he saw Heps only steps away, then walked over and wrapped his arms around his front legs. Heps bent his head down to Dilahn and gently nuzzled the boy.

"See, Mima, he does love me!"

"Yes...I think you are right," she answered as she smiled.

Dilahn looked up to Heps and whispered, "Will you wait for me, Heps? Will you be my friend?"

Heps snorted and rubbed his hoof in the ground.

Many years passed and Kettiajya settled into the routine of sharing her time between supervising Dilahn with the Misha leader and going with Paterson to wander the mountains. Still, she never stayed away from Dilahn for more than three days at a time.

It was on her return to the Misha dwellings after one of her longer stays away with Paterson that leader Misha told her that the next stage of Dilahn's training could involve him being alone for a long period of time.

"Alone?" asked Kettiajya.

"Yes, Kettiajya, he needs to absorb a lot of information and come to conclusions without the influence of anyone," she said. "Not me and not you!"

Kettiajya turned away from leader Misha and looked over the valley below before turning back to face her.

"Where are you going to send him?" she asked. "At least tell me that."

"He's going to the vault."

Kettiajya gasped and said, "Oh no, leader Misha, he is only nine years old! He can't go there alone."

"I think he is ready, Kettiajya. He is very strong and has a curious mind; I am sure he will cope very well."

212

Kettiajya sat down on the ground with her head between her hands and shook her head.

"I think he has had enough of this," she said in a low voice, thinking out loud. "Leader Misha," Kettiajya continued. "I have been without my son for long enough and I believe the debt has been paid. I want this to stop now and let Dilahn live a real life of his choice."

Leader Misha stood silently, watching Kettiajya. "I agree with you, Kettiajya, but the decision has to be with Dilahn."

"You won't send him to the vault?"

"He must decide."

Kettiajya stood up and took a few steps towards leader Misha, reaching out, but leader Misha stepped away. Kettiajya stopped and smiled as she nodded her head.

"OK," Kettiajya said, "What's next?"

"Call the boy."

Kettiajya headed for the hut that had been Dilahn's home all of his life and began calling for him. "Dilahn, today is a happy day. We are going home to the mountain where you were born," she cried. "You are finished here but we need to say goodbye to leader Misha."

Dilahn met her at the door of the hut. "Is it true, Mima," he asked. "Am I really going to leave here?"

"Yes, sweetheart, but first leader Misha wants to ask you something. I know you are going to say no so we will be home tomorrow night," said Kettiajya excitedly. "Just think Dilahn, only you, me, Paterson, and Heps."

After Kettiajya had gathered Dilahn's few possessions they both went to say goodbye to leader Misha.

"Is it true, Big M?" asked Dilahn. "Am I finished here?"

Leader Misha reached out and put her hand on Dilahn's shoulder. "Yes, you have finished with me but there is one more thing I want you to do. It is your decision, son of Yondalin," she said as she raised his chin to direct his eyes to hers. "There is a place here under the mountains that I think you should

213

visit. It is a large cavern full of information about life on this planet and how different people from many lands dealt with change to their lives and their environment." She paused and put both hands on Dilahn's shoulders to turn him to face the valley below.

"The information covers many hundreds of thousands of years, and how it is presented to you may be traumatic because you will see and experience many things that you and everyone but a few have never seen."

Dilahn turned to face his mother, who was smiling, knowing he would choose to go home.

"Dilahn," continued leader Misha. "You do not have to go. I will release you from my bond as soon as you say no. However if you decide to go, I will immediately gather you and take you to the place, but you will still be free to turn away and not continue at any time."

"How long will I be there if I choose to go?" he asked.

"Dilahn!" cried Kettiajya, realising that Dilahn was considering his options. "Please do not go. I know that place and please listen to me. If you go there you will not be the same when you return." She pulled Dilahn into her arms and held him tightly. "Please come home now!"

Dilahn moved away from his mother and leader Misha and walked to the edge of the ravine, taking in the view of the river below and the mountain peaks covered in snow. He rubbed his arms as the cold wind sent a shiver through him.

He turned and joined his mother.

"Please understand, Mima, I need to go to the cavern."

Kettiajya struggled to hold back the tears as she once again grabbed her son and held him close before leader Misha approached them.

"What is your decision, young Yondalin?"

Dilahn looked up to his mother and said, "I want to see the vault."

214

Leader Misha swept Dilahn away on a grid before Kettiajya could say goodbye.

She was once more left alone with the silence of her loneliness.

Once more she mounted Paterson and began another journey back to her home alone.

The Vault

Dilahn found himself alone on a ledge which was halfway up on the side of a deep ravine. A large waterfall falling from a great height above was only a few steps from him where it formed a pool before continuing its fall to the bottom of the ravine.

Leader Misha had taken him there and left him without saying a word. She only held his hand and smiled as she brushed his hair out of his eyes and disappeared onto a grid before he could ask any questions.

He stood taking in his surroundings, knowing that the entrance to the vault would be very close. He remembered that his mother had said it was a cavern which would need an entrance. He ventured close to the edge of the ledge and looked down into what looked like a large circle of rock where the ravine appeared to begin; centuries of water flowing down had carved a large abyss.

Dilahn began to explore the area high upon the ledge. He found an area where the stones had been laid to form a pathway, leading to an area under the face of the cliff where many smaller caverns beckoned him into the belly of the mountain. Dilahn knew that leader Misha would not have made it difficult for him to find the vault but the wrong choice of entry here could take him to the wrong place, so he sat down to think about his next move. He smiled and jumped to his feet when the midday sun caused a reflection of light to shine onto a pattern on the wall above one of the cavern entrances. He stared at the pattern, wondering what it meant. It was a spiral pattern divided into five sections with engravings of animals, plants, and stars enclosed in a five-sided border.

He approached the doorway with great caution, remembering his mother's words pleading with leader Misha not to send him here. As he entered, the ground beneath his feet began to glow showing him the way. He stopped and stepped backwards to see the light follow his feet back and then forward when he stepped forward. He was feeling frightened but not threatened, so he continued with the light as his guide. He quickened the pace when he started to feel confident but stopped suddenly when the pathway opened into a large cavern. He was high in the cavern looking down into a very large area lit very faintly by the light on the ground, which had continued on down many steps into the cavern without him. He smiled as he watched the light become a life unto itself and moved down each step one at a time, enticing him to follow.

Dilahn began to follow the descending light but moved very slowly. His heart was beating very fast and perspiration formed on his hands as he contemplated going back. However, curiosity urged him to continue. Taking one slow step at a time, Dilahn followed the light on the ground into the large, empty space where he could only see his hands reach in front of himself. He stopped when the light began to move very fast, covering the whole floor, which caused a soft glow to engulf the cavern. He watched as many strange shapes and objects became visible and noises were slowly penetrating the environment. It sounded like music but not like any music[1] he had heard before. He looked around for the musicians, curious about the instruments that could make such strange but beautiful sounds.

---

1   *Los Hermanos Roque: Generacion Andina – "San Juan Bonito"*

218

The music became louder as all the walls became alive with colours and shapes that appeared to reach out into the space of the cavern as they moved in rhythm with the sounds.

He could feel himself shaking with fear and looked around for the entrance into this place in anticipation of leaving very quickly, but his feet would not move. He fell to the ground and covered his face with his robe and began to cry, wishing he had taken his mother's advice.

After many minutes, Dilahn found the courage to slowly peek out from under his robe at his strange surroundings and push himself up to a sitting position. He did not know what he was looking at, but the walls were shiny and like nothing he had ever seen.

The music changed to a different tune which was hauntingly beautiful, and again he could not guess the instruments but the voice singing the song was exquisite.[2]

He sat for a long time, looking and wondering what he was supposed to learn from this, but he was gaining confidence quickly. He rose to his feet and began walking towards the walls, but jumped back quickly as he saw his reflection in the shiny surface. He felt safe but still looked around for clues to what this all meant. He wandered around, looking and touching, until he found a strange object much larger and different from everything else in there. When he touched it, it was soft. It was shaped like a person sitting down, but there was no shape of a head. He found it to be much softer than the ground, so he climbed up onto it and sat looking at the large flat shiny wall in front of him, still not knowing what he was supposed to learn in here or what his mother was frightened of.

Dilahn felt comfortable and was considering finding his way out of there when the large wall in front of him began to glow a beautiful blue colour. His heart began to beat faster again when the stars that he knew so well appeared. The blue wall became as dark as the night and the stars moved very quickly through their

---

2   *Micheal Jackson – "Will You Be There"*

annual patterns before slowing down and eventually stopping. He jumped out of the large, comfortable sitting object and ran to the wall and touched it expecting to find space, but his hand hit the hardness of the wall. He ran back to the sitting object when the images began to change. Now the image of the stars was moving to focus on one star only, getting closer to the constellations that he knew very well. He held onto the sitting object very tight as he felt like he was being thrown through the stars. He laughed and clapped his hands until the image movement stopped and focused on a beautiful blue and green planet.

"My home," he whispered. "That's my home!"

He watched in awe as the blue planet slowly turned, following a path around the sun.

The magic he was seeing was hard for him to comprehend even though he knew that what he was looking at was true. He had studied the stars and the constellations for many years with leader Misha, but he could not understand how it was all here on a flat wall with no depth. He was intrigued by the music[3] which changed as the subject on the wall changed.

As he watched, the scene moved closer to the planet, showing images of many beautiful places full of wonderful animals and forests. The seas were crystal-clear and he saw more species of life in the water than he ever thought would be possible.

He saw lands with large river systems, mountains, and deserts, and he cheered and clapped his hands with joy and jumped up and down on the sitting object.

"Thank you, leader Misha," he called. "This is the best!"

The image on the wall continued with closer views of humans roaming the countries in family groups, stopping in one place for only days at a time before moving on. Dilahn was shocked to see them trapping and killing animals for food and was surprised to see them thanking the animal after killing it. He began to understand but did not agree when he saw that the animal meat was eaten and any excess was dried and carried, the bones

---

3   *Enigma – "Return to Innocence"*

used for instruments and decoration, the skins for clothing and warmth.

The many lands on the planet had similar living habits and customs and a general respect for the planet and its gifts.[4]

As the images progressed, Dilahn began to understand that he was watching a history of people but did not understand the significance; he sat back and let the images entertain him.

He saw the progress of humanity as they slowly began to stop the roaming and stay in one place, building solid structures to live in.

He saw that ownership of structures, claiming hunting lands for one family's sole use, and the imprisonment of animals created conflicts.

He saw the families unite to build larger structures and walls around their structures to keep other people out. Other people who would have been welcomed to share food and stories were now feared and often became victims of the conflicts of ownership.

These groups now had conflicts based on ownership the groups. This led to individuals declaring themselves to be the decision makers on behalf of all, saying that they had to be united to survive the now-predatory environment they had made for themselves.

Children and daughters were traded for goods with neighbouring tribes, and young men were kidnapped to do the work of maintaining crops and herds of animals.

The self-appointed leaders became more and more greedy and lazy and began to lose respect for the planet and their fellow human.

The imprisonment of animals became a sign of wealth and their welfare deteriorated rapidly, causing immense stress and illness upon them.

Dilahn began to get anxious as the story unfolding before him was becoming very hard to keep watching, but he now felt

---

4   *Los Hermanos Roque: Generacion Andina – "Suncuima"*

221

that he was at a point of no return; he needed to see what happened and learn the reason for him to know about the history.

He watched the growth and destruction of many civilisations, large and small. The civilisations were governed by greed and ignorance and destroyed by other civilisations to feed their own greed and ignorance. Dilahn wondered why the majority of people were eager to follow and obey without question.

He saw many amazing inventions that changed people's lives and minds.

He saw people become like the machines they sought to own, machines made to make a few very wealthy under the guise of making lives easier but eventually becoming a burden—the burden of ownership.

He saw greed extend to powerful nations using political reasons to invade and destroy, using incredibly vicious tools of war.

He saw people stolen from their countries to serve greed in foreign lands and forced to live in unspeakable conditions where women and children were used for pleasure and men flogged consistently.

He saw millions of people starved, tortured, and killed by chemicals because of their race or beliefs.

He saw religious zealots and institutions abuse the people trusting in them for care and protection.

He saw children become the target for despicable adults seeking to satisfy a vicious and horrendous mind.

Dilahn's face was wet with tears as he continued watching. He cried, "No, no," as he sobbed. "How can it be?"

He saw animals suffer unmentionable horrors as they were forced to breed and live in unnatural and unspeakable conditions for the greed of man.

He saw animals shipped to foreign lands in large seagoing vessels to die on the way or to die terrible deaths in foreign lands under the name of religion.

He saw religion become a force within itself to govern by fear: fear of their god and fear of retribution by their god.

222

He saw humans go to extremes to cure human illnesses and extend life of the individual, adding to the overcrowding of the planet and not allowing natural attrition to restrict human numbers on the planet.

He saw the planet covered with more people than it could sustain, but still the leaders proclaimed human life more precious than animals or the environment.

Humans became the ultimate life form to be preserved at all costs—even at the cost of the planet itself.

He saw the beautiful blue planet become consumed by smoke, fire, and destruction at the hand of humans.

Dilahn was left exhausted and shocked.

Kettiajya Claims Dilahn

Kettiajya travelled with Paterson and Heps every day to the place of the vault, hoping to find Dilahn waiting to come home. Every day she returned alone.

It was after three weeks that she decided enough was enough. For the first time since the wars with the shorthairs, she dressed with all her weapons attached to her belt and wrists and asked Paterson to take her to the entrance of the cavern complex.

"Wait here, baby," she said. "We're taking our boy home."

She climbed the steps up to the entrance and felt her way using the walls until she found the round doorway. She had no fear this time; Dilahn was foremost on her mind.

As she approached she heard a song. It was a song asking the listener to "imagine all the people living life in peace."[5] The cavern was covered with a soft blue light but the image on the wall was a large ball on fire. Dilahn was nowhere to be seen. She called his name but no answer was forthcoming. She ran to each of the large, shiny objects, calling for Dilahn. She stood in front of the large wall with the fiery ball and turned to see Dilahn curled up in the large, soft sitting item.

"Dilahn," she cried as she reached out to him.

---

5   *John Lennon – "Imagine"*

She was shocked to see him emaciated and not responding. Kettiajya scooped him up into her arms and started to run into the passage leading to the outside.

"Paterson, here, quickly," she called.

She lowered Dilahn to the ground near the water and began splashing him with the cold mountain water as she brushed his arms and face with her hands.

"Please wake up, please!" she cried.

She then sat on the ground and dragged Dilahn onto her lap, holding him in her arms with his head on her shoulder as she scooped up water in her hand and dripped it into his mouth.

He coughed and opened his eyes before sobbing and shaking.

"Oh, Mima," he cried as he put his arms around her and held her very tight.

"Shh, my baby, it's all over now. Misha, the vault, it's all over now."

Dilahn then collapsed into Kettiajya's arms.

Paterson and Heps were waiting at the top of the steps for them. Heps nudged Dilahn as Kettiajya lifted him onto the back of Paterson and wrapped her large robe over him, holding him onto Paterson's back as she pulled herself up next to him.

Paterson took one step at a time carrying them down the side of the ravine as Heps followed close behind.

"OK, Paterson, take us home," she said softly.

When they were up out of the ravine, Paterson settled into a rhythmic walk and Kettiajya reached into her kutcha bag and took out her flute.

She held Dilahn's head close to her breast and kissed his forehead. "I'll never let you go again." she said. "Never!"

She wrapped her robe around her waist, enclosing the sleeping Dilahn tightly, and began playing the song of Yondalin as Paterson carried them over the mountains and rivers to the comfort of her home.

226

Kettiajya laid her son down on a bed of grasses and woven mats, undressed him and covered him with her robe. She then prepared a fire to heat the rocks and a large gourd of water ready for the hot rocks.

She sorted through her baskets of dried plants, selected maracuja and mulungu, and added them to the water. When the rocks were hot, she placed them into the water with the plants. She then took the plants from the water and commenced washing Dilahn's body. He opened his eyes and cried; Kettiajya placed her hand over his eyes and said, "Shh, rest now. We will talk tomorrow."

Kettiajya awoke with a fright when she saw that Dilahn was not in the cavern. She ran outside and was relieved when she saw him sitting on the edge of the river with his feet in the water. She went to sit next to him and put her arm around his shoulders, and he responded by leaning into her. He was quiet and his eyes were sunken and dark.

Kettiajya sensed a deep sadness within him but did not want to force him to talk until he was ready. She rose to her feet leaving her hand on his shoulder and said, "I will prepare some food my dear, just a little," she said. "Will you eat it?"

Dilahn nodded his head.

Kettiajya returned to the cavern and began to prepare a small meal of flat bread and a paste of tubers and seeds while keeping her back turned to the direction of Dilahn. Tears flowed down her face and her body shook with grief. "Oh, leader Misha, what have you done to my son!" she whispered. "What have you done?"

She returned to Dilahn with the food and a tea of graviola and sat with him.

Dilahn turned to face her, looking into her eyes.

"Don't cry for me, Mima!" he said. "I need time to think about the things I have seen, that's all."

Kettiajya pulled him close to her. "OK, my dear, I will wait. But please promise me that you will eat and rest and let me care for you until you are ready to talk to me?"

227

"Of course," he said, and paused before saying, "And, Mima, I knew you would come for me when the time was right."

It did not take long for Dilahn to recover physically. He followed Kettiajya's instructions and ate when she requested him to eat and took the teas of amargo, papailla, and manaca when she handed them to him.

Kettiajya was standing with Paterson overlooking the valley below when Dilahn approached her and stood with her.

"Mima? I don't know what to do with the knowledge I now have."

"You are still a boy, Dilahn," she said. "You have many years to think about all of this. Now is the time to not think about it all and just be a boy for a change."

"That is another question for me. Am I a boy, Mima? Maybe I am a girl!"

"Do you need to be anything, sweetheart?" she answered. "Why don't you just be Dilahn?"

Dilahn thought about her answer for a moment. "Uh huh," he finally said as he threw his arms into the air. "I am Dilahn," he said softly. "I am Dilahn!" he shouted as he laughed. "I am Dilahn!"

Kettiajya laughed with him and then they both became silent as Dilahn sat on the ground and offered his hand to his mother. She took his hand and sat next to him.

"Mima? I believe we are all destined for self-destruction."

Kettiajya didn't answer, feeling that it was time for him to talk.

"This planet has seen many attempts by man to survive peacefully, but every time the result is the same. Self-destruction and a willingness to destroy everyone and everything, including their own children and the environment, rather than lose a conflict."

"What do you mean when you said that there have been many attempts?"

"Over a period of many millions of years, man has had the opportunity to try again but the story is always the same. They

228

begin as nomads and progressively destroy themselves and the planet. Every cycle it is the same. It is like they have been programmed to destroy themselves."

"Surely not every person, Dilahn," said Kettiajya. "Surely everyone does not willingly do this?"

"That is what I don't understand, Mima. A few people make all the decisions for everyone else and the masses just go along with all the decisions of the few, even if they do not agree. They will go to war and kill millions of innocent people for the leaders. They destroy the forests and poison the oceans, killing magnificent creatures. They make the air so dirty that every living thing cannot breathe fresh air!"

Kettiajya looked at Dilahn in shock. "How do you know these things?"

"The images I saw in the vault were like I was there, seeing it all happen. There have been many times that this beautiful planet has given humans another chance, but every time it is the same! Mima...why do you think the Misha chose me to receive all this information and training? Who are the Misha?"

Kettiajya readjusted herself and straightened her robe as she thought about the things Dilahn had said.

"Well, my dear, I really can't answer that question," she said. "You were taken from me as payment of a debt that the Misha thought I owed them. I used trickery to get the help of leader Misha when your father was in trouble." She continued, "I knew there would be a price to pay but I didn't think that you would be the price. Now, after all these years that you have been with leader Misha and what you have experienced in the vault, I think Misha are trying to educate the human race. Maybe this is our last chance to get it right."

"But who are they, Mima, who are the Misha...really?"

"I don't know what you mean, Dilahn. They have always been there doing what they do. They do not harm anyone—in fact they go out of their way to help but they do not tolerate dishonesty

229

as I learnt," she said as she raised her eyebrows and nodded her head.

"I think the leader Misha has all the answers, but what do I have to do with it?" said Dilahn.

"You will know in time. You are only nine years of age and you are different in many ways, my dear."

Kettiajya was only just realising that her son was a lot more mature in his mind than she had thought, and it worried her when she thought about his future. She raised her arms into the air to stretch and gazed across the valley and laughed as she nudged Dilahn as she pointed.

"Look, sweetheart!" she said.

Dilahn looked in the direction she was pointing and jumped to his feet, laughing, as he called, "Heps, Heps, you are still here!"

They both stood and laughed as they watched Heps and Paterson trot along a narrow pathway on the side of the mountain across the valley. They were a sight to remember with Paterson in front and Heps following very close behind him. The contrast between the tall, glowing ebony of Paterson trotting with his head and tail held high emphasised the short, stocky, golden-coloured body with black tail and mane of Heps was striking. Heps trotted with a gait that threw his legs to the side but like Paterson, his head and tail were held high.

Kettiajya and Dilahn watched as the father and son worked their way across the river and up the steep ascent to approach them. Dilahn ran to Heps and the mutual affection was obvious. Kettiajya watched but was concerned when Dilahn turned to face her. His face was that of pain.

"Mima, do you know what humans do to animals?"

"Please, Dilahn, don't upset yourself now."

"I need to tell you, Mima."

"OK, I will listen."

"They kill animals. They make them stand in lines and they have to watch as the one in front of them is slaughtered. They can only wait for their turn. They smell the fear, Mima, and then

230

they die to be cut into pieces and eaten. All animals suffer; they are carried in machines and vessels to terrible deaths. Even the ocean animals suffer at the hands of humans. Large, beautiful creatures that give birth and breastfeed in the oceans are hunted and slaughtered, filling the sea with the red of their blood." He cried. "Humans breed animals for killing, Mima; they are kept in small cages where they cannot move, forced to have babies, and then killed."

"Dilahn, Dilahn! I find it hard to believe but I believe you," she said.

"It is children also, Mima."

"They kill children?" exclaimed Kettiajya.

"Many children die at the hands of humans. They are stolen and used for terrible things." Dilahn's voice was now monotone with no emotion as he described more to his mother. "Even the parents of some children do terrible things to their own children. The leaders of countries make decisions that destroy futures for their own children." He paused and Kettiajya sat silently with him. "Why don't they love their children, Mima? No one loves the children. Everyone follows instructions of the leaders knowing that the children will have no future. I don't understand."

"Why do you think this happens, Dilahn? You saw the images, why do you think it happens?"

"Greed."

"Greed?"

"Yes. Possessions, ownership of things make humans want more, and the more they have the more they want, and the person with the most possessions begins to feel powerful and becomes the envy of other people."

"We have seen some of this in our time, Dilahn," said Kettiajya. "You know about the shorthairs and the war when your father died? Those people sound like the ones you speak of. They killed some of our boys and treated Taisha very badly."

Dilahn embraced his mother and ran past Heps, challenging him to a race down to the river.

231

Kettiajya watched and smiled as Dilahn dealt with the information in his own way and felt that he was indeed different and special. She also worried that her son's time on this planet may have many unpleasant experiences for him. She made a silent promise to always be by his side.

Reunion

For three years after Dilahn's release from the Misha; Kettiajya, Dilahn, Paterson and Heps lived the nomadic life that Kettiajya loved, and Dilahn finally enjoyed each day just being a child.

Kettiajya heard him whistling the song of Yondalin many times and asked him who the song was for.

"Anyone special?"

"It is for everyone," said Dilahn.

"It can't be for everyone."

"Why not, Mima? Why not for everyone?"

Kettiajya paused. "Yes, why not for everyone," she answered.

They often found Icemon, who sometimes joined them for a week or two before going her own way again. Times of meetings with the Misha were anxious times for Kettiajya, who worried that leader Misha might call on Dilahn to spend time with them; but never a word was mentioned about the past training and no questions asked about the present.

During one of the meetings with Icemon, they decided to take time to find the tribe of Tsulib, whom they had not seen for twelve years.

It took many months before they arrived at the place on the edge of the mountains where Icemon left the tribe many years before. Icemon insisted upon staying overnight to enable Dilahn to experience the spectacular display which was presented every morning when the sun first appeared through the mists.

Dilahn cried with joy as he watched Mother Nature in her finest glory unfold before his eyes.

It was a slow journey following the river as it descended into the jungle, as new sights and sounds distracted them for hours at a time. The birds were many and the colours so magnificent that they all sat for hours just watching and listening. As they continued their journey into the jungle following the course of the river, they stayed for days in places which were incredibly beautiful with animals like they had never seen before scurrying across the tops of trees and strange creatures hustling through the jungle floor.

As they progressed, signs of old habitations were becoming more prevalent. They decided that these sites were not left by Tsulib's tribe because they found animal bones and beautiful feathers. Many trees had been cut and the destruction of the surrounding forest had exposed the land to erosion and rotting vegetation. They all agreed that their people had more respect for the earth and would not leave any place like this.

Their happy anticipation of meeting their old friends again quickly turned to sadness as they travelled deeper into the jungle. The destruction appeared to get worse with larger areas destroyed and sections of small waterways blocked with walls of clay and fallen trees. Behind the walls were rotting and stagnant pools with putrid fish remains.

Dilahn would not allow Kettiajya and Icemon to proceed before breaking the walls and freeing the waters. They also found small structures made from vines entwined through each other. Some of these structures had skeletons of creatures inside.

"What do you think this was, Mima?" asked Dilahn.

"I don't know, Dilahn, but it is not a natural thing for an animal to make a structure for nesting if they can't get out."

They sat and looked at the destruction and tried to come to a conclusion about what had happened there.

234

"It's made by humans," stated Icemon. "I hope Tsulib and the others are OK. Looks like there are other humans here; bad humans."

The destruction seemed to intensify with the discovery of each site.

It appeared as though these people destroyed their own environment and were forced to abandon their camp to find new grounds.

It was after five weeks of following the river that they came upon a large area of sandy riverbed exposed by low waters. It was a pleasant surprise and a change from constant battling against the jungle. Paterson and Heps were elated to be able to run free and roll in the loose sand. They galloped the full length of the sandy riverbed and sometimes disappeared around the bend of the river, only to reappear moments later.

Icemon asked for a few days to recuperate, and Kettiajya and Dilahn agreed that everyone, including Heps and Paterson, deserved a break.

Dilahn awoke early on the second morning sensing that something was not right. He whistled for Paterson and Heps and began to prepare food for everyone. He was concerned when they did not appear and woke his mother.

"Mima," he said as he touched Kettiajya. "Mima, Paterson and Heps have not come back yet."

Kettiajya jumped to her feet, also sensing that something was not right.

She whistled for Paterson and waited silently hoping to hear his familiar canter. There was nothing.

"We must follow the riverbed, maybe the sandy section goes for a lot further around the bend," she said calmly. "They will be there enjoying the morning."

Kettiajya and Dilahn woke Icemon, told her what they were doing, and asked her to follow at her own pace.

"I am sure we will find them just around there," she said, pointing downstream.

Kettiajya and Dilahn began walking but progressed to a run as they saw no sign of Paterson and Heps downstream where the sandy riverbed had ceased.

They stood and listened after whistling many times.

"Mima, do you think they do not want to be with us anymore?" asked Dilahn.

"No, I feel that something is wrong. This is new territory for them as well as us."

"What can we do?" asked Dilahn.

"We'll sit quietly, sweetheart. Sit and listen and watch for anything."

"Watch for what."

"I don't know. I don't know what else to do," said Kettiajya.

Icemon eventually caught up with them and lay on the sand, exhausted.

"We'll have to wait here for them to return," she said. "We can't leave them."

"Wait, Mima!" said Dilahn. "Did you hear that?"

They all sat silently and then they all heard a distant sound of a horse in trouble.

"Sorry, Icemon, we have to leave you behind again," said Kettiajya. "Our boys are in trouble."

Dilahn began running before Kettiajya had a chance to discuss how they would handle this. She followed Dilahn as he crashed through the jungle, falling and picking himself up again as he followed his heart instinctively.

They stopped exhausted after many minutes and Dilahn began to cry.

"What do you think is wrong, Mima?"

"There are animals here, Dilahn, maybe large enough to challenge them," she said. "Come, we'll walk. We need to keep moving toward them."

They did not get very far when a group of men appeared from out of the jungle and knocked them both to the ground.

Being outnumbered, Kettiajya whispered to Dilahn, "Don't fight, sweetheart, just do as I say."

Dilahn was too frightened to object as he was pulled to his feet and pushed with Kettiajya towards a track leading downstream.

They were constantly taunted by being pushed in the back and prodded with long sticks with sharp ends. Kettiajya told Dilahn not to speak and to try to be cooperative.

Distant noises of excited people and distressed horses became louder and Kettiajya realised that Paterson and Heps were more than likely in a similar situation as she and Dilahn were.

"Oh, Mima," cried Dilahn. "It's Heps and Paterson. I can hear..."

He was silenced by a sharp jab in the back by one of the captors.

Blood began to run down his back as they approached a camp with many people and structures in a large cleared area.

Everyone was gathered around teasing Paterson and Heps who were tied by their necks to a tree. They were covered in white froth and whinnying frantically.

Kettiajya whistled.

When Paterson saw her, he became more frantic until she whistled again. He calmed down but his eyes reflected the fear that he and Heps were experiencing.

Dilahn cried out loud. "Heps, I am sorry. I am so sorry for bringing you here."

Suddenly, the attention changed to another distraction.

It was Icemon stamping into the clearing with her signature hop-step walk and screaming at an old man crouched nearby.

"Arthur, is that you?" she screamed. "What the hell is going on here?"

"Sorry, I am not permitted to speak," he answered.

"What is this place? Who says you cannot speak?"

The old man pointed to a large central dwelling and said, "Tsulib."

"Is this the tribe of Tsulib?" she asked in disbelief.

A group of men approached Icemon and tried to grab her arms.

"You don't want to do that," she said quietly as she lifted her stick.

They stepped back as she began walking toward the large dwelling. Icemon stopped when she was close to Kettiajya and Dilahn.

"Let them go," she said slowly. The men stood staring at Icemon still holding sharp sticks against Kettiajya and Dilahn. Icemon walked very slowly up to one of the men and said, "Let them go... now."

After eye-to-eye contact with Icemon, the man waved to indicate to the other men to free their captives.

Dilahn ran to Heps and proceeded to untie the restraining ropes.

"I am not frightened by an old, crippled woman," called a young man as he knocked Dilahn to the ground.

The old man, Arthur, who spoke to Icemon suddenly found courage and came forward.

"You should be afraid," he said.

"Where is Tsulib?" interrupted Icemon.

Arthur pointed to the large dwelling where three young women were standing in the doorway. They stepped aside to let a big man adorned in many colourful feathers in a headpiece and a robe covered in bones and coloured stones.

"Tsulib? Tsulib is that you?" called Icemon.

"Icemon!" he called as he walked towards her with his arms outstretched. Icemon stepped back, preventing him from embracing her.

Kettiajya and Dilahn had followed Icemon to the dwelling, freeing many birds and animals that were imprisoned in structures or tied to trees. Dilahn was very distressed when he saw the suffering and fear in their eyes, reminding him about the things he had seen in the vault.

238

"Mima, it's happening again," he said as he wiped his nose and eyes on his arm.

"Yes, I can't believe what I am seeing," she said. "These are the people from the mountains, your grandfather. I didn't recognise them."

Kettiajya stood watching Tsulib, not believing what he had become.

Icemon gestured towards Kettiajya and Dilahn as she said, "Kettiajya and your grandson wanted to visit you."

"My grandson? Dilahn?"

"Yes, Tsulib, the son of Yondalin."

Tsulib put his arms around Dilahn and held him away from him as he looked at him. He was a beautiful boy, tall and slim like his mother, but his hair and eyes were black like his father's. His skin was lighter than Yondalin and his face had gentle features that made the onlooker stare in wonder at the beauty of him.

Tsulib forced his gaze away from Dilahn to invite everyone into his dwelling.

When they were all seated, Kettiajya noticed that Tsulib's seat was much higher and more ornate than the other seats. Tsulib clapped his hands three times and the three young women who were outside at the entrance quickly entered with dishes of food, including pieces of cooked animal. They then stood behind him.

"You must be hungry," said Tsulib as he waved his hand over the food.

Icemon, Kettiajya, and Dilahn sat silently, looking at the food but not taking any.

Tsulib waved a hand to one of the young women signalling her to chase insects away from his face. She moved quickly and silently.

"Tsulib, what has happened to you?"

"You've noticed the changes?" he answered. "Isn't it great how we have progressed since we left the mountains?"

"You now kill and eat animals?"

"It's an easy food source, Kettiajya, and it really is delicious."

239

He clapped his hands again and a woman brought drinks, but not quick enough for Tsulib, who chastised the woman. She ran quickly from the dwelling.

"Who are the women?" asked Icemon.

"My charges for now," he said.

"For now?"

"Yes, I, being the leader, need to teach the young women the ways of men before they..." He stopped talking and appeared to be embarrassed.

"Before what?" continued Icemon.

Tsulib looked at each of them.

After an eternity of silence, Icemon, Kettiajya, and Dilahn stood and turned to leave.

"Hey, you need to understand," he pleaded. "We needed to adjust to this environment. Things are not the same here."

The three visitors did not answer Tsulib. They walked out of the dwelling without saying goodbye and walked through the gathered crowd towards Paterson and Heps, who were very agitated and waiting near the pathway into the camp.

Kettiajya stopped when she recognised Sinai.

"Is Taisha still here?" Kettiajya asked.

"No," answered Sinai. "She left years ago."

"Alone?"

"No, Brodie, Carlos, and some others went with her."

Kettiajya reached out to Sinai, touching her shoulder.

"You are not prisoners here, are you?"

"No."

"Then why are you here with all of this?" asked Kettiajya.

Sinai just shrugged her shoulders.

Kettiajya looked at her in disbelief before turning to join Dilahn and Icemon.

They walked for days towards the mountaintop without saying much to each other. They were shocked by what they had encountered and did not know what to say about it.

240

Paterson and Heps were nervous and stayed very close to their companions. They had also learnt a nasty lesson.

When they reached the mountains, they stopped and prepared to stay for one night before heading back to the comfort of their beloved mountains.

Kettiajya awoke early the following morning but was surprised to find Dilahn already prepared to move on.

"Keen to get going?" she asked.

"Yes, Mima. Please don't be angry with me but I am going back that way," he said as he pointed down to the jungle.

"No, Dilahn. Please don't go back," she pleaded.

"I need to go back, Mima."

Kettiajya walked to Dilahn and put her hands on his shoulders. She realised that he had made up his mind and would not be persuaded to change it.

"I know now. I must begin with big pa Tsulib," he said. "I need to know what happened to make them change."

He approached Heps and said goodbye. "I would never ask you to come back there with me, Heps," he said. "Thank you for being my friend. I will never forget you. I love you."

Kettiajya watched as Dilahn began his descent into the jungle one more time and was not surprised to see Heps trot after him.

Icemon watched silently. She sighed as she realised that Dilahn was going back to the jungle. She knew that Kettiajya would not leave him alone again and wherever Kettiajya went, Paterson would follow.

Well, she thought, *I am not going back there, it's the mountains for me. I didn't climb all the way back here to turn around and go all the way back again.* She continued mumbling to herself, "The things they have me doing, you'd think I was a fit and able youngster. So goodbye, you lot, see you sometime down the track."

She turned to begin her long trek back to the mountains, but she paused to watch her companions going in the opposite direction down the mountain to the jungle.

"It'll be good to not have to bother with all their silliness," she muttered.

She smiled as the silhouettes of Dilahn, followed by Heps, Kettiajya, and then Paterson disappeared into the golden pillow of clouds illuminated by the rising sun over the clouds.

"Bugger!" she mumbled as she turned to add her silhouette to the troupe descending through the mists down into the jungle. "Bugger!"

Glossary for the music references

Yondalin's song – Oliver Shanti and Friends: "Chief White Bear's Trance Dance"

Kettiajya's song – Oliver Shanti and Friends: "Axtu Leman Sumix Sacred Mountain"

Acknowledgements

I want to thank the music for inspiring me.

Thanks also to:
My children, Tim, Shane, and Kelly, for their undying faith in me and my projects.
My mentors Noelle and Maggie.
The local people of Cahuela and Shintuya in Peru for their friendship and for sharing their knowledge with me.